The Children of Punjab

Inspired by true events

Ishar P. Singh

ISBN: 9798725936773

Cover design by: Ishar P. Singh

Created in the United Kingdom

Waheguru Ji Ka Khalsa, Waheguru Ji Fateh!

This book is dedicated to my daughter, Harkiya.

I would also like to thank my family and especially my 'Peeps', who have believed in me from the beginning.

- Ishar

Chapter 1

It was a burning summers day in the great city of Lahore, as the minister's youngest son Mir Mannu, played idly by the well in the cool shade of their great marble courtyard. Mir was a scrawny boy compared to his older brothers, Akbar and Ahmed. His brothers often taunted and humiliated him at every opportunity, so Mir had grown accustomed to spending time alone. He preferred it that way anyway. No one bossing him around or telling him what to do. Anything was better than attending religious studies, which is where he should have been.

Instead, he liked to sit by the well and play with his toys whilst watching the hustle and bustle of his father's great house. All manner of servants and maids quietly weaved their way in and out of the grand hallways and interconnected rooms that circled the great courtyard. They all seemed busier than normal today and for good reason. The prime minister of Delhi, Wazir Qamar udDin Khan, was returning home today after a lengthy absence. Mir knew his father was an important man, but he knew nothing of what his father did.

"Mir betah, where are you?" called out the voice of a young woman. Dressed in the finest Persian silks and embodied with gold, stood a radiant young woman of no more than twenty years in age. Her lips were painted ruby red, and her eyes were underlined with a hint of Kohl. With her long brown hair flowing openly, the young bride stood on the upper balcony and scanned the courtyard below for her son. She didn't have time for this. Her husband was due to return any moment now and everything had to be in its proper place, including her son.

"What's the matter Hira Didi (sister)? Lost something?" Miriam's stern yet insincere attempt to be playful, cut across the air. As the minister's first wife, Miriam was the lady of the house. As she emerged from her chambers on the other side of the large hallway, the stark difference between the two wives became clear. Dressed far more conservatively than the younger bride, Miriam was adorned in a Jade coloured silk Sari and draped with fine jewelry that could have almost been reserved for royalty. Only the wrinkles around her eyes betrayed her true age.

"The boy should be with the Imam, studying the Qur'an with his brother's," she said disapprovingly, as she made her way along the decadent hallway.

"Yes, Didi. My apologies, I…" Hira began to reply, but was cut off by her elder.

"Make sure it does not happen again. Qamar Sahib is not as forgiving as I am."

Miriam passed the young bride without making any eye contact. Hira was everything that Miriam once was. Young, beautiful, and desirable and it burned Miriam inside that she was no longer enough for the minister. She had given him her whole life. She had borne him two strong and healthy sons. What more did he want of her? What more did he expect of her? Whilst it was

6

not uncommon for a man of his status to have multiple wives, Miriam took her husband's taking of a second wife as a personal insult, especially one so young.

A noise from below drew the women's attention. Raja, the housekeeper, entered the courtyard and addressed the mothers on the balcony above. "My ladies, forgive the interruption. Qamar Sahib has arrived and has requested that his sons greet him by the stables."

Both wives hid their joy from one another as they received news of their beloved's return. Hira immediately covered her head with the Chunni resting on her shoulders, and both wives descended down the marble staircase and headed towards the centre of the courtyard.

"Akbar and Ahmed's lesson with the Imam should be finishing now anyway. Recall them immediately Raja and escort them to their father," instructed Miriam. Just as Raja was about to enquire about Mir, the young boy instantly spotted his mother and ran towards her for a loving embrace.

Raja nodded and went to collect the other boys. Hira smiled at her little boy. "Your father is home, follow Raja to the stables and leave your toys here," she said lovingly. But Mir was apprehensive. He had tried his best to avoid the stables ever since his brothers had warned him that they were haunted by the ghosts of dead slaves.

Outside, a tired looking man in his mid-forties stepped down from his carriage. He was dressed in an immaculate ivory coloured

Jama coat, that draped almost the entire length of his trim frame. From the hand stitched patterns woven into his luxurious clothes, to the creamy pearls wrapped around his neck, it was clear that the minister was a man of great importance and wealth.

It had been a long journey from the capital and Qamar was looking forward to finally spending some time in his own home. No longer was he to be burdened by the attendance of court, or stuck hearing the woes of the local peasants. He was sick of it. This was not his homeland, and these were not his people.

They were all insects as far as Qamar was concerned. Slowly draining his life-force one bite at a time and keeping him away from the warmth of his bed and the touch of his wives. Working for the empire had exacted a heavy toll on the Wazir's family life. But they were all far safer here than in the capital. Insurgent strikes had the emperor on edge and by default, this meant the minister's life was on edge too.

Following the law set out by the great and almighty Prophet (peace be upon him) was no easy task, especially in this land of kafir's. No matter how much the emperor had tried to show the people the light of Islam, the infidels continued to struggle and reject the truth. But no such people disgusted the minister more than the Sikh's. They were a weed, a plague that had rotted this land to the core and had forever been a thorn in the empire's side. It was time to pluck this weed once and for all.

Towed behind the minister's carriage and covered by a large dark stained cloth, sat a large iron cage. But it was the contents of the cage that pleased the minister the most. Inside, lay a present for his sons unlike any other that they had yet received.

As the minister stretched his legs, Raja appeared from the haveli (mansion) closely followed by Qamar's three sons. "My children!" Shouted the minister happily. Each of them ran towards their father and embraced him tightly.

"Pitha Ji, you are home!" Qamar beamed with joy at seeing the faces of his sons. Almost six months had passed since he had last gazed upon their faces.

"My, you have all grown!" he said, unable to stop smiling. Qamar then bent down to Mir's level and ruffled his hair. "May Allah bless you all."

Mir was happy to see his father, but yet knew enough to be a little afraid of him too. "I have a present for you boys." And with that, Qamar nodded to his accompaniment of guards who then approached the trailing carriage and removed its filthy cover.

Blinded by a sudden burst of light from above, four Sikh prisoners recoiled from the sun. Each one was bound by metal chains, tied from their wrists to the top of the iron cage. Their blood-stained and tattered clothes clung to their near naked bodies, whilst the smell from their various open wounds and rotting flesh blended with the oppressive heat of the summers air and the manure from the stables nearby. Mir covered his face in horror at witnessing such a terrifying site. These shadows of men were unlike anything the boy had ever witnessed before.

Overcome by the assault on his senses, Mir moved to hide behind his father's legs in a bid to cleanse his mind from what he had just seen. Akbar and Ahmed laughed at their younger brother's reaction. "Who are they Pitha Ji?" asked Akbar with excitement.

"This my son, is taste of the cancer that has plagued these lands for far too long. They are a gift from the emperor himself. But for you my children, they are also a lesson." Akbar and Ahmed now hung on their father's every word, but Qamar could also see the confusion on their faces. He continued...

"These swine attacked your emperor's guards. If it were up to them, each of *your* heads would be placed on spikes outside this city. Given a chance, these pigs would rape our women and plunder our wealth for their pagan way of life. It is therefore our farz (duty), bestowed by almighty Allah himself, to rid ourselves of these vermin. Our beloved Prophet (peace be upon him) has shown us the path. And as his children, it is our farz to execute the almighty's will upon this earth."

Qamar's words fell upon his children like a sermon from the Imam himself. Standing between the iron cage and his children, Qamar instructed his guards to unload the prisoners and have them tied up against the stable walls. Still bound by chains, each prisoner was dragged from the carriage across the muddy floor and then dumped unceremoniously against the edge of the stables.

They were all but hours from death, as they had all clearly been beaten and starved. But what was most unsettling was how none of the prisoners made a sound. It then became clear as the guards moved away from their stinking bodies, as to why. Hanging around each of their necks by a single black string, were their severed tongues.

Satisfied with the arrangement, Qamar turned his attention back to his boys. "Today, my children, you will become men and you will all join our family and faith in Jihad. Jihad is not simply a fight against the enemies of Islam, it a fight against all evil and sin in this world." Qamar paused to let his children process his words.

"It is the most noble of causes. Jihad is about the spiritual struggle each man must go through in their lifetime. We are the chosen people and our path to salvation is long, hard and treacherous. Chetan (the devil) lurks around every corner and if your will is weak, he will devour you and our entire family along with you. Do you understand my children?"

Each of the boy's nodded slowly in silence. Akbar and Ahmed looked into their father's eyes with love and admiration as his words flowed over them like a river. Mir on the other hand was still terrified inside and could barely contain his emotion. Qamar could see the struggle within his youngest child and smiled. "Each of us has a duty in this life, betah. The sooner you realise your duty, the sooner you will have peace."

Qamar then unsheathed his Talwar and moved closer to one of the prisoners. His sword shone like a beacon of light as the curved blade reflected the sun across the earth below. "Swine like this do not deserve our mercy. They do not deserve your love or kindness.

Remember, these kafir's are not human." And with that, the minister swung his sword in one swift stroke across the throat of the nearest Sikh prisoner.

Barely conscious and still bound to the wall, the prisoner was unable to clutch his own throat. As his life force now pulsated freely out of his neck, the prisoner's eyes rolled back and he fell forward into the dirt with a dull thud. Blood continued to flow from his final wound and formed a pool around his now very dead body. The other prisoners now fully alert, began mumbling a single word in unison. "Vah-gru, vah-gru, vah-gru…"

"Silence swine!" shouted the minister. With warm blood still dripping from his sword, Qamar gazed into the eyes of the other prisoners. Yet in a final act of defiance, the Sikh's prisoners did not head the word of their captor, instead they continued their muffled chanting. Their insolence enraged the minister further.

"Do you understand now my children? These, infidels have no remorse, no feelings, no worth. There are maggots who seek to destroy everything you love and hold dear!"

Turning to his guards and with his patience wearing thin, the minister commanded them to prepare the next prisoner. Unable to stand or put forth any resistance, the next 'kafir' was dragged forward and held into position for execution.

With a single gesture from his father, Akbar understood what was expected of him. Without hesitation, the eldest of the brothers drew his sword and swiftly repeated the action of his father. As the air fell silent, another thud greeted the floor.

Pleased with his obedience, Qamar praised his son. "Shabash betah! Today you have made your father proud!" Also eager to gain his father's acceptance, Ahmed unsheathed his sword and dispatched the third prisoner in the same fashion as his father and brother before him. All eyes then fell upon the youngest of the three, Mir.

Tears began to fill Mir's eyes as he stared at the last Sikh warrior bound to the wall by chains. The last prisoner was not much older than his own brothers, yet he looked nothing like them. With his long-knotted hair dangling by his shoulders and an open beard soaked with dry blood, Bhajan Singh resembled more of a rakshasa (demon) from the old Hindu myths and legends, than a man.

But the thing that upset Mir the most was Bhajan's eyes. There was not any anger or fear or hatred looking back at him. If anything, it was pity. Still mumbling the syllables 'Vah-gru', Bhajan prepared himself for his death. As his brothers before him, he was at peace with his 'Maharaj's hukam'. The command of his Guru, the Granth Sahib.

Understanding the importance of the moment. Qamar took Mir by the hand and presented him with a handmade Pesh Kabz (small dagger). Mir looked down at the exquisite weapon now in his hand and admired its beauty. The hilt had been expertly carved from bone and had been decorated in a floral pattern that flowed towards the edge of its cold steel blade.

Softening his tone for his youngest son Qamar continued. "This Pesh was my fathers before me and now it is yours my love. You have always been a part of me and now we are bound by the same purpose. Do you understand my son?"

Mir tried his best to compose himself and nodded in acceptance. His hands began to shake at the thought of what he may be asked to do next. But his father continued. "This blade is now a part of you and shall be used to wield the will of almighty Allah. As he commands, we must act. Now... remember your training and join your family as liberators of this cursed land."

Steadying the dagger in his hand, Mir approached his captive. The stench of his prey filled his nostrils, making the boy's stomach churn, yet he knew what was expected of him. Mir also feared what would happen to him if he did not act. His heart held him back from thrusting the dagger forward into the prisoner. 'What could this poor soul have done to deserve such a fate?' the boy asked himself.

Once again Bhajan looked up at the small child in front of him, but then did something none of the other spectators expected. He attempted to shuffle forward, closer to his child executioner and with his head, he gestured for Mir to proceed.

Aiming for Bhajan's neck, Mir raised the dagger into the air. But before he could complete the forward thrust, a voice cut through the air from behind them, startling them all.

"Stop!" Mir turned around and faced the haweli to see who had saved him from becoming a murderer. Running towards them followed closely by Hira, was the lady of the house, Miriam. "Qamar Sahib, he is but a child!" she bellowed, with a combination of authority and annoyance in her voice.

Both wives hurried towards their husband and the scene that was unfolding before them became clearer. This was not the homecoming any of them had expected.

Qamar's surprise at being disturbed quickly turned from anger to joy at seeing his heart's desires. But he was also determined not to show it. He did not like to be interrupted, especially by a woman.

But then Miriam was unlike any other woman he had ever known. Regardless of her faults, he loved her even after all these years. Her strong and outspoken ways are what drew him towards her in the beginning. He was now beginning to regret that, yet his love for both of his wives was as resolute as ever.

What he did not understand, is why Miriam of all people was objecting to this execution? She was not Mir's mother, nor did she know these vermin. Eager to complete the lesson for his sons, Qamar indulged his ladies if for only a moment. "Speak," he said through gritted teeth, whilst trying to control his temper.

"My husband, whilst I am overjoyed to see you, this spilling of blood in our home is not right. It is not righteous, nor just. Where is the honour in killing defenseless men? Why do you slay these men like dogs in our home?" Miriam's voice echoed around the stables surrounding them.

Unwilling to start a debate in the baking hot sun and surrounded by death and manure, the minister aimed to put an end to what had now developed into a drama. "My love, my heart is filled with joy at seeing you too, but do not speak to me about matters of which you know not and do not concern you. Today is a joyous occasion, as today, all of my son's will become men."

Satisfied that the 'discussion' was now over, Qamar turned to his second bride. "Hira Begum, watch as our son joins his older brothers and see our family truly unite as one."

Unable to challenge her husband's authority, Hira nodded in acceptance. The conflict within her tore her apart. She could not bear to see her baby turn into a killer, yet she felt powerless to stop it. Her only hope lay in the arms of her senior companion.

Unable to let the matter pass, Miriam attempted to steady her husband's temperament one last time. "Tell me oh wise one, where is it written in the Qur'an that my children should butcher the defenseless enemies of their father?" Miriam saw a flicker of anger stir within her husband.

"Are you done?" Qamar spat out the words in a deadly tone. Knowing not to push the matter any further, Miriam turned to her younger companion and gestured her to withdraw.

Ignoring the women, he turned his full attention back to his youngest son once more and bellowed a final command… "Mir!"

Holding back the tears once more, Mir turned away from his mother and faced the condemned man before him. Once again, the boy raised his arm only this time, he thrust his new blade forward into his victim's windpipe.

As he withdrew the blade in a jagged motion, the final Sikh prisoner spluttered blood onto Mir's white pajama bottom before slumping to the ground and choking on his own blood.

Each second of Bhajan's death felt like a lifetime to the newly adorned murderer. As a pool of blood formed around his feet, tears fell from Mir's face into the puddles below. The deed was done.

Overjoyed with his son's accomplishment, Qamar lifted Mir into the air. "Well done my boy! Tonight, we celebrate!" Hira watched helplessly as her husband spun her son around in celebration. As the family retreated from the stables back towards to the cool shade of their haveli, four corpses remained behind in the blood-soaked mud and dirt.

Upon entering their courtyard, Hira pulled her son to aside and hugged him tight. "Are you ok my baby?" Mir looked up at his mother. Without uttering a word, he stared soullessly into her eyes and for the first time in her life, Hira did not recognise the boy staring back at her. It was then that she realised her son had also died that day. Hira embraced what remained of her boy tighter than ever before and wept silently for their loss.

Chapter 2

Almost three hundred years later, far across the lush green fields of the Punjab, a beautiful young Sikh woman dressed in the traditional clothing of a native Punjaban, made her way along the winding banks of the mighty Sutlej river. Her plastic sandals left a dusty trail behind them, leading all the way up back to the sleepy village of Tehara, from which she had come.

Surrounded by nothing but farmland for miles, Tehara was an unremarkable tiny farming village, nestled deep within the heart of the Punjabi countryside.

Ruhi Kaur loved walking along the snaking riverbed. Just listening to the sound of the flowing currents, calmed her ever-racing mind. It was the first time she had been back to her Dhaddha Ji's (grandfather's) homeland in over a decade. And whilst nothing had really changed, everything was different now that he was gone.

With every step forward came the whisper of a memory from her childhood. It was here by the riverside where Ruhi and her older brother Jaikaar, were often brought as children to spend their long summer days. Ruhi was but only a child when her grandparents decided to leave the cold and damp of the British Isles behind them. Despite having put down roots and having started a family in an often hostile and foreign land, Ruhi's grandparents Kirpal and Kuldeep, always longed for the warmth and greener pastures of the Punjab, from which they had once come.

Whilst it was not her home, Ruhi had always felt a deep connection to this land. It was almost as if she had lived here in another life. But sadly for the young lady, the reason for her journey back to land of her ancestors was not a happy one. Her duty as a granddaughter had bound her to create one more memory here, to say farewell to her Dhaddha Ji once and for all.

"Ru, we're over here!" Interrupting her thoughts came the voice of a person Ruhi knew all too well. Standing in the distance by the east bank of the winding river, stood a handsome and broad-shouldered Sikh gentleman waving to his younger sister. Even without her older brother's strong home county accent, there was no mistaking this figure for a local.

Dressed in a plain white kurta pajama and towering above the locals around him, stood Jaikaar Singh. With his long flowing black beard, piercing brown eyes and immaculately tied blue turban, Ruhi could have recognised her brother from a mile away. "Quick! They're waiting for us," yelled Jai impatiently, whilst he gestured for his sister to hurry up.

"I'm coming, I'm coming," replied Ruhi, as she hurried along to her sibling. As Ruhi caught up to her older brother she stretched out her arm and handed him his phone. "Next time, you go back for it," she growled, clearly annoyed at having been asked to rush around at her brother's command.

"Thank you, sis," Jai replied sheepishly, as he quickly scanned his phone for a signal.

"We're in the pind, you aren't going to get a signal out here," muttered Ruhi in annoyance.

Jai attempted to defend himself. "I promised Mum I would take pictures, remember?" Ruhi rolled her eyes at her brother's lack of sensitivity.

"You sent me back so you could take pictures? Seriously Jai? This is not the kind of event you take photos at. I can't believe I actually have to tell you that." Conscious of the time, Ruhi now grew impatient with her brother. "Let's just go, we better not have missed anything," she added hastily.

The siblings left the main trail that ran alongside the river and headed down a small pathway that led them towards the river's edge. Making their way through overgrown shrubbery, they came across a wooden pier that stretched out from the bank, right into the heart of the turbulent water.

The pier was a strange sight to behold. It was almost as if someone had attempted to build a bridge but had given up halfway through Ruhi thought to herself. In the centre of the wooden platform, a small number of villagers had gathered in a group. They too had come to pay their final respects to the siblings Dhaddha Ji.

Furthest from the river's edge with her head covered in a royal blue Chunni, stood a tall elderly lady. The passage of time had etched wrinkles around her eyes, yet they still conveyed a message of beauty and strength. Holding a wooden urn in her arms, Kuldeep Kaur watched her grandchildren approach her. "I'm glad you two could join us," she said sarcastically, with a disapproving look upon her face.

"Sorry Dhaddhi Ji, it was my fault." Ruhi replied quickly, covering for her brother. Without trying to draw any more attention to themselves, Ruhi and Jai moved to take their place by their grandmother's side.

Ignoring their tardiness, Kuldeep turned her attention back to the Giani (priest) and instructed him to begin the final Ardas (prayer). As the Giani began reciting the words he had spoken a thousand times before, Ruhi and Jai could not help but feel a sense of deep sadness at having lost the head of their family.

After the short prayer concluded, Kuldeep stared at the urn one last time and then poured the ashes into the river. The three of them stood in silence as they watched the ashes of the recently deceased Kirpal Singh, melt away into nothingness.

After the moment had passed, Kuldeep turned to her grandchildren and gestured to them that it was time to go. "That's it we're done. Anyone hungry?" she asked her grandchildren with genuine curiosity. Seeing the look of confusion on their faces, Kuldeep took a moment to explain.

"The moment your Dhaddha Ji's heart stopped beating he was gone." Pointing to the river behind her, she continued, "Those ashes behind us, were simply that, Ash. They were not your grandfather any more than the grass beneath your feet is or the sky above your heads is."

Ruhi whispered the words 'Satnam Waheguru' to herself, whilst Jai stood there with a look of indifference upon his face. It had been a lifetime since he had last heard one of his Dhaddhi Ji's little sermons on Sikhi, but he was in no mood to be lectured today.

Oblivious to her grandson's lack of interest, Kuldeep pressed on. "Once we die, our soul will leave our body. If your Dhaddha Ji's actions were enough and if he lived his life in line with the Guru's hukam, then he will have ended this cycle of life and death and have become one with the almighty. If not, then perhaps we shall be meeting him again one day!" Kuldeep chuckled at her own little joke.

Jai wanted to contradict her right there and then, but he held his tongue. He knew better than to openly challenge his grandmother's beliefs, especially in public. Whether Jai agreed with her logic and reasoning or not, he owed his grandmother far too much to ever disrespect her. It was only his love and respect for her, that had compelled him to keep his appearance as a Sikh for this long. Cutting his kesh (hair) and openly disregarding his faith would have broken her heart and this was not something he could bring himself to do.

Despite them being close in age, Ruhi's beliefs differed greatly to her older brother's. Whether it was the long summers she had spent with her brother and grandparents in Tehara or simply her kismet (destiny), Ruhi found comfort in the teachings of her Guru, the Granth Sahib.

Seeing her grandfather's ashes scattered in the open water was a deeply humbling experience for the young lady. As her grandfather would have said, 'today was simply the conclusion of another small chapter in the great tapestry that is existence.'

As the villagers left the pier and began to return to the village, Jai discreetly checked his phone again for any kind of connection to the outside world. Unlike Ruhi, he could not wait to leave and return home to the UK. "Seriously? Nothing? Why am I not surprised?" Jai muttered to himself.

"What's wrong?" interrupted Ruhi. As usual, Jai could not hide anything from his sister.

"Nothing. Are you ready to go?" he replied, stuffing his phone back into his pocket.

Conscious of not being overheard by her grandmother, Ruhi lowered her voice so that only Jai could hear. "What are you in hurry to get back to? We are here for Dhaddhi Ji, remember?"

"She's fine, look at her. Look, you may love it out here Ru, but this…. this ain't my home," said Jai, as he turned away from his sister.

"Relax! We'll be out of here tomorrow. At least pretend you're interested, for *her* sake," replied Ruhi, whilst looking at their grandmother.

Jai sighed in defeat, "Okay." Eager to change to topic to anything else Jai continued talking. "How are you not dying in this heat?" he said, wiping his brow.

Just then, Kuldeep approached her grandchildren. "Let's go beteh, we are done."

Having concluded matters with the Giani, the trio left the pier and retraced their steps through the bushes until they reached the main road leading back up to the village. Their dusty path led them up a hill and through a small forest made up of great banyan trees. Their giant tree trunks and tall branches cast great shadows over the forage below, giving all those seeking shade, a welcome break from the scorching sun above. But more than that, the forest was a sign that they were almost home.

As they exited the shade, Ruhi and Jai stood at the top of the hill and looked down towards the village of Tehara nestled below. Even from that distance, they could easily recognise their ancestral home located at the outskirts of the village. The silhouette of a large farmhouse imposed its size over a clutter of smaller buildings that surrounded it. The Singh family home was a welcoming site for the siblings.

The house always reminded Ruhi of a mother hen surrounded by her baby ducklings. Whilst the main building had barely changed over the last hundred years, there were signs of modernisation everywhere. Two electric generators and a large, filtered water tank had been added to the roof. But Jai was most thankful for the new air conditioning units that had been installed throughout every room in the house. Clearly, their Dhaddha Ji had been busy making improvements over the last few years.

In the traditional Punjaban layout, the entrance of the main building led towards an open courtyard. Scattered around the tiled floor were a series of tables and chairs that circled a great fire pit that lay in the center. Lined up along the right-hand side wall, were pair of manji-sahibs (beds), for when the family would lay out at night and stare up at the stars above.

Seeing her husband's favorite chair, Kuldeep felt uncharacteristically emotional, "Let's have dinner outside tonight. Your Dhaddha Ji loved it out here and besides, I have made your favourite," said Kuldeep, looking at her grandchildren.

"Sure Dhaddhi Ji, do you need any help?" offered Ruhi.

Kuldeep waved her hand as to stop Ruhi. "Dyal will help me. But that reminds me. There is something I need to talk to you both about tonight before you leave tomorrow. Remind me again if I forget. Dinner will be ready soon. You two get washed up," instructed Kuldeep, as if they were both children again. Kuldeep then ordered her housekeeper Dyal, to prepare their evening meal as she made her way to her bedroom and closed the door behind her.

"Do you think she's OK? Maybe I should stay for a few more days?" Ruhi asked her brother with concern.

"I don't know Ru, it's up to you. I would if I could, but I have to get back. If I wasn't joining a new practice next week then…maybe." Jai's voice trailed off. This was the last place he wanted to spend any extra time, but he also felt a pang of guilt for leaving his grandmother alone. "Why don't you just ask her?" he added.

"You know what she'll say. She'll say she's fine," replied Ruhi. Both siblings knew that neither of them could change their grandmother's mind once it had been made up.

"Let's have a chat with her tonight, after dinner. If she agrees then I'll change your flight. Who knows we might even be able to get her to come home with us for a bit," Jai added optimistically.

"Ok bro, sounds like a plan." Ruhi hesitated for a moment. She wasn't sure whether it was too soon to bring up the topic of her Dhaddha Ji again. Ruhi knew her brother's belief about life and death and how it differed greatly to her own. Softening her tone, she made an attempt to bridge the spiritual divide between her and her sibling. "How are you *feeling* about today?" she asked her brother cautiously.

Jai knew what his sister was up to. "Fine. You know me." Jai said in a manner that indicated that he did not wish to discuss the topic further, especially with his younger sister.

"Ok, well… I'm here if you ever need…" began Ruhi, before Jai stopped her.

"I know sis, but I'm good. I'm gonna go get changed, I'll be down in a bit." And with that, Jai ended the conversation and went up to his room to pack his belongings.

"Good talk Ru," Ruhi said to herself. "I guess I better start packing too, just in case." Ruhi left the empty courtyard and disappeared into her own old room, to prepare for their departure the next day.

As the sun set outside and the evening cooled, the stars began to light up the evening sky. Ruhi, Jai and Kuldeep sat around a large mahogany dining table, that sat adjacent to the great fire pit in the centre of the courtyard. As the gentle glow of the flames lit up the courtyard around them, the family feasted on a fresh pot of steaming hot Saag and Makki Ki Roti (Spinach and Cornmeal bread).

Of all of Jai's complaints about India, the food was most definitely not one of them. Nobody cooked Saag quite like his grandmother. Despite growing up on a western diet, nothing else could quite compare to the fresh cuisine of the Punjab for him.

After reminiscing about their Dhaddha Ji and filling their bellies, Ruhi and Jai helped Dyal to clear the table. The siblings then enjoyed a hot cup of adarak-wali cha (ginger tea) and warm gulab jamen. It was the perfect dessert to end the meal and it just so happened to be their grandfather's favorite.

Sensing the time was right. Ruhi tested the waters with her grandmother. "Why don't you come back with us now Dhaddhi Ji? probed Ruhi gently. "Jai and I can look after you now. And before you say anything, Mum won't mind and we have plenty of room." Ruhi tried her best to think of any other excuse that her grandmother might use to not accompany them.

Kuldeep just smiled as she looked at her granddaughter. "Ru is right, we would all feel a lot better knowing that you weren't out here alone," added Jai.

"Don't you two worry about me. I am fine and I am not alone. The Guru is with me always," replied their Dhaddhi Ji. Seeing that they were not convinced. Kuldeep continued. "Listen, I love you both and I am very proud of the people you have grown to be, but this is my home, and it is where I choose to be. Besides, what am I going to do back in England? Drink watered downed cha and knit sweaters in the cold and damp? I have a life here too you know," she added, hoping to end the conversation.

Ruhi and Jai knew it was not going to be easy to change their grandmother's mind. But Ruhi wasn't done quite yet. "How about I stay for a few more days? Jai has to go back tomorrow, but my Uni won't start for a few more weeks."

Kuldeep raised a hand to calm her granddaughter down. "Beti, you are both welcome here always, but…" Kuldeep paused, uncertain whether to finish her sentence. Setting down her cup, Kuldeep leaned forward and grabbed each of their hands and held them tight. "Your journeys are only just beginning my children. Both of you will face challenges in your lives that your Dhaddha and I have tried our best to prepare you for. But… we have taken you as far as we can go. *Both* of you must now walk your own paths without us." Kuldeep looked for understanding in their eyes, but only saw blank stares reflected back at her.

Jai spoke first. "Dhaddhi Ji, that doesn't make any sense," he said with a puzzled look upon his face. "What path? What journey? What are you talking about?" Jai said impatiently.

"Patience betah," said Kuldeep, as she smiled and leaned back in her seat. "Go to my room. On top of my cabinet there is a wooden chest. Please bring it to me Jaikaar," requested Kuldeep, in an authoritative tone.

Accepting defeat, Jai stood up and glanced at his sister before answering his grandmother obediently, "Han-Ji Dhaddhi Ji."

Moments later, Jai returned to the courtyard with a large wooden chest in his hands. "Just lay it here on the table betah," instructed Kuldeep, as she pointed to an empty space before them.

Complying with her command, Jai placed the incredibly old chest onto the table. With splintered panels and dark scratches across all sides, the case looked as if it had been through hell and back. "You sure you don't want this on the floor Dhaddhi?" inquired her grandson skeptically.

Kuldeep nodded her head from side-to-side as to gesture 'no'. "Your Dhaddha Ji and I wanted to give you these together but, it was not meant to be." Kuldeep's voice trailed off as she positioned herself over the chest. She then removed the lid to reveal a pair of magnificently sculpted Kirpan's (daggers), fixated into the very centre of the chest.

They were unlike anything the siblings had ever seen before. Both were covered in swirling patterns of black and silver that spread across their dark metal sheaths. Only one detail separated the pair of fourteen-inch blades, their hilts. A lion had been carved into the end of a lapis-blue marble hilt, that belonged to the top Kirpan.

In an exquisite craftsmanship that matched the Kirpan above, the second blade had a hilt made of pure jade with the head of an eagle sculpted into the end of it. Both were elegant in their design, yet they both had an air of absolute beauty in their simplicity. Reaching into the chest with both hands, Kuldeep picked up the lapis blue hilted Kirpan and raised it to her forehead as to bow down before it.

Mumbling some words under her breath, she swiftly withdrew the blade from its cover. The sound of the metal withdrawing from its sheath seemed to vibrate the air around it. Kuldeep then gently placed the weapon into the hands of her grandson.

From the moment the cold blue marble touched his skin, Jai felt a surge or energy flow throughout his body unlike anything he had ever experienced before. Every sense in his body sharpened and focused upon that moment in time. It was as if the world around him had stood still for a moment.

Both Ruhi and Jai were taken back by the beauty of the razor sharp, gun metal grey blade. The swordsmith who had created this weapon had clearly designed it for one purpose only, to part human flesh.

"In honour of our sixth Guru, Hargobind Ji, this Kirpan is called Miri and she belongs to you now betah. Miri is bound to you from now, until your final days." Kuldeep's words resonated in Jai's ears.

For the first time that day, Jai was at a loss for words. "This is mine?" he asked with skepticism. Kuldeep nodded 'yes', and then turned back to the chest and took out the second Kirpan. As with the first, Kuldeep repeated the process of bowing to the weapon before unsheathing it and displaying the curved metallic blade in all its glory.

Placing the elegant weapon into her granddaughter's hand, Ruhi felt the same surge or energy flow throughout her body, from the moment the cold jade touched her skin. Kuldeep could see the wonder in her granddaughter's eyes. "She is called Piri, and she now belongs to you my Betei," said Kuldeep lovingly.

Ruhi mimicked her grandmother and bowed her head to the Kirpan in her hands. The power she felt was unmistakable. It was as if every cell in her body had been supercharged with electricity. Everything before that moment, felt like it was a dream to the young woman.

"What just happened to me Dhaddhi Ji?" asked Ruhi, who was clearly mesmerised by the weapon in her hand.

Kuldeep smiled at her grandchildren. "Miri and Piri are to remain with you at all times and will serve you both faithfully for the remainder of your lives." The siblings stared at their weapons in wonder as their grandmother continued. "They are a rare mixture of Sarbloh (wrought iron) and Damascus steel. These Shastar (weaponry) are imbued with the power of Gurbani (the

Guru's word) and as you progress in your spiritual development, your individual Kirpan's will help you to focus your energy and help you to defeat your enemies in battle. But always remember, a Kirpan is meant for the defence of those who cannot defend themselves."

"Wait, what? Enemies in battle?" Trying his best not to be overcome by the blade in his hand Jai pressed on. "What are you talking about Dhaddhi Ji? I'm about to start a new job on Monday and Ru is going back to Uni in two weeks. When are we ever going to be slicing and dicing agents of evil?" asked Jai. Snapping back to reality, Jai sheathed his new blade. "It is a beautiful gift Dhaddhi, but I can't accept this. Besides, I don't really need it," said Jai, as he placed Miri back into the chest.

Ruhi looked at her brother with disbelief. She knew he had been questioning his faith recently, but she never thought he would reject a piece of their heritage like this. Ruhi sheathed her own blade and held onto it tightly.

Kuldeep smiled at her grandchildren's innocence and naivety and sat back in her chair. Her legs were tired from walking up and down the banks of the river and it felt good to rest her bones after such a draining day. She thought for a moment how to best explain her intentions to her grandchildren. Kuldeep closed her eyes for a second and spoke to herself. 'They are your children Guru Ji, please guide them.'

After taking a deep breath, she decided to try a different approach. "Why do you think your Dhaddha Ji and I brought you

32

to this farm all those years ago? Why do you think we wanted you to learn about Paat (prayer), Kirtan (hymns), Seva (selfless service), Simran (meditation) and Gatka (martial arts)?" she asked them both. There was a silence, as both Ruhi and Jai were trying to decipher what their Dhaddhi Ji was trying to get to.

"To learn be a better person?" queried Jai.

Kuldeep then looked at her granddaughter. Ruhi tried next. "To learn about God and our history and to serve our Guru?"

"Those are both good answers, but… they are not the reason." Kuldeep chose her next words very carefully. "As Sikh's, we are students first and foremost and our topic of study is the whole Universe. We but introduced you to the only teacher you will ever need in this life, the Guru Granth Sahib. What it means to be a Sikh is a question you must both answer for yourselves. Another person cannot tell you who or what you are. Only by walking the path the Guru has laid out for you, will your truth be revealed."

Jai tried his best not to roll his eyes. 'Oh great, more riddles,' he thought to himself.

Kuldeep concluded. "Within every lifeform in this Universe, lives the light of the lord and it is his hukam that binds and guides us all. But beware, Kaljug (evil) will pull you now more than ever before as this is *his* time. You must both resist his maya (illusion) now more than ever before."

Thinking about the wisdom their grandmother had just departed upon them, Ruhi replied obediently, "Han-Ji Dhaddhi

Ji." Jai on the other hand was less convinced but nodded to his grandmother in acknowledgment.

Cautious of not wanting to overwhelm her grandchildren, Kuldeep returned Miri back into the hands of her grandson and repeated her instruction, but this time in a stern voice. "She is to remain with you at all times Jaikaar."

"Yes Dhaddhi Ji," replied Jai in defeat. Kuldeep's face lit up.

"Good. Then there is only one last thing I must ask of you both, before you leave tomorrow."

"Of course Dhaddhi Ji, what is it?" replied Ruhi instantly.

"Join me again by the river, but this time, we leave at Amritvela (before dawn) together," requested Kuldeep.

Although he was now frustrated at the notion of having to wake at 3am, Jai nodded in agreement. "Yes Dhaddhi Ji, of course," he said in compliance.

"Excellent! Then it is settled! I will see you both in the morning." Rising to leave, Kuldeep opened her arms. "Come, give your old Dhaddhi Ji a hug. It has been a long day for us all." Both grandchildren obliged their grandmother, who then retreated back to her room for the night. "Don't worry, Dyal will lock up. Just don't stay up too late," said Kuldeep, as she closed the door behind her.

As soon as she heard her grandmother's door close, Ruhi turned to her brother. "What the hell was that Jai? Do you realise how important these are?" said Ruhi in frustration. She then raised Piri up into the light. "They must be well over two hundred years

34

old," she said, staring up at her Kirpan in wonder. Regaining her train of thought, Ruhi looked at her brother and waited for a response. "Well?"

"Chill woman, it's just a Kirpan. Just like the zillions we shouldn't have been 'training' with years ago. Child-line anyone? Maybe I can eBay it when I get back?" Jai said jokingly. Seeing the look of horror on his sister's face, Jai quickly realised that Ruhi was not in the mood to joke. "I'm kidding! I'll wear it. Look…" Jai reached into the chest still on the table and took out two gatra's (straps) that accompanied each Kirpan and handed one to his sister. "I have never seen a gatra like this before… strange," said Jai, genuinely taken back by the black suede patterned weapon holder.

Eager to change the topic, Jai pressed on. "So what is this whole riverside Amritvela thing about? I don't remember needing to trudge along in the dark to a questionably safe pier in the middle of the night before?"

Still annoyed with her brother's idiocy Ruhi replied. "I don't know, but we told Dhaddhi Ji we're going to go, so just be ready. And if you forget something this time, you can go back and get it yourself!"

"I was just following orders!" protested Jai.

"Shush! You're going to disturb Dhaddhi Ji," replied Ruhi, not wanting to be drawn into another pointless argument with her brother. Ever since he had left home, Ruhi had noticed that her brother had grown more distant from her, and she could not understand why.

Even though Jai was only older than her by eighteen months, Ruhi often felt like the elder sibling. Lowering her voice, she continued. "Ok, truce. We've both got an early start tomorrow. I need my beauty sleep and you damn sure need yours!" Ruhi couldn't help but add one little taunt for her brother before heading off to bed.

Left in the courtyard alone, Jai looked down at the contrasting black and silver cover of the Kirpan in his hands. "It's going to be a long day tomorrow. At least I'm going home. Thank god for that," he said to himself. Placing the Kirpan in its holster, Jai too left the courtyard in the hope of catching a few precious hours of sleep before the dawn of another day.

The buzzing of the alarm on his smartphone startled the young man awake. 'It can't be 3am already, I just fell asleep!' Jai thought to himself. Memories of the night before started coming back to him as he reached out to hit the snooze button.

Packing his suitcase had taken far longer than expected and no matter what improvements his Dhaddha Ji had made to the house over the years, Jai could never get comfortable sleeping on a manji sahib. He suddenly remembered his promise to his Dhaddhi about meeting on the pier. "Oh god…fine, let's get it over with," he said out loud to himself.

Jai rushed about his room getting ready. He slipped on his navy-blue kurta pajama and just finished tying his royal blue coloured keski (short turban) when his eye caught his 'present'. He contemplated for a moment whether to take the weapon with him or not. Unwilling to take any more grief from his sister or grandmother, Jai once again strapped Miri to his chest and hurried along to join the ladies waiting for him in the courtyard.

Upon his arrival, Ruhi greeted Jai with a look of surprise upon her face. She was surprised that he was actually on time for once. She too had chosen to dress in blue today by coincidence, and her Kirpan was concealed by her matching navy chunni.

As they were all ready on time, the trio departed the farmhouse and made their way back up the hill, through the forest and along the dusty road towards the pier. With only an oil lamp to guide them, Ruhi was grateful for the extra light shining down from the moon. She loved the silence of the night, even the crickets and the birds seemed to be asleep at this hour.

As they approached the pier once again, it suddenly dawned upon Jai that it really wasn't safe for them to be out there in the dark, all alone. Unable to hold his curiosity back any longer, Jai questioned his grandmother. "What are we doing out here Dhaddhi Ji? There is nothing out here and I can't see a thing."

Kuldeep smiled to herself and carried on walking until she reached the edge of the pier. It was the same spot she had stood upon less than a day before. Turning to face her grandchildren, Kuldeep's voice was suddenly heavy with emotion. "I love you both so very much and I am very proud of the people you have become."

Unable to look at them anymore, Kuldeep turned to face the river. She then closed her eyes and took one large step forward, falling straight off the pier and into the deep, dark water below.

"Dhaddhi Ji!" Screamed Ruhi, as she ran towards the edge where her grandmother had stood only seconds before. "Jai, we have help her!" The oil lamp was insufficient at lighting the water below. The normally calmer younger sister watched the rushing currents for any sign of their grandmother. Tears formed in her eyes as Ruhi turned to her brother who was now stood by her side. "I can't see her Jai!"

Without waiting for his response, Ruhi put down the lamp, kicked off her slippers and dived headfirst into the cold water below and just like her grandmother before her, she disappeared below the surface. "No! Wait! It's too dark!" shouted Jai in vain, but it was too late. Ruhi could no longer hear her brother's voice as she was far beneath the surface of the water, desperately searching the pitch-black abyss for her grandmother.

Unable to see his sister or grandmother, panic began to overcome Jai as he desperately tried to think of a way to save his family. He reached into his pocket and pulled out his phone in an attempt to call for help. But just as before, there was no signal. They were over five miles away from the nearest town with a cell tower, Sidhwan Bet. It was in that moment, Jai realised he was completely alone.

The flashlight. Jai suddenly realised he could use the flashlight on his phone to scan the surface of the flowing river. He waved the light from his phone over the water in the hope that he would catch a glimpse of life. But it made no difference. Nothing here made any sense. "Ru! Dhaddhi! Where are you?" he yelled out into the night. He had already lost so much, his father and grandfather. He could not stand to lose his sister and Dhaddhi Ji too, not like this.

"Help! Please somebody help me!" he shouted out in desperation. But his cry for assistance went unheard, as there was no one nearby to hear his plea or to aid him in his moment of need. "Please God, don't take them too," he pleaded out loud.

Just then, something caught the corner of his eye, a light beneath the surface. Jai could not make out the source of the light, but if there was any chance that it was his sister or grandmother, he knew he had to take it.

Without a further thought, Jai too kicked of his slippers and leapt forward into the water, towards the source of the light and like his sister before him, he too was swallowed by the darkness below.

Chapter 3

The shock of the cold water seemed to electrify every cell in his body. Jai opened his eyes in a desperate bid to find any sign of the light that drew him into the water. But there was nothing to be seen. With his sight failing him in the chilling darkness of the Sutlej, Jai's survival instinct to draw breath forced him to the surface. Gasping for air, the young Sikh realised that his search for his sister and Dhaddhi was futile in the darkness. The light that he had chased was now nowhere to be found and the first light of day was still over an hour away.

Jai tried his best to tread water as the current pulled him along. He could feel that he was floating further away from the pier with every second that passed by. "Ru! Dhaddhi!" he shouted once again, but there was no one to answer him back. Using his powerful arms, the young man swam forward with only the light from the moon to guide him towards the banks of the river.

As he floated towards the edge of the muddy river, the water became shallower, and Jai felt the reassurance of some loose earth beneath his feet. He stumbled his way through the reeds and surrounding foliage, dragging himself up the steep bank until finally, he reached dry land.

Tired and soaked from his head to his toes, Jai once again reached into to his pajama pocket for his phone, but this time it was nowhere to be found. The realisation that he must have dropped it in the river behind him quickly sunk in. "FUCK!" he yelled out in frustration. "Dhaddhi Ji! Ru! Can anyone hear me!?" he said as loud as he could. Only the silence of the night and the sound of rushing water answered him back.

Jai grasped his head in his hands. "Think god damn it, think!" he said to himself, trying to hold back his tears. Jai began to realise that not only did he not know where his sister or grandmother was, he also did not know where he was either. As he squinted into the darkness surrounding him, Jai padded down his other pockets for anything else that could help him.

All that remained was a soggy tissue and a stick of chewing gum. His wallet and keys were back at the house along with everything else. It hadn't occurred to him that he would need anything other than his phone. Other than the clothes on his back and Miri strapped across his torso, Jai had nothing and was alone.

The sound of his father's voice began to echo in his mind as panic began to take a hold of him. The words he had heard every day for the last ten years began to repeat themselves over and over again in his head. 'Look after your sister and mother son, they are your responsibility now...' Jai tried his best to banish the distant memory of his father, bleeding out on the tarmac in the middle of the street. But the harder he tried, the stronger the memory became.

He could sense every detail of it now. From the cold wind, to the way in which the droplets of rain mixed with the ruby-coloured blood spilling out from his dad. Jai remembered the warmth of his fathers' blood as it seeped through his fingers. No matter how hard he pressed, it just continued to flow from his father's open head wound. One moment, they had been crossing the street and the next, he was cradling his father's head in his arms.

With one involuntary action, Jai had learnt the hard way, that flesh and bone were no match for steel and glass racing down the street. What should have been a normal journey home from the gym with his father, had turned into the worst day of his life, until now.

Jai forced himself back to the here and now. Once more, he looked out across the river in a desperate attempt to find any sign of life. Jai realised that with every second that passed, it was less likely that his sister and grandmother would be able to survive in the strong currents of the Sutlej. He needed to get help because searching alone in the dark was futile.

Turning around to face the dark fields behind him, Jai looked for any signs of a path that could lead him back to the village. Far into the distance just above the horizon, a faint amber glow lit up the sky above. 'That light must be coming from the village,' Jai thought to himself. Without a clear path forward, Jai stumbled into the fields before him and once again disappeared into the darkness.

With only the faint glow of a distant light to guide him, Jai ploughed through the curtain of maize before him until finally, a clearing opened up. A feeling of relief washed over him as he recognised a row of great banyan trees that his sister and he used to play by as children. It was the forest.

"Ruhi," Jai said out loud. The idea of never seeing his little sister again sent a pain into his chest. Just the thought of losing her made it hard for him to breath. With no more time to lose, Jai sprinted through the trees and towards his Dhaddhi Ji's village.

As Jai cleared the tree line, the first light of a new day began to creep across the yellow and pink sky. That is when Jai's eyes fell upon the village. As he stared down from upon the hill at the collection of buildings nestled closely together, Jai could instantly see something was very wrong.

What had once been a soft guiding light, now fiercely illuminated the sky above. A raging beast of fire and wind was devouring the entire village before him. Multiple fires were consuming every building in sight, sending thick plumes of black smoke high up into the skies above.

Jai could not comprehend what he was seeing. "Holy shit bags!" Jai blurted out loud, before he sprinted down the road towards the village. Jai could just about make out the outline of what remained of his ancestral home. It burned bright in the early morning sky and radiated a heat that made looking at it directly, difficult to sustain.

As the smell of burning materials polluted the air around him, Jai began to cough. The thick black smoke threatened to fill his lungs. He backed away and squinted for any sign of life around him, but it was difficult to see anything through the smoke. With his Keski still dripping wet from the river, Jai removed it from his head and tied it around his mouth and nose to protect himself from the smoke.

He turned to the centre of the village and looked for any kind of a path forward. But as the direction of the smoke moved with the wind, the carnage became clearer. The floor was littered with the charred remains of the villagers and their livestock.

All that they were and everything that they had owned was turning to ash before him. It was unlike anything he had ever witnessed before in his twenty-four short years. The smell of charred corpses seeped through his Keski and filled his nostrils, making his stomach churn. The sensory overload was too much for his mind and body to assimilate. Only moments before, he had lost all trace of his sister and Dhaddhi Ji and now his ancestral village was burning to ash before his very eyes.

Fighting to process the images around him, Jai struggled to breathe. Between the burning village, inhaling smoke and the shock of losing his family, Jai began to hyperventilate. It was a sensation that he had never experienced before. Unable to take in any deep breaths with the Keski covering his face, Jai desperately pulled it down and instinctively ran away, towards the fields outside the village.

As soon as he cleared the outer perimeter wall, Jai dropped to his knees and forcefully coughed in an attempt to fill his lungs with fresh air. With each gasp, the world around him began to swirl in a circle. Images from the last few minutes rushed through his mind like a nightmare. Unable to sustain a clear thought, Jai's eyes rolled back and he fell forward into the grass, losing all consciousness.

Deep within the darkness, Jai saw his Dhaddhi Ji. She was alone and walking into the entrance of her farmhouse. Before she crossed the threshold, Kuldeep turned around and looked straight at him, before being swallowed by flames coming from the room behind her. Everything around him now was beginning to burn. The inferno engulfed the farmhouse and all the interconnected buildings.

Waves of fire now washed over the floor towards Jai, but then a girl's scream filled the air, "Jai! Don't leave me! Jai!" Jai felt a stinging sensation in his arm. The pain pulled him away from the heat and a bright new light began to sting his eyes. As his sight slowly began to return, a voice echoed throughout his ears. "Jai! Wake up!" A young woman knelt over him and prodded his arm in an attempt to wake him up.

"Ow! I'm awake!" he said, in an instinctive annoyance. Suddenly the reality of his situation came flooding back to him and Jai sat up abruptly. The sunlight shone bright and stung his eyes. It took him a moment before he recognised the face of his beautiful younger sister. "Ru!" He said, grabbing her by the arms and hugging her tight. "I thought you were dead!"

"Relax, relax! I'm ok," she said, struggling not to be squished by his hug.

Still holding her by the arms, Jai continued in relief. "I had this crazy dream. I thought I had lost you and Dhaddhi Ji." Realising he hadn't seen his grandmother yet, Jai let go of his sister and looked behind her. "Wait, where is she? Is she with you?"

Jai looked at his sister properly for the first time. Her hair and clothes were still wet from the river. Ruhi looked at her brother straight in the eyes. "It wasn't a dream Jai. She's… gone," whispered Ruhi, with a sadness in her voice.

"What?" he replied in confusion. "What do you mean gone?" But Jai already knew the answer to his question. Ruhi took a deep breath and recalled her experience.

"I saw just as much as you did. One minute she was talking to us on the pier and the next, she had fallen into the river." Ruhi explained calmly.

"She didn't fall Ru, she jumped." The idea that their Dhaddhi intentionally jumped into the river did not sit well with Ruhi.

"She wouldn't have done that Jai; it must have been an accident." Sensing that he was about to protest, she raised her hand in a gesture to stop him from interrupting her. "Either way, I couldn't find her. I tried. I looked everywhere." Ruhi's eyes narrowed as she thought back to her hopeless attempt of searching for her Dhaddhi Ji in the cold, dark currents of the river.

"Why didn't you answer me? Couldn't you hear me calling for you? I jumped in straight after you both and I couldn't see anything or find either one of you. What happened to you Ru?"

queried her brother, in an attempt to make any kind of sense of what had happened to them.

"I don't know. The moment I went under, I couldn't see anything. The water was freezing. I tried my best to resurface but the next thing I remember… I was waking up on the banks of the river and it was daylight. It was as if nothing had happened. I tried looking for you both back at the pier, but it wasn't there Jai. It's as if it was never there. I looked up and down the banks as far as I could, but I couldn't find any sign of Dhaddhi Ji or you or anyone else. I figured you may have found her and brought her back to the village for help. Luckily, I found the path to the Banyan trees, but then I came upon… this."

Ruhi pointed over Jai's left shoulder to the wispy clouds of grey smoke that were still rising up into the air. "What the hell happened here Jai? Who did this? Are you hurt?" asked Ruhi with genuine concern, as she looked him up and down for any wounds.

Jai felt a quick wave of embarrassment as he realised that he must have passed out from inhaling the smoke. He didn't like to appear weak in front of anyone, even his sister. "I'm fine," he said dismissively. "I don't know what happened here anymore than you do." Jai looked away and then started to get up from the ground.

"What do mean? How did you end up here then?" Ruhi enquired, as she too stood up from kneeling down. Jai replayed the series of events in his mind and then explained to his sister how he had dived in after them, only to lose them both in the river. He also explained how he lost his phone and finally made his way back to the village, only to find it burning down to the ground.

"Did you see what caused the fire?" questioned Ruhi.

"I don't know Ru. But something isn't right here. There is no way something like this was an accident."

"Why? What makes you say that?" replied Ruhi. Jai looked past his sister and pointed into the distance. "Well, I'm pretty sure they weren't there before," he said sarcastically.

Ruhi's eyes followed the direction of Jai's finger to a row of wooden spikes that were poking out from the ground, near the entrance to the village. Each of the spikes had been hammered into the ground recently and carried a severed human head at its end.

Ruhi turned to her brother. "What the hell Jai? Who? What...? Dhaddhi Ji..." It only just occurred to them both that their grandmother could have been one of the heads on the spikes. Ruhi ran forward towards the ghastly new monument, followed closely by Jai. To their relief, they didn't recognise any of the heads on the spikes, but then neither of the siblings had ever seen a mutilated body before, let alone a severed head on a stick.

"Jai... we need to get away from here right now. We need to get help." She said, with as much calm as she muster in her voice.

"Ru, I know you are scared, but we need to check the rest of the village first. There might be survivors... *she* could even be over there," Jai said cautiously, referring to one of the many charred remains, scattered across the village floor.

Ruhi stared at her brother and knew he was right. She nodded in acceptance. The duo moved away from the morbid display and proceeded deeper into the ruins of the village. The air was thick with the stench of death and whispers of grey smoke still rose from the ashes.

Ruhi gasped when the full picture became clear to her. The entire village had been decimated. Not a single structure had remained standing. It was almost as if someone had tried to remove all evidence of its existence from the earth.

But had that been truly been the intention, the ground would not have been littered with the bodies of the dead. In every direction she looked, Ruhi saw the charred remains of the peaceful humans that had lived there only hours earlier.

It was now clear to both Ruhi and Jai, that this was no accident. These people had been butchered and burnt alive. Tears began to form in Ruhi's eyes, as the horror of the scene in front her began to sink into her heart.

"This can't be real," she whispered to herself. Jai stared at the ruins around him too and then looked at his sister's reaction. Sensing her distress, Jai led his sister away from the centre of town, towards the shell that had once been their grandparents' house.

Just outside the remains of the property, a pair of bodies lay huddled together. "Ru, look at their hands," Jai said, pointing to the corpses. From the position of their arms and legs, it was clear to see that the villagers had been bound by some kind of rope before being executed. "They didn't stand a chance," he added, as he struggled to come to terms with his new reality.

"Who could have done this? Why would anyone want to hurt these people?" Ruhi replied in distress, as she examined the remains of a man in closer detail. Jai did not answer as he continued to move throughout the rubble, lost in thought.

"Wait, something is wrong here. Something is missing," said her brother with a puzzled look upon his face.

"No shit bro, look around!" Ruhi replied shakenly.

"No," Jai replied in annoyance. "Where are the cars and bikes? Look around, there is nothing left. The AC units that Dhaddha Ji installed, the water tank? Everything is gone. That stuff wouldn't have just melted away without a trace." Ruhi didn't have a clue what her brother was trying to get at. All she could think about, was whether their Dhaddhi Ji was still alive or not.

"Ru... the stables," said Jai, as he pointed to an area adjacent to the house.

"What are you talking about Jai? Whoever did this probably robbed the place and took everything of value before burning the place down. So what?"

"No you Aloo (potato), you can't just take a whole building. Even if it had burnt down, we would be looking at ash and wood just like this place." Jai had a point. It was enough to divert Ruhi's attention away from the deceased and she too began to take in her surroundings in a different light.

Coming to think of it now, the whole layout of the village was not as she had remembered either. "What are you saying Jai, that this is not Tehara? That this place just kind of looks like Tehara?"

"I'm not saying that. This was clearly Dhaddha Ji's house, but something else here just doesn't make any sense Ru."

"None of this makes any sense Jai! All I know is that we have to find Dhaddhi Ji right now and we need to get some help." Jai knew his sister was right. They weren't going to get any answers from just standing around in the ruins. He could speculate all he wanted to, but the truth was, neither of them knew who had butchered these people or why. All he knew, is that it wasn't safe to stay there any longer. Ruhi was correct, they needed to get help.

"You're right sis, we can't stay here. But let's check the rest of them first. We need to know whether Dhaddhi Ji was here when this happened or not." Jai looked at his sister for any sign of resistance, but there were none.

He continued… "We'll stick together. We need to salvage anything we can. Keep an eye out for clean water and anything else you think we can use." Jai looked down at his feet. "And some shoes would be great too," he added, trying to force a smile.

Ruhi looked down at her bare feet too. "Without a car, we'll have to walk to the nearest town, right?" she asked her brother.

Jai nodded. "I reckon Sidhwan-Bet is about five miles west of here. Going by foot, that's probably an hour and a half at the least and that's if we don't stop."

The siblings shared a look. Neither of them looked forward to the prospect of walking down the road to Sidhwan barefoot, especially in the searing heat.

It did not take long for the siblings to work their way through the village debris. It seemed as if everything of value had been taken. The only evidence that there had once been a thriving community there, was now in the form of eighteen charred remains.

The low number of villagers also concerned them both. "Eighteen people and no women or kids? Whoever took them may have taken Dhaddhi Ji too..." Ruhi reasoned out loud. She wasn't really expecting an answer from Jai, but he replied anyway.

"I don't know Ru, I'm just glad we didn't find Dhaddhi Ji in this pile," he said, pointing to one of the corpses. The fact that they hadn't been able to salvage any clean water, food or any other resource was of far more concern to Jai.

Worse still, upon closer examination of the dead, it was clear to Jai that all of them had either been stabbed or bludgeoned to death before being burnt. This was not a fact he wanted to share with his sister, but from the expression on her face, she knew the truth. This was no simple robbery; it had been nothing short of a massacre.

Ruhi and Jai looked at each other with a fear and uncertainty in their eyes, but it was Ruhi who spoke first. "We need to leave now Jai. Once we get to Sidhwan, we can call the police and then call home and let Mum know what has happened. She'll be able to send us some help from Ludhiana or something…"

"Ok Ru, that sounds like a plan. Let's just keep our eyes peeled on the way. The people who did this are still out there. I know India isn't the safest of places at the best of times, but all of this shit, is on another level," said Jai, as he looked around at the remains of the village.

"I don't want us to take any unnecessary chances, ok?" Ruhi nodded in agreement and both she and her brother began their long journey westwards, towards the village of Sidhwan Bet.

Chapter 4

The scorching sun bared down bright across the summers sky and continued to bake the land below. Only the occasional gust of wind gave the siblings a brief respite from the relentless heat. The path to Sidhwan was no riverside walk. Whilst the neighboring town was only a relatively short distance away, neither Ruhi or Jai had been prepared to trek along a dusty trail in the baking Sun, without shoes or water.

"This trip is seriously beginning to suck," said Jai, trying to cheer up his little sister and lighten the mood.

"Oh really? What makes you say that?" she replied sarcastically.

"I could totally kill for some water right about now. And some shoes…or better still a car…with air conditioning and food. Oh I could murder a pizza right about now!" Jai said enthusiastically.

"Seriously!? How can you be thinking about food at a time like this?" Ruhi asked in bewilderment.

"How can you not? I haven't eaten anything since last night, and I am starving mate! The first thing I'm doing when we get to Sidhwan, is getting some bloody food." Jai looked over at the disapproving look on his sister's face. "*After* we call for help of course!" he added quickly. A small smile broke on Ruhi's face for the first time that day. No matter how she was feeling, she could always rely on her brother to cheer her up.

Just as she was about to reply, something caught her eye about a quarter of a mile directly ahead of them. For the last hour, they had passed nothing but fields of overgrown grass, muddy earth, and scatterings of trees. It was as if time had forgotten this area of Punjab completely.

"Jai, what is that?" asked Ruhi, pointing up ahead. A small group of shadows seemed to be moving very slowly towards them. It was difficult to make out their shape from the rising heat washing over the surface of the road.

Ruhi and Jai proceeded cautiously down their path, and everything became clearer to them as they moved closer to the objects. A herd of sheep wondered aimlessly across the empty dirt road before them. "Now *that* is bizarre. Well, I guess it would be if this wasn't bloody India or any other freaky day," Jai stated, annoyedly.

"Where do you think they came from?" asked Ruhi, but just as soon as she had asked the question, she received her answer. A few lambs trailed the pack from an overgrown path leading off from the main road.

The siblings followed the new path towards a single clay hut hidden amongst a collection of rosewood trees. If it had not been for the trailing lambs, the siblings would have never even noticed it. With its sand-coloured walls and wonky lines, the building looked as if it had been built by hand. There wasn't a single straight line visible on the entire structure.

Unfazed by its shabby appearance, Jai felt a sigh of relief at their first opportunity to get help. "Finally, a sign of life! Do you think anyone is home?" he said, turning to his sister who was looking slightly drained from the heat.

Ruhi shot Jai a disconcerted look. "I don't know. We should be careful though. You still have your Kirpan right?" she queried, as she reached down for her own weapon. Ruhi wrapped her fingers around Piri's cool jade hilt and a felt surge of reassurance. Jai nodded 'yes' as he looked down at his own unique weapon, nestled discreetly in its gatra.

"Relax, we'll check it out first. Just stay close," instructed her brother, as he led them carefully towards the haphazard structure.

Upon closer examination, it was clear that the cottage had seen better days. It had a shabby wooden door, hay thatched roof and no visible windows at the front. The whole building could not have been more than five meters wide. "I'm beginning to think we got our hopes up for nothing Jai, this place doesn't even look like it has electricity let alone a phone line," said Ruhi, as she tried to manage her disappointment.

Jai quickly glanced around for any sign of transportation that they could use, but he too was disheartened to find nothing of value amongst the overgrown trees and bushes that surrounded the hut.

"I don't remember us ever driving past this place before Jai. Maybe we should just carry on to Sidhwan?" whispered Ruhi quietly. Jai understood her skepticism. Nothing about the building was welcoming or showed any sign of life. And coming to think of it, he too could not remember ever passing a house like this before, even if it was a little hidden away from the main road.

As they slowly crept towards the structure, a new collection of sounds became apparent, including some raised voices, emanating from the rear of the property. Ruhi and Jai exchanged a look. There was only one way to find out who it was and where it was coming from.

Without speaking, Jai gestured them to head to the left side of the house. The side of the property had a window on it, but it was covered with a cloth making it impossible for them to see inside. Ruhi could hear a faint moan coming from inside the house but, Jai did not want to stop until they had reached the back of the hut.

As the siblings peered into the back garden, they were both astonished to find a large open field filled with an array of livestock. They were all sectioned off into their respective pens. There were goats and bulls and an empty pen with its gate wide open.

"I guess we know where the sheep came from," Jai whispered to his sister. Opposite the empty pen in the middle of the field, stood a tall wooden barn larger than the house itself. It too had its door open wide and it was clear that the voices they had heard were coming from within the rickety structure.

But before either of them could take it all in, a lean bearded man suddenly appeared in the doorway of the barn. From his leathery tanned skin to the worn sandals on his feet, it was clear that this was a person of modest means. His once white kurta pajama was stained with sweat and mud, and a mustard-coloured turban sat loosely upon his head.

Even from where the siblings were hiding, they could see that the young man was distressed. But just as quickly as he had appeared, the unknown stranger began walking briskly towards the main house, whilst struggling to balance a large terracotta pot in his arms.

Right behind him, another far shorter person emerged from the barn and began to run after the scruffy man in haste. It was a little girl of no more than six years in age. "Hurry Baani, get the door love!" yelled the man, as he struggled not to spill the contents of his pot.

The little girl sprinted past the man and pulled on the makeshift handle attached to the backdoor of the house. As soon as the door opened, a female voice could be heard from within. "Quickly!" she called out, before being silenced by the closing of the door, as both the man and girl entered and disappeared into the property.

Ruhi and Jai looked at each other, but it was Jai who spoke first. "Someone's in a rush. What do you reckon?"

"Well, they are the first people we've seen all day and by the looks of them, I don't think they are the blood thirsty killers who attacked Tehara. They obviously have their own issues, but maybe they could still help us..." reasoned Ruhi.

Jai considered his sister's logic and nodded in agreement. The siblings made their way back around to the front door and could now hear a muffled commotion coming from inside. "Are you sure about this?" questioned Jai, as they tried to listen to the raised voices from within.

"It's sounds like someone's in trouble Jai," and without waiting for his response, Ruhi knocked on the door.

The voices inside fell silent. Ruhi knocked once more, but this time more loudly. "Hello?" She called out. Footsteps moved their way towards the door followed by the sound of a latch unlocking. The door cracked open several inches to reveal the young girl from the garden, standing before them.

Her hair was split untidily into two ponytails on either side of her head, and she was dressed in a yellow and green Punjabi suit. By the look on her face, she was clearly upset. But before she could utter a word, a voice bellowed out from behind her. "Daai Ji! Hurry please, she's in here!"

The young girl opened the door wider, and the dimly lit room flooded with sunlight. The only other source of light came from a series of candles scattered around the room as the few windows there were, had been covered up with disheveled rags.

Ruhi and Jai entered the stuffy house, but they were not prepared for the scene that was unfolding before them. Laying on a wooden manji sahib in the far corner of the room was a heavily pregnant lady. She was covered in sweat and withering in pain.

Her husband tried his best to comfort her as he knelt by her side and attempted to feed her some water from the terracotta pot, he had just carried in. The only other person in the house was the little girl, who was stood quietly by the door with a look of fear upon her face. She was not used to seeing her mother in considerable pain.

"Who are you? Where is Daai Ji (the midwife)?" asked the man in frustration. From the look in his eyes, the husband was clearly overwhelmed by the situation before him.

"I'm sorry, I don't know who that is," replied Ruhi, before she turned to her brother.

"Jai, you have to help her. You've studied medicine, right?" she said, hoping to aid the expectant mother in any way that she could. Jai looked at the husband and wife before him and felt his level of anxiety rising again.

"Ru, I studied dentistry! I'm not a pediatrician or obstetrician or whatever. I haven't delivered a baby before, that's a completely different type of extraction!" he said, trying to disguise his discomfort.

"Jai!" Ruhi responded in annoyance. She was not in the mood for his silly humour.

"Ru, I know just as much about delivering babies as you do!" Jai said in his defence. "Besides, I don't think hubby here is going to appreciate me looking at his wife's under carriage. He doesn't exactly strike me as the progressive type," he added.

Ruhi took a deep breath. On one hand, she knew he was right and on the other, she knew she was not going to get anywhere further with her brother. Ruhi turned to the man and woman before her. "I can help," she said, whilst raising her hands as a symbol of reassurance.

The husband's stern expression softened as he looked to his wife for her approval. Whilst they were both surprised by the sibling's sudden appearance, the wife nodded to her husband, before groaning loudly in pain.

Ruhi addressed the husband first. "I'm going to need some clean blankets, some water and scissors." The husband stood up and hurried across the room towards a cabinet to retrieve the items Ruhi had requested, whilst Jai looked around the cabin for anything else that Ruhi might need.

It was sparse to say the least. In one corner of the room there were a few manji sahib's cluttered together and on the other side, there were several wooden stools, a table, and some makeshift cupboards. "I need some more light in here," instructed Ruhi, as she knelt beside the woman in pain.

"I'll open these windows," offered Jai.

Ruhi looked down at the woman laying beside her on the manji sahib. The lady's green suit was drenched in sweat, and she could see the pain in her eyes. The lady couldn't have been any older than Ruhi was. "Didi (sister) my name is Ruhi. What is your name?"

"Suhadna," came the reply through gritted teeth.

"Suhadna? That's a pretty name" replied Ruhi nervously. She glanced at her brother who was across the room struggling with the curtains. "Ok Suhadna, I'm going to have a look and see how far along you are." Suhadna nodded. She was exhausted and tried her best to reserve her energy.

"Guy's, where are my blankets?" called Ruhi out loud. Baani moved over to the terracotta pot that her father had brought in only minutes earlier and began to scoop out a bowl full of water. She presented it to Ruhi without a word and then sat down beside her. Suhadna's husband returned next with a few blankets and a pair of iron scissors and then handed them to Ruhi. Ruhi looked at the blades "Are these clean?"

"Yes," the husband replied.

"Thank you. But you guys need to go now. I need to check how far along she is."

Jai looked at the husband. "They'll be fine, my sister knows what she is doing," he said reassuringly. The husband looked at his wife and before he could speak, she told him it was ok. The nervous father and Jai made their way out of the back door and into the garden to wait.

As the door closed behind her, Ruhi whispered to herself. "Satnam Waheguru Ji," and she lifted the shawl that was covering Suhadna's lower body.

Suhadna was almost fully dilated and Ruhi could see the top of the baby's head. Ruhi took a second to compose herself. "Suhadna, I can see your baby. I'm going to need you to take some short breaths and the next time you feel the urge, I'm going to need you to push, ok?" Suhadna moaned in agony as another contraction began to torment her lower body in pain.

Ruhi quickly laid a blanket before the pregnant mother and instructed her to push. Within moments, the baby's head began to emerge from Suhadna's body. "Perfect, you're doing great!" Ruhi reassured her. "Just a few more pushes and we're there!"

A few agonising moments later, the rest of the baby emerged from its mother and for the first time in her entire life, Ruhi held a newborn child in her hands. She looked down at the goo covered child and examined every feature of his squished little face. "He is beautiful," she said, smiling down at the baby who then began to cry at being separated from its mother.

Ruhi placed the baby gently into his mother's arms and then proceeded to cut the umbilical cord. 'Binge watching Grey's Anatomy wasn't such a waste of time after all,' Ruhi thought to herself, as she wrapped up the placenta and cleaned her hands on a spare piece of cloth.

"Thank you Ruhi," muttered Suhadna as a tear fell upon her cheek. Suhadna was overjoyed and exhausted at same time. Holding her new baby in her arms, she turned to her daughter who had been standing beside them the whole time. "Meet your baby brother Baani." Baani cautiously stepped forward and looked at her new baby brother in awe, as he attempted to open his eyes for the first time.

"Thank you, Guru Ji," whispered Ruhi to herself, as she witnessed that beautiful moment. Suddenly aware of her surroundings, Ruhi stood up abruptly. "Um, I better go. I'll tell the guys the good news."

"It's ok, Baani can go," replied Suhadna, as she looked at her daughter who instantly understood her mother's instruction and bolted towards the back door without hesitation. Ruhi was impressed. "Wow, you have her well trained."

Suhadna smiled. "She knows her duties, as did I at that age."

The noise from the back door opening and slamming shut, caught the attention of Suhadna's husband and Jai who were sitting on a bench beside the entrance of the barn, deep in conversation. A jubilant Baani sprinted towards her father who had since stood up and had begun taking enormous strides across the garden to meet her halfway.

"Papa Ji, I have a new baby brother!" she yelled, as she leapt into her father's arms and hugged him tight. Her father was overjoyed and swung her in a circle before turning to his unexpected guest. "Come Jaikaar Singh, come meet my son with me!" he said joyously, as he carried his daughter back into their house.

Jai too rose up and joined his host in a rare moment of happiness, in what had otherwise been a nightmare of a day. As his eyes once again adjusted to the light, Jai walked straight over to his little sister. "Are you ok?" he asked with genuine concern.

Ruhi smiled at her brother's overprotectiveness. "He is a miracle Jai," whispered Ruhi, as she stared down at the newborn being cradled in his mother's arms.

Suhadna's husband walked over to his wife and picked up his son for the first time. After a few moments, the man looked up from his new offspring and spoke directly to Ruhi. "My wife and I are in your debt. How can we ever repay you?"

Ruhi glanced at her brother with embarrassment before answering. "You don't owe me anything Bhai Ji (brother). I'm sure my brother must have told you by now what brought us here. If we could just use your phone, we can call our Mum and maybe get some help from Sidhwan or somewhere else." Suhadna looked at her husband in confusion.

"Yeah, I hadn't got to that part yet," added Jai, who quickly updated his sister on what she had missed. "I was just telling Harjit here about how we lost Dhaddhi Ji by the river. But that's when Baani came out to tell us about the baby. They don't know about Tehara yet…"

"What about Tehara?" interrupted Harjit.

"I think we need to finish our talk bro. Maybe just not around her," Jai said, nodding to the six-year-old sat on the bed beside her mother. Harjit and Suhadna exchanged a worried look again.

"Come Pehn Ji (sister), Baani and I will help you get cleaned up while my brother talks to Bhai Ji. I could really do with washing my hands too," said Ruhi, as she looked around for any kind of a sink to clean the dried blood and goo from her hands.

Suhadna turned to her husband. "We'll be down by the river. I'll get washed up and prepare dinner when I get back." Without waiting for her husband's response Suhadna looked up at Ruhi and Jai. "Do not worry, it is not far. You can see the edge of the river from the barn in the yard and you two are staying for lunch. That is not a request," instructed Suhadna sternly. The siblings could tell she meant business and they were in no mood to argue with their unexpected hosts.

Feeling a little reassured, Ruhi helped Suhadna up from the manji sahib and accompanied her and the children to the riverside, leaving Harjit and Jai alone to talk outside.

"What do you mean the whole village is gone?" Harjit asked in disbelief.

"I know how it sounds, but I saw it burn with my own eyes. I was there..." Jai's voice trailed off as flashes of his grandparent's home burning and images of heads on spikes, haunted his thoughts. "My sister and I checked for any survivors, but there weren't any. At least half of them had been butchered and the rest were just missing." Jai's words sat heavy in the air as an emotionless Harjit stared off into the distance and processed Jai's words.

Jai continued... "Do you have any idea who could have done this?"

Harjit continued to stare forward. "I do not know. But I have heard stories." He looked at Jai. "Firstly, you have to understand, we are mostly alone out here. We only go into town once or twice a month to trade and to sell our goods. But a few weeks ago, some travelers from the villages up north came into Sidhwan, talking about how some groups of bandits had raided their villages and taken their women and children. Our Zamindar accused them of lying and exiled them from the town and we never saw them again."

"Zamindar? Who is that?" asked Jai.

"He is the chief of our town. He owns most of the land in Sidhwan and collects all the taxes for our province. If what you say about Tehara is true, then we are no longer safe here."

"Wait, if there are groups of people going around burning towns and villages and kidnapping people, shouldn't we just avoid towns and villages? Why not just call for help? I know you guys are pretty out of the way here, but you must have access to a phone or some other way of calling for help right?"

"What is this word… phone?" Harjit asked in confusion. "I do not know this word." Now it was Jai's time to be surprised.

"You're kidding right? How bloody remote are we? Ok, forget the phone. How do you communicate with the outside world?" Jai could feel his anger level starting to rise. 'Was Harjit just trying to wind him up? How could this guy not have heard of a phone? Fucking India man,' Jai thought to himself.

"There is a scribe in Sidhwan. He writes our letters, and a courier delivers them to other the villages." Harjit answered, as if stating the obvious. "Once the women are back, let us break bread and then we will load up the cart and leave for Sidhwan. Even with a loaded cart, we should arrive by the evening."

Whilst this wasn't the plan Jai had envisaged, it did make sense. There was strength travelling in numbers and Harjit's plan beat walking to Sidhwan barefoot in the baking heat. But one aspect of the plan still niggled at Jai.

"What makes you think you wouldn't be better off hiding here? Ruhi and I have no choice, we have to get help from Sidhwan. But you guys are out of the way here. If it hadn't been for some roaming sheep, we probably wouldn't have even spotted the trail leading up to this place."

Harjit seemed to be lost in thought. "My son Ajay, left for Sidhwan two days ago and should have returned yesterday with the Daai Ji and some supplies. I am now worried about him."

"You have another son?" Jai asked in surprise.

"Yes, Ajay. He has seen ten winters and is quickly becoming a man," said Harjit unable to hide the pride in his voice. Jai quickly did the math in his head. 'Harjit and Suhadna couldn't have been older than their mid-twenties, so she must have had Ajay when she was about fifteen years old. That meant Harjit fathered a child, as a child, with another child.' The realisation shocked Jai to his core. "Wait, how old are you?" he blurted out.

Harjit looked puzzled at Jai's reaction. "This will be my twenty sixth year, why do you ask?"

"You became a father when you were fifteen? When the hell did you get married?" Jai struggled to hide his shock and started to physically distance himself from Harjit who was almost amused at Jai's reaction.

"Suhadna and I were promised to each other from birth, and we were married when I became a man at the age of fourteen," said Harjit, as he reminisced with pride at his wedding day.

Jai struggled to process what he was hearing. "You guys got married when you were fourteen years old? What the hell bro? You guys were just kids! That is totally messed up."

"This has always been the way of our people. It was the same for me as it was for my father and his father before him." Harjit explained in a calm manner. "Is this not the custom in your village too brother Jaikaar?" asked Harjit, with genuine curiosity.

"No bro, where I am from, that shit is illegal. I must have been crazy to think it was illegal here too, but I guess I was wrong," said Jai, trying to rationalise his thoughts before his brain imploded in on itself.

"You do not have children of your own?" Harjit asked a bewildered Jai, who chuckled at his response.

"No bro, I'm only twenty-four. I only finished Uni a few months ago. Besides, you need a wifey to have kids and that is a long way off yet! Anyway, forget about me. We need to focus and get back on track. Let's start by prepping this cart of yours because from the sound of things, the sooner we leave here, the better."

"Agreed brother Jaikaar," responded Harjit, as he stood up and stretched.

"Just call me Jai bro, all my friends do." Harjit smirked at the odd behavior of his new acquaintance and led the way to the barn where the men began to load up the bullock cart.

Just as they had finished attaching the oxen, a refreshed Ruhi Kaur came walking towards them. She was holding Baani's hand followed closely by Suhadna and the baby. The ladies had finished freshening up by the river and it was not long before Harjit and Jai brought them up to speed on their plan to travel to Sidhwan together.

The new friends sat outside on the floor, under the shade of a makeshift tarp and dined upon a simple yet nutritious meal of brown dhal and rice. Ruhi and Jai felt lucky to have met some strangers willing to aide them in their quest for help.

Everyone was unusually quiet as they quickly finished their meals and made the final preparations for their departure. Harjit and Suhadna tried their best not to focus on their missing son. Once the children were ready, everyone boarded the bullock cart. Harjit and Jai sat up front nearest to the pair of white oxen that would take them to Sidhwan. Whilst the women and children nestled safely in the back on a bed of hay.

It wasn't the most comfortable of transportation, but it was far more efficient than walking. With their bellies full and an air of uncertainty around them, Ruhi and Jai departed for Sidhwan, accompanied by their newfound friends.

Ruhi wasn't sure if it was the rhythmic rocking of the cart or simply her blood going to digest her meal, but she felt very sleepy sitting in the back of the cart. Suhadna nursed her newborn child, whilst Baani slept on the floor in the space between them. "Any ideas on a name?" Ruhi asked, trying to stay awake and alert.

Suhadna smiled and looked up. "We haven't decided yet. Any suggestions?" Ruhi had never been asked for her opinion on naming a baby before. She felt honoured at the gesture.

"Well… I've always liked the name Veeraj. It was our father's name," replied Ruhi.

"A brave king?" interrupted Harjit from the front. "I like it! What say you my wife?" Harjit called out, over his shoulder.

Suhadna ignored her husband and shuffled closer to Ruhi. Would you like to hold our son, Veeraj Singh Khalsa?" she asked, as she passed the sleeping baby gently into Ruhi's arms. Ruhi examined every feature on his little face, from his tiny nose to his full head of black hair.

She couldn't help but feel a sense of love and protection over the child, yet it made no logical sense. She held no blood connection to the boy, yet his very existence seemed to weave its way into her heart. As did the sleeping child who lay beside her feet.

Ruhi looked down at Baani's arms wrapped around her leg for comfort, as Jai turned around and looked at his sister holding a baby. "If only Mum could see you now," he laughed, as the cart continued on to Sidhwan.

After an uneventful hour, Jai began to recognise certain parts of the landscape, but something wasn't quite right. It was only now

71

that they had begun to pass small houses and other buildings similar in shape and size to Harjit and Suhadna's home.

"Bro, are you sure we're on the road to Sidhwan? I don't remember seeing any of these building before and we haven't passed a single other person on this road yet. It's like we're living in the twilight zone or something," Jai said with concern.

His observations had caught Ruhi's attention who was playing a game with a recharged Baani. "I am sure brother Jai. Look over there," said Harjit, pointing at the fields to his left. In the distance, dozens of people could be seen working the fields. "The people are busy harvesting their crops. Only when the sun sets, will their work for the day be done," he added.

Jai was embarrassed to admit he knew nothing about farming, but he was relieved to see some normalcy again after everything they had just been through. "Once we clear that tree line on the hill ahead, the town of Sidhwan will await us," Harjit said with certainty.

Whilst the hillside did look familiar, the trees did not. Jai looked back at Ruhi with a look of concern upon his face that was starting to become all too familiar to her. This was the latest in a line of incidents that were not adding up. Jai did not need to speak for her to understand his worry, as it was a concern that she too was beginning to share.

As soon as the cart cleared the hill, the siblings cast their sight upon the town. The first thing they saw was a giant tree standing twice as tall as a house, deeply rooted by the entrance of the town.

It had the words, 'Jee Aiya Nu (welcome) to Sidhwan' painted upon its wide trunk in large white letters. But that is not what shocked the siblings the most. Sidhwan Bet looked nothing like what they had remembered.

The road ahead went straight through the centre of town where it divided dozens of wooden and clay buildings that sat upon each other, as if they had all been squished together. Dozens of different carts being pulled by oxen and cattle moved slowly up and down the muddy streets, whilst food vendors cooked all sorts of delicacies on their open fires. The townspeople were dressed in dirty white and grey clothes, and they hustled and bustled through what looked like organised chaos.

It looked more like a town from the wild west rather than one from the 21st century. There were no cars or bikes in sight. There were no electricity pylons or telephone poles or giant trademark Bollywood posters advertising the latest blockbuster, soda drink or skin lightening cream. This was a town unlike any the siblings had encountered before. "Stop the cart! Blurted out Jai, as he struggled to absorb the sights and smells that were assaulting his senses. Ruhi on the other hand was stunned into silence.

"What is the matter brother Jai?" asked a puzzled Harjit, as he and Suhadna looked at the shocked expressions on the sibling's faces. Harjit pulled on the reins gently and the oxen ground to a halt by the entrance of the village.

"What the hell is going on here? This is not Sidhwan Bet, this is the bloody dark ages!" exclaimed an erratic Jai.

Just then he felt a hand on his shoulder. "Jai…" Ruhi struggled to speak, she didn't have the words to process what she could see and hear. Whereas Jai had no shortage of words.

"Seriously guys, ha fucking ha, where are we really? Oh I get it, you guys are just messing with us…right?"

Harjit and Suhadna exchanged a worried look. "This is Sidhwan Bet, Bhai Ji," came the calming voice of Suhadna. Ruhi examined her face for any signs of deception or trickery, but there were none.

Ruhi tried her best to calm her racing mind and to remain rational. "How can this be Didi? This is not the Sidhwan we remember. Half the town is missing and what remains here, is nothing like what we had expected."

Suhadna did not know how to answer Ruhi's question. "This is how the town has always been," said Harjit, trying to aid his wife. Meanwhile Jai had begun to regain control over his thoughts.

"Ok, ok, ok. Let's just assume this is Sidhwan Bet for argument sakes. If the *what* and *where* aren't the problem, then it must be the *how* and *when…*" Even Ruhi looked puzzled at Jai's ramblings this time.

"What do you mean *when* Jai?" she asked, trying to hide her annoyance.

"What is the date? Today's date?" he asked, turning to both Harjit and Suhadna.

"It is halfway through the month of Bhadon," replied Harjit.

A puzzled and annoyed Jai turned to his sister. "Bhadon?" he asked impatiently.

"End of August, just like it was yesterday," she answered sarcastically, as he should have known that already.

"But *when*? What year is it?" he said out loud, staring at Harjit who answered just as quickly as Jai had asked the question.

"1753."

Chapter 5

The date '1753' seemed to echo in their ears. Ruhi could just feel that her brother was about to lose his shit, so she spoke first. "Yep, ok that makes sense," she said, shrugging her shoulders and looking at her brother who looked as if he were about to explode.

"1753?... 1753?... 17 mother-fucking 53!" Jai said, getting louder each time. Jai felt a crushing pain in his chest as he began to hyperventilate again. But this time he kept repeating the same word over and over again. "1753, 1753..." and that is when Ruhi slapped him hard across the face, in a sudden burst of violence that shocked them all.

Even Ruhi gasped at her own action as she immediately covered her mouth in shock. "I'm so sorry!" she blurted out quickly. But Jai did not react to her in the way she had expected. He immediately stopped talking and snapped back to the present. Holding his burning cheek, he looked at his sister with astonishment and then cracked a smile.

"Thank you. I think I needed that. But don't slap me no more woman!" he said, smiling at her.

Everyone felt an instant sigh of relief, but no one understood what was happening. Jai turned to Harjit and looked into his eyes. He sensed no deceit. Jai started talking again, but this time to everyone and in a controlled and calm manner as if he were just thinking out loud.

"Almost everything that has happened from the time we woke up by the river, until this moment has made no sense... until now. IF we are *truly* in 1753, then everything that has happened since the river, does make sense. Except for the *who*... and the *why*... and the *how*. Like who were the people who destroyed Tehara and why did they do it? Why are *we* here in 1753? And how are we here in 1753? And what the hell happened to Dhaddhi Ji? Is she here too? Is she a part of all of this?"

Jai looked at a blank Harjit and Suhadna who had no idea what Jai was rambling about. "How do we know any of this is even real? OW!" Jai yelled out in pain, as he quickly grabbed his arm.

After pinching her brother, Ruhi replied. "It looks real enough to me."

Before her brother could reply Ruhi cut him off. "Look it doesn't matter Jai. It doesn't matter *who* or *what* or *how*. It doesn't change anything right now, does it? Whatever the reason, we are here in this moment right now. Dhaddhi Ji is still missing and IF she is still out there, she needs our help. We owe it to her to find her Jai."

"Ru, we *both* looked everywhere that we could, and we saw no trace of her. If we have no idea how we even got here, how do we know that she is here too? In order to help her, we need to get help ourselves first. If all of this is not some kind of crazy collective pipe dream, then we need to find a way of getting back home."

Harjit interrupted Jai's flow. "Brother Jai, I do not understand your situation, but we cannot stay here in the middle of the road. Nightfall is only a few hours away and we really must look for our son. You both clearly have some issues, and we are happy to aid you in any way that we can, but Suhadna and Veeraj also need to be seen by the Daai Ji and then we must find Ajay."

Ruhi and Jai looked at one another and agreed to put their conversation on hold as neither of them had any tangible answers to any of Jai's questions or any ideas on what to do next. The least that they could do was to help Harjit and Suhadna find their son, whilst they worked on a way of getting back home and back to their time.

With a temporary truce in place, Jai turned to Harjit. "Don't worry, we'll help you find your boy. It is the least we can do for your hospitality and for the lift into town. Even if it wasn't quite the town that we expected!"

"Thank you both," chimed Harjit and Suhadna, as the group proceeded into the centre of town. This version of Sidhwan was unlike anything the siblings could have imagined. There were a multitude of sights, smells and sounds surrounding them. From the shop merchants selling everything from spices and clothes to the vailed ladies drawing buckets of water from the well, it was truly a sight to behold.

Even though they were both still adjusting to their new reality, the siblings couldn't help but be mesmerised by the commotion around them. Smaller roads and pathways interconnected to and from the main road and snaked away around corners and bends, becoming almost indistinguishable from the chaos around them. 'It was like being on a surreal history trip,' Ruhi thought to herself.

The bullock cart ground to a halt outside an ancient looking building that was being held up by a series of tall wooden beams and large clay bricks. If it hadn't been for a red tarp hanging over the entrance, Ruhi and Jai would have never even given the place a second look.

Harjit turned to the others and spoke in a hushed voice so that only they could hear him. "This is the Daai Ji's house. Hopefully, she will have some news about Ajay. Suhadna and I will speak to her whilst she examines Veeraj." Harjit looked up, as the background noise around them seemed to fade. He sensed an air of unease as he felt the gaze of wondering eyes upon them. "I think it is best that you both come too, but it is up to you," he added.

Ruhi and Jai exchanged a look. Their appearance seemed to have drawn some attention and neither of them were comfortable being left alone in a strange town, especially one from the past. "We'll come too," Ruhi added quickly, whilst Jai nodded in agreement.

"Excellent. Let's go," instructed Harjit, as the group descended from the cart and made their way towards the entrance of the Daai Ji's home.

Harjit led the way and walked through an open door which turned out to be a walkway that led towards a small courtyard. As the group filed into the open space one by one, they came across an elderly lady with her back turned towards them. She seemed to be lost in concentration, whilst hovering over a cooking pot and stirring in some herbs and spices.

Behind her, in the centre of the yard, was a garden patch filled with flowers and plants of all different shapes and sizes. The fragrance from her cooking and the greenery was almost as calming as it was alluring. "Daai Ji?" Suhadna called out.

The elderly lady was startled and almost dropped her wooden spoon into her cooking pot completely. As she turned around, Daai Ji instantly recognised the Khalsa family. "Suhadna Beti?" A look of surprise overcame Daai Ji's face as she glanced down at the baby in Suhadna's arms. "What are you doing here? The baby has come already?" Daai Ji asked, with a mix of surprise and joy. Ruhi instantly took a liking to the woman. She had kind eyes and a wrinkled nose and seemed to be a woman who spoke her mind.

"Mubarak ho! (congratulations)" Daai Ji said with excitement, as she rushed towards Suhadna and the others. Without asking permission, she lifted the baby out of Suhadna's arms and examined him closely in the light. Veeraj began to stir at being separated from his mother. "Don't worry little one, you will soon be back with your mother," she whispered to the newborn as if he understood her every word.

Daai Ji took Veeraj to a small manji sahib nearby and lay him down whilst she examined his body. "Who delivered this child?" she asked, without looking up. Unsure whether to answer, Ruhi looked at Suhadna who answered for her.

"This is Ruhi Kaur, Daai Ji. God sent her to us just when needed her."

"Allah be praised! It is a good clean cut." Daai Ji replied, as she examined Veeraj's belly button. "He will need Keshya oil mixed with turmeric for his navel and Bala oil for the rest of his body. Come, you are next," she instructed Suhadna, without looking up. "The rest of you can wait in my room," Daai Ji commanded, as she stood up and went to retrieve the necessary oils from a shelf.

Harjit was used to her sharp manner and did not take offence. "Daai Ji, Ajay was sent to retrieve you two days ago, but he did not return home. Did he come to see you? Do you know where he is?" Harjit asked respectfully, whilst trying to disguise the worry in his voice.

Daai Ji was now in the middle of crushing turmeric into a bowl when she glanced up at Harjit for the first time. "Your boy has not been to my door since the splinter in his foot from the last harvest." Daai Ji continued to prepare the oil and focused once again on Suhadna. "I must attend to your wife now. We can discuss your other concerns once we are done. Go now," ordered

Daai Ji, as she walked back to Veeraj and applied the new lotion onto the sleeping baby.

Suhadna shot Harjit a look, willing him to comply with the Daai Ji's orders. But Harjit already knew better than to argue with the lady who had delivered him. He looked over to Ruhi and Jai. "Come, I will show you the way," he said dejectedly, as he led them and Baani to an adjacent room which was clearly the Daai Ji's living quarters.

It was a small room with no windows and very little in terms of furniture. There were two manji sahib's and a small chest where Daai Ji kept her ointments and a few grooming pieces. Ruhi also noticed a quaint little shelf for what looked like her prayer books.

After Daai Ji had finished treating Veeraj and Suhadna, she called Harjit and the others back into the yard, where they sat around her garden bed and drank the cardamom tea that she had prepared for them. Whilst their introduction had been a little uncomfortable, Ruhi and Jai felt relaxed whilst drinking the chai. It was almost as if they were back with their own Dhaddhi Ji. "Do you have any idea what could have happened to him?" Suhadna asked Daai Ji with concern.

Jai noticed that Daai Ji was avoiding direct eye contact with both Harjit and Suhadna. It was as if she were looking just past them. It was bizarre enough for him to notice, but not enough for him to say anything, especially as he was a guest in her house. "No," replied Daai Ji, as if she did not wish to discuss the topic of Ajay.

"In fact, you should all go now before it gets dark," she added. Harjit and Suhadna exchanged a look of concern, as even they had noticed Daai Ji was acting rather hastily, even more so than normal.

But Harjit was undeterred. "Please Daai Ji, we have come far and we..."

"You must discuss the matter with the Zamindar! If anyone knows where your son is, it will be him. Now go, I have other business to attend," said Daai Ji abruptly, cutting him off. She stood up and motioned them to leave. Harjit looked away from the old woman with disappointment and signalled to the others that it was time to go.

But before they exited the courtyard, Harjit turned back once more. "What do we owe you for the treatment?" he asked, slowly reaching into his pocket.

"Nothing." Came the abrupt response, as she once again turned her back to them and begun stirring her cooking pot. "Now go, alavida (goodbye)," Daai Ji ordered, without looking back.

Suhadna led the group back towards the cart. Once everyone was onboard, Suhadna was the first to break the silence. "Something is wrong." The others nodded in quiet agreement.

"She definitely wanted you guys out of there. I say she's hiding something," said Jai.

"Well, what do you suggest? That they go back in and interrogate an old lady?" Ruhi asked sarcastically.

"No, I'm just saying, something was off about that woman, and I just met her," replied Jai.

"We have known Daai Ji all of our lives" added Harjit. "She has probably delivered half of the people living in this town. If she wanted to harm any of us, she would not have treated Suhadna and Veeraj," he reasoned.

"I agree, I don't think she would ever hurt any of us, especially Ajay," said Suhadna supporting her husband.

"So what next? Where does that leave us?" asked Jai.

"We go talk to the Zamindar" responded Harjit, as he shot a brief look of concern over to his wife.

"Wait, what was that?" Ruhi caught their interaction. "What was that look?" she repeated, pressuring them both for an answer.

"The Zamindar is not a good man," Suhadna explained diplomatically.

"The guy is a bastard," Harjit added bluntly. "He owns half of the damn town, and he struts around the place like he is some kind of god king. The reality is, that he is bleeding us all dry. He has risen taxes to over sixty percent this year alone. And if anyone complains, he takes their land and leaves them to starve. We have barely held on. Another year of this and we…" Harjit stopped himself from finishing his last sentence. The truth is that he didn't know what would happen to any of them if their taxes rose again. He was scared, but this was the first time he realised just how much the last few years had affected him and his family.

"Don't worry, we've got your back," said Jai, trying to inspire some confidence in his companions. "We said we would help you find Ajay and we will. If this Zamindar guy is the person to see, then what are we waiting for? Where does this guy live?" asked Jai.

A skeptical Harjit looked over to his wife for reassurance, who then nodded in agreement. Harjit faced forward and pointed at a large haveli that towered above all the other buildings in the town. "Over there," he said, as they all looked up at the impressive stature of a mansion, sitting high upon a hill at the very end of the town. Without a further word, Harjit lifted the reins and drove the oxen forward, towards the imposing house on the hill.

The haveli had its own pathway that connected it directly into the center of town. As they passed the market stalls and headed up the hill, the oxen began to slow as the gradient of the land below their hoofs increased. With every step forward, the true size of the Zamindar's property became clearer.

Both Ruhi and Jai were taken back by the sheer size and scale of the building up close. It was at least two stories high and the intricate patterns and carvings in its stonework seemed hundreds of years old. The entire ground floor had large, beautiful archways with flowing curves and floral patterns interwoven into its design. Every part of the haveli looked as if it belonged to a local king rather than a local landowner.

Harjit drove the bullock cart up to the main entrance of the mighty building where they were greeted by two burly sentry guards. Both men held five-foot spears and were dressed in matching red and white pajama outfits. 'Whoever this guy is, he ain't taking no chances,' Jai said to himself.

Harjit addressed one of the guards. "We are here to meet Raichand Sahib. Tell him Harjit Singh Khalsa is here to see him and hurry up, it is important," instructed Harjit, in a commanding voice.

At first the guards did not react, they simply stared at everyone in the cart almost as if they were counting the occupants. The guard on the left stepped forward first and then called out to behind him for the housekeeper. "Kaka! Visitors for the Sahib Ji!" he yelled.

Within a minute a small yet tidy bald man, dressed in a simple white shirt and matching dhoti (loincloth), approached the large open entrance of the property, and greeted Harjit.

"Pranam Khalsa Ji, how may I assist you?" asked the housekeeper respectfully. Harjit sighed at having to repeat himself but kept his manner and tone in control.

"Call your master Kaka. I need to speak to Raichand Sahib."

Kaka did not take any time to process Harjit's response and immediately responded. "Sahib Ji is busy right now, perhaps I can be of assistance?" offered the housekeeper with a hint of insincerity.

Harjit was not deterred by his response. "You are correct, you can help. You can go get Raichand down here right now," said Harjit in a stern, no nonsense tone.

Kaka was about to spout another lie when a voice from within the property called out from behind them. "Harjit Singh Khalsa? Come in son! Welcome to my home!" came the loud and joyful voice of a happy and elderly gentleman. Everyone looked around and turned their attention to the master of the house.

A man of short stature adorned in gold jewelry and with a black ponytail, shaved head, and a peppered moustache, stood in the centre of his extravagant courtyard. He struck Ruhi and Jai as an odd-looking sort of fellow. His peculiar look was exaggerated by the brightness of his gold and blue jacket and the matching dhoti that he wore.

Raichand Das Kumar held his arms wide open as walked over to his guest standing in the entrance of his mansion. "Welcome betah," said Raichand, as he walked up to Harjit and embraced him like a son. Harjit awkwardly allowed the hug and then turned to face the cart and nodded to his wife.

That was the sign that it was ok to get down. As Suhadna stood up, she signalled to Ruhi and Jai to join her. Baani held onto Ruhi's hand tightly as they passed the guards, as neither Ruhi nor Baani liked the looks the guards were giving them.

"Suhadna beti, it great to see you again and you too little one," Raichand continued, as he looked down at Baani who became instantly uncomfortable and hid behind Ruhi's leg. Raichand then pretended to notice Ruhi and Jai for the first time and turned back towards Harjit. "And who are you friends? Family from Sirhind?" enquired Raichand playfully.

Harjit was skeptical of Raichand's sincerity and replied in a cautious and level tone. "Cousins from out of town. They have just come to see the new baby," he said, pointing to Veeraj who was nestled cosily in Suhadna's arms.

"Oh congratulations! Another boy! Jai ho Mata Parvathi! (Glory to the goddess of fertility) said Raichand, as he turned his attention to his housekeeper. "Go fetch us some matai (sweets), we must celebrate!"

Kaka scuttled off immediately as Raichand escorted his new guests through the walkway and into his large open courtyard. The walls and balconies were sculpted equally as beautiful inside, as they were out. In the traditional haveli layout, large open rooms surrounded a stone-coloured courtyard. It was decorated with fine wooden tables and chairs and a variety of furniture reserved only for the wealthy. "Please take a seat, Kaka will be along shortly," reassured Raichand.

In all his years, Harjit had never been treated with the level of hospitality that Raichand was now showing him, his family and new friends. Something was wrong, but he couldn't quite put his finger on it. Following his lead, Jai and the others copied Harjit and took their seats beside Raichand.

"Raichand Ji, thank you for having us in your home. We do not wish to inconvenience you, as we know you are a very busy man. But we are here looking for our son Ajay. Have you seen him?" asked Harjit earnestly.

"Ajay, the tall boy, right? I am afraid not," Raichand replied. "What makes you think that I would have seen him? If I remember correctly, your whole family hasn't been into town together since Lohri almost seven months ago, correct?"

Raichand's demeanor had shifted slightly. His jolly persona had suddenly been replaced by an inquisitive one. It was a change that had not gone unnoticed by his guests.

"Yes, that is correct, we have had a difficult year as you know," Harjit replied, cautious as to not give away anymore information than was entirely necessary. "We sent Ajay into town for some supplies two days ago, but he never came back. We just thought you might know what happened to him, as you know everyone in town," reasoned Harjit.

"Ah, if it were only that simple. I am sorry. I do not know where he is. But rest assured, my men will find your boy." Raichand turned to the table beside him and hit a metal gong with the steel rod that sat beside it. Within seconds, four guards entered the courtyard with their sheathed Talwar's tied to their waists. They promptly approached their master.

Raichand stood up and faced his men. In a complete contrast to his jolly disposition and tone from only moments earlier, Raichand lowered his voice and barked a command in a tone more akin to a master ordering his slaves. "Find the Khalsa boy. He has not been seen in two days. Start with the marketplace…" Raichand stopped mid-sentence and reverted back to a soft tone before addressing Harjit directly.

"What was your boy looking for in the market?" Harjit quickly glanced at his wife. Jai could tell that lying did not come as naturally to Harjit, as it did to Raichand.

"Clothes and supplies for the baby," Suhadna blurted out. Raichand acknowledged Suhadna's input by continuing to bark commands at his men. "And check in with Wariq Uddin, the dharjee. If the boy came in for clothes, he will have gone to the only tailor in town."

"Ji Sahib," came the instant reply from his guards in unison, who then immediately turned around and left the courtyard to undertake their master's commands.

"Thank you, Sahib Ji," came the voice of Suhadna, as Raichand returned to his seat.

"Please, the boy is like my own son," said Raichand smiling, as he reached down for a goblet of water sitting on the table beside him only to find it empty. Raichand could not hide his annoyance anymore. "Where is that damn…"

No sooner had he spoken those words, Kaka appeared with a tray full of cups, a copper jug full of water and some matai. The housekeeper immediately began to serve everyone refreshments, whilst Raichand observed his guests with a curious gaze.

"Where are my manners? Raichand began. "You all must all join me for dinner tonight." But before Harjit could object, Raichand raised his hand as to squash any objections they might have and then carried on talking. "You must all be tired from your travels. Speaking of... where exactly have you travelled from my boy? You moved closer to Tehara if I remember correctly?"

"No. My brother lives in Jagraon, so we moved closer to him. It is only few miles south of here," Harjit replied cautiously. Whilst Raichand seemed to accept his answer, Harjit wasn't sure whether his lie was good enough, so he quickly changed the topic.

"Raichand Ji, I appreciate you helping us out, but we really must head back into town before darkness falls. It has been a long day for us, and my wife needs to rest," said Harjit, as he forced a smile and stood up to leave.

"I am afraid that won't be possible," Raichand replied. Ruhi and Jai who had remained silent throughout the whole conversation began to brace themselves for whatever was about to come next. "The evening is already upon us, and your oxen are probably resting in my stables by now."

Harjit shot Raichand a look of concern. "Do not worry, I promise you they will be well catered for. They are being watered and fed as we speak." Raichand looked over to Kaka who confirmed this by nodding his head.

"It must have been a long journey for you all, and I can see by your faces that you are all exhausted. Please, do me the honour of staying here for the night. Consider my home as your own home for this evening. Kaka will show you to your rooms and then prepare dinner for us all. And if by morning, you are still in a rush, then you can leave at first light. No one will stop you. In the meantime, my men will keep searching the town for your boy.

There is nothing more to be gained by leaving now." Raichand had made a convincing argument and presented them with an option that made it almost impossible for them to turn down, without arousing further questions and suspicion.

Harjit sat back down and raised up his cup of water as if to make a speech. "In that case, we graciously accept. Thank you Raichand Ji." And with that he drank the cup of water in his hand and the others followed his lead.

"Excellent! Kaka will show you the way and I shall see you all at dinner within the hour. If you need anything, Kaka will be at your disposal. Now, you must excuse me as I have some business to attend to before dinner."

As Raichand stood to leave, everyone else also stood up as a sign of respect. But before he walked away, he turned and spoke directly to Ruhi and Jai. "It was nice to meet you both," and without waiting for a reply, Raichand left the yard. Baani was relieved that the strange man had gone and Veeraj had begun to stir. "It's time for his feed," Suhadna said to Harjit.

Kaka walked over to the Raichand's new guests, who had been left standing by their chairs and offered to show them to their rooms. As the group followed the housekeeper, Jai caught up to Harjit. "Are you sure about this? Can we really trust this guy?" he whispered quietly, as they headed towards a grand staircase in the middle of the courtyard.

"For now. We have no choice. Besides, it would be more dangerous to head into town after dark."

Jai looked back to make sure his sister was ok. Ruhi seemed to have made a new best friend. Baani stuck close to her as they made their way up the stairs to the first floor. Ruhi's eyes widened when she saw the full size of the passage before her. 'Wow, this place isn't so bad for the dark ages,' she thought to herself. The lengthy hallway followed the same rectangular pattern as downstairs and looped around the affluent courtyard below, completing one giant circuit.

On the left-hand side of the great walkway, were decorated walls and grand doorways leading into various chambers and on the right was a marble-like balcony that protected the upper occupants from falling twenty feet onto the hard stone floor below.

Kaka continued to lead them towards two empty guest chambers, situated at the end of the mansions west wing. Harjit and Suhadna took the lead and entered the first room. It was a surprisingly spacious area. Sitting in the centre of the room was a luxurious manji sahib big enough to accommodate four people. To Suhadna's relief, it also had clean sheets and soft looking pillows.

There was also a grand dresser filled with clean clothes and a wash basin in the left corner for freshening up. "We'll take this room. You boys can have next door," Suhadna told Harjit, as she laid Veeraj down on the bed and began to get ready to feed him.

"That is our cue to leave," Harjit said to Jai, as he began to exit the room.

Jai glanced at Ruhi. "Are you ok?" he began asking her. Ruhi had just finished examining the room. She walked over to her brother and pulled him aside.

"I've been thinking about what you said before. We really do need to talk about what's going on here and what we're going to do next. The implications of us being here in this time are completely crazy. If we are *truly* in 1753, then what we say and do here in this time, could alter the future forever. Do you have any idea what that could mean?"

Whilst Jai too had been pre-occupied with their time travel predicament, he didn't have any more answers for her now than he did a few hours ago. "Let's talk about this after dinner. We'll all feel better once we're fed and watered," he said, conscious of Suhadna who was waiting for him to leave.

"Ok bro," Ruhi agreed, "Just don't be late!" she teased, as she pushed him out the door and closed it behind him.

Jai found himself in the hallway facing a lingering Kaka who was stood quietly observing them all. "Over here," came Harjit's voice from the adjacent room. Jai walked past Kaka and entered the second guest room. It was almost identical in setup to the first room, except for a balcony that ran the entire length of the room.

"Nice!" Jai said out loud, as he peered over the balcony and observed the view of the gardens and forest outside. The sun was setting, and it illuminated the skyline in an array of yellows, pinks and blue. "Don't show my sister this or she'll kick us out just for the view," Jai joked to Harjit, who was busy trying to ignite the oil lamps beside the cabinet.

The housekeeper who had been stood by the door peered inside. "Dinner will be ready within the hour," he said, as he took his leave from the guests and closed the door on his way out.

"So now what?" Jai asked Harjit, who was now stood by the door listening for any unusual sounds. Satisfied that Kaka had left, he turned back to Jai. "Now we change and get ready for dinner." Harjit replied calmly, as he began to remove his dirty clothes.

"Bro, that Raichand is one shady fucker if I have ever seen one. Are we seriously having dinner with this guy?" Jai asked skeptically.

"I understand your concern brother Jai, but right now, we do not have a choice. Besides, if he had meant to harm us, we would know by now," said Harjit, as he walked towards to the closet.

"How do you know that?" asked Jai.

"Because, we would be dead already," explained Harjit. Whether Jai liked it or not, Harjit made a good point. Jai looked at the bed and fought the urge to just crawl up into a ball and sleep away his new nightmare. "Here, I think you could use these," said Harjit, as he passed Jai a clean white kurta pajama set with leather sandals.

After Harjit and Jai had washed up and changed into some fresh clothes, they went to check on the ladies next door. Harjit went first and gently knocked on the wooden door. After a few seconds, a refreshed looking Ruhi Kaur greeted them. She too had changed her suit and was now dressed in a dark purple suit with a green chunni that almost matched the hilt of her concealed Kirpan, Piri. She had also used to opportunity to tie her hair back into a neat plat, as to mimic the fashion of the time. Ruhi did not want to stick out in the past anymore than she had too.

"You guys are looking well," said Ruhi, as she let them into the room. Veeraj lay asleep peacefully on the bed, whilst Suhadna plated Baani's hair in the same style as Ruhi's.

"Are you ladies almost ready to head down?" asked Jai, who was now eager to eat once again.

"We just need a few more minutes," said Suhadna as she finished Baani's hair. "I forgot our ointments in the cart. Would you mind getting them for me?" Suhadna asked her husband.

"Sure. Brother Jai and I will be back in a few minutes. Baani, do you want to come with Papa Ji?" asked Harjit with a smile upon his face.

Baani chuckled and nodded a 'no'. She then pointed to Ruhi. "You want to stay with Didi?" he asked his daughter, who had suddenly become shyer than normal. She nodded 'yes' this time. Harjit looked at Ruhi.

"It looks like you have a new best friend. Do not worry, we will not be long," he said, as they exited the room and closed the door behind them.

Harjit and Jai made their way down Raichand's grand staircase. As they reached the empty courtyard below, they both looked around for a path to the stables outside. Jai couldn't help but wonder why one guy needed such a big house. 'Doesn't he have any family?' Jai asked himself.

Whatever the reason, something about their whole situation made Jai feel uneasy. "Which way?" he asked Harjit quietly. But Harjit kept wandering around as if he was lost deep in thought. "Hey!" Jai said louder, hoping not to attract too much attention.

Harjit woke from his trance like thought process. "Sorry, I was just thinking about Ajay and how none of this makes any sense."

"Welcome to my day," replied Jai sarcastically. Just then a door opened and closed behind them. The duo turned around to find Kaka standing behind them.

"Can I help you Khalsa Ji?" asked the housekeeper, without expressing any real emotion.

"Where are the stables? I need my things," Harjit replied. Kaka hesitated for the briefest of moments, but then agreed to lead them to the stables himself.

"Follow me."

The trio walked back through the main entrance of the haveli and outside into the dark and muggy evening air. Jai noticed that the guards who were posted at the entrance earlier, were no longer there. A series of oil lamps now lit up the path towards the east side of the property, where the stables were located.

As they got closer to their destination, a scruffy nokar (servant) came limping out of the dimly lit structure to greet them. "This is Ramlal. He is the stable master. He will retrieve whatever you need." Kaka then turned to Ramlal and spoke to him in a bitterly harsh tone. "Bring them whatever they need from their cart and escort them back to the house. And do it quickly, the Sahib Ji does not like to be kept waiting."

Having completed his objective, Kaka promptly left Harjit and Jai with the stable master and returned to the haveli. "Please Sir Ji, tell me what you need, and I will get it for you," requested a timid Ramlal.

"Take me to my cart. I will get my items myself," commanded Harjit. Ramlal considered protesting, but then backed down when he saw the intimidating expression on Harjit's face. Ramlal led them both inside without further protest, whereupon Harjit instantly recognised his cart, parked at the rear of the stables. The building was far larger on the inside than they had first thought. 'It was more like a warehouse than a stable,' Jai thought to himself.

All along the right-hand side of the building were giant pots large enough to hold ten men. All of them were neatly lined up against the wall. They seemed to be filled with an assortment of old furniture and clothes. It was a very unusual site to behold, even for Harjit. On the left-hand side of the stables were all the cattle and livestock that were being housed and fed for the night.

Harjit proceeded to his cart and began to rummage around his belongings, whilst Jai stood back and observed a nervous Ramlal. His shifty deposition caught Jai's attention and for the second time that day, Jai felt the presence of imminent danger. He wasn't sure if it was his lack of sleep or the extreme stress of having woken up over two hundred and seventy years in the past, but either way, something definitely had Jai feeling on edge.

He reached inside the pocket of his kurta top to feel the hilt of his Kirpan under his clothes. Every time he held Miri in his hand, Jai felt a sense of comfort and empowerment.

"Got it," came Harjit's voice, as he stood up on his cart and held up two vials of ointment in his hand. But just as he was looking at Jai, something caught his eye by the cattle enclosure. The expression on Harjit's face turned from happiness to concern within the blink of an eye.

Harjit jumped down from the cart and stormed over to the cattle pen. In that moment, Ramlal seemed to understand exactly where Harjit was headed and moved to intercept him. Ramlal was now stood between Harjit and the cattle.

"Move!" ordered Harjit, with a seriousness in his eyes that let Ramlal know he was not going to ask twice.

Ramlal started to panic. "Sahib Ji, only I am allowed to tend to the horses," he said, pressing his hands together as if to plead Harjit to stop.

But Harjit was unfazed by the stable master's request and instead ploughed straight through Ramlal, pushing him to the floor in one swift motion. Ramlal crumbled like a leaf and pleaded with Harjit to stop, as Jai stood by and watched the father enter the pen and call out to a ginger-coloured horse.

"Billo?" Harjit asked the horse gently, as if talking to a long-lost friend. The horse immediately recognised its owner and trotted over to Harjit, who instinctively began to stroke her mane.

It was clear to Jai that this was not just any random horse. It must have belonged to Harjit, which meant that it was probably the horse Ajay had ridden into town.

'But what was it doing here in Raichand's stables?' Jai feared he already knew the answer to that question. Harjit turned around and faced Jai, who could see the anguish and confusion on his face. Harjit then spoke one word, "Ajay."

Chapter 6

"Where is my son?" bellowed a furious Harjit, as he grabbed Ramlal by the scruff of his shirt and lifted him inches of the ground. Jai was taken back by Harjit's upper body strength, as Ramlal tried his best to wriggle free from the young father's grasp. But there was no breaking the iron grip on the stable master.

"Speak now! You will only get one chance." threatened Harjit, who was trying his very best to ignore his paternal instincts to tear Ramlal apart.

"I don't know, I swear! Please Sir Ji, let me go. I am just a simple servant, I do whatever they tell me to do," pleaded the stable master, as his body began to shake with fear.

"Not good enough! My horse didn't just magically appear here. What have they done with my boy?" yelled Harjit, as he slammed Ramlal's body into the floor. The small man took the brunt of the force on his back, but his head also flung backwards and struck the ground. Ramlal cried out in pain as he grasped the back of his head and began sobbing. "I don't know Sir Ji, I don't know," he whimpered.

Harjit looked down at the nokar and felt an uncontrollable rage rising up from within him. He looked around for anything he could use as a weapon and saw a metal pitchfork with a wooden handle, laying upon a bundle of hay. Harjit reached for the lethal weapon when Jai interrupted him.

"Bro! Footsteps… somebody is coming," he said, with a worried urgency in his voice. Harjit proceeded to grab the fork and then turned around to face the entrance of the stables. He was surprised to see Kaka standing before them, blocking the doorway.

But the housekeeper was not alone. He was accompanied by the two guards who had been stationed by the main entrance earlier. But this time, they had their spears lowered and were stood in an attack formation.

It was Kaka who spoke first. "Sahib Ji, requests that you *both* accompany us back to the courtyard…immediately." The housekeeper's curt voice grated on Harjit who was not in the best of moods. He glanced over to Jai who had slowly begun to reach down for his concealed Kirpan. Jai did not know what was going to happen next, but he could feel the adrenaline starting to course throughout his veins. The idea of being skewered like a kebab did not appeal to him at all.

Jai reached under his shirt and wrapped his fingers around the cool marble hilt of Miri. Instantly, he could feel his fear and anxiety being replaced with focus and calm. Jai looked at Harjit and gave him the tiniest of nods to show that he was as ready as he would ever be, for whatever came next.

"Where is Ajay!? What have you done with my son?" bellowed Harjit. But Kaka was not fazed by Harjit's anger. If anything, he just looked disappointed.

Kaka turned to the guards and issued a single command before taking a step back. "Take them," he ordered. Both guards immediately began walking forward at the same time. One headed directly towards Jai and the other straight for Harjit, whilst Kaka stood back to observe.

The first of the two lunged at Harjit with his spear and in a great feat of athleticism, Harjit side stepped the attack at the final moment and countered the lunge by thrusting his pitchfork directly into the chest and neck of the guard with one hand. The four pincers of the fork pierced the guard's skin like needles and stopped the charging guard dead in his tracks.

There was a mix of confusion and pain on the guard's face as he dropped his spear and fell to the floor. But Harjit did not have time to celebrate his victory as he looked over to his friend who was busy wrestling with the other attacker for his life.

Jai had drawn his blade and held Miri in his right hand. It was as if she had become an extension of his arm. But the charging guard held the advantage as the reach of his spear far exceeded that of the fourteen-inch blade. The attacking guard thrust his spear towards Jai's torso. Jai instinctively swung his Kirpan down, hard against the shaft of the incoming spear, deflecting it mere moments before it could pierce his skin.

Annoyed that he had missed his target, the guard closed the gap between them and once again thrust his weapon forward. This time, Jai was unable to parry the full force of the attack and the spear head cut across his right shoulder, slicing open his skin as it passed through the air.

The pain of the blade cutting into his flesh, felt like fire causing Jai to cry out in pain. Jai dropped Miri involuntarily and the Kirpan fell to the floor with a dull thud. He immediately reached down with his left hand to regain his weapon, but his opponent had sensed the opportunity.

The guard had regained his footing and prepared to deliver a killing blow when two metal pincers exited the front of his throat. The guard died even before his brain could process what had happened. Harjit's pitchfork had been thrust into the back of his neck and had severed his spine. As the second guard slumped to the ground, Harjit looked around for any other threats. Kaka was gone, but Ramlal was still cowering in the corner.

Harjit turned his attention to Jai. "Are you ok brother Jai?" Jai was oddly warmed by his new friend's concern. He looked down at his own shoulder and saw a two-inch gash. Whilst it burned, Jai had been incredibly lucky as it was only a flesh wound. He still had mobility in his arm which meant that it hadn't been deep enough to injure any muscle.

"It stings like hell, but I think I got lucky. Thank you for saving my ass bro," Jai said to Harjit with gratitude.

"This is not over yet. Kaka will be back here any moment now with more guards. We must get to the women and lea…" A distant cry cut Harjit off mid-sentence. Harjit paused and looked back at Jai who was now binding his wound with his ripped sleeve. The voice faded as it seemed to be muffled out by some louder shouting. Harjit ran to the entrance of the stables to investigate where the commotion was coming from.

Meanwhile, Jai picked up Miri and placed her back in her sheath. For a moment, he was grateful that his Dhaddhi Ji had forced him to take the weapon. But Jai needed to focus on the here and now. He turned his attention back to the matter at hand and walked over to Ramlal.

Taking some rope from the wall, Jai dragged Ramlal to the cattle gate and began tying him to it. He then yanked on a long scarf that had been wrapped around the nokar's neck and stared into his eyes. "Make a sound and you die. Try to escape and you die. Nod if you understand me," he warned the stable master. Ramlal looked at Jai in terror and nodded several times before Jai stuffed the scarf into his mouth.

"Brother Jai, come quick!" called Harjit, from the doorway. The urgency in his voice worried Jai.

Jai ran up to the doorway to join his new friend who instantly pulled him to the side, so that neither of them could be seen from the outside. Harjit pointed in the distance, but Jai did not need directions to see the crowd of riders, making their way up the hill towards the main entrance of the haveli.

All of them carried flaming torches and they seemed to be escorting a carriage of some sort. Even with the oil lamps illuminating the pathways, it was still difficult to make out how many there were or what they were doing out there. "Who the hell are they?" Jai asked Harjit skeptically. But before Jai could get an answer, another scream cut across the air followed by shouting, coming from within the haveli.

This time Harjit instantly recognised the voice of his wife and both men knew something was very wrong. "Suhadna!" cried out Harjit, as began to run towards the house. But before Harjit could sprint away, Jai pulled back on his arm.

"Wait!" he said urgently. "We'll never make it that way, not before those riders arrive. It's suicide!"

Harjit growled and gritted his teeth at Jai. "Let go!" he snapped. Although Harjit was strong, Jai was the stronger of the two. But he decided to let go of Harjit's arm.

"We'll go around the back," Jai replied sternly and undeterred. "Over the balcony remember!?" he said, trying his best to hide his annoyance. Without waiting for Harjit to comply, Jai turned towards a path that led to the back gardens and sprinted off, knowing full well that Harjit would follow him.

Jai kept looking up at the first floor from the outside, as he ran around to the side of the house. He was looking for any kind of leverage or entrance point into the building that would make their climb up quicker. Just as he turned the corner, he entered the garden and spotted some patterned grooves carved into the brickwork that they could use to climb up.

Jai leapt forward onto the wall like a panther climbing a tree and scaled the side of the building with ease. As he predicted, Harjit was right there behind him and had followed him every step of the way. Within a minute, both of them had climbed over the balcony and found themselves creeping into a dark and empty bedroom chamber.

Luckily, the room they had broken into was unoccupied. But unluckily for them, they had climbed up into the wrong side of the haveli. Their bedrooms were at the other end of the house in the west wing, which was at least a hundred and fifty feet away.

As Jai carefully opened the bedroom door to check whether their pathway was clear, Harjit pushed past him without a word and proceeded to sprint down the hallway without thinking. He had been overcome by a single purpose, to find his family. Whilst Jai too was concerned for his sister, he was also very conscious of running into a trap.

But it was too late for stealth now. Jai had no choice but to run out after Harjit at full speed. 'If they weren't going to be quiet, they could at least be quick,' Jai thought to himself, as his heart pounded in anticipation. Just as Harjit reached the halfway point, he came to an abrupt stop. It was the echo of his daughter crying and the sound of his wife pleading with the guards that had stopped Harjit dead in his tracks.

"Let us go!" came the distressed voice of Suhadna. Harjit glanced straight ahead, but their voices were not coming from in front of him, they were coming from the courtyard below. Jai caught up to his reckless new friend and instantly understood what had just happened. In a twisted turn of fate, Baani's crying and the commotion below had drowned out their footsteps, allowing Harjit and Jai's presence to go unnoticed.

Harjit and Jai exchanged a look of concern before they both cautiously peered through the columns of the first-floor balcony. But it was the top of the staircase on the opposite side of the corridor that caught their attention first.

They could see a trail of fresh blood leading all the way down from the top of the stairs to the very centre of the courtyard below, where Raichand was stood over the body of one of his dead guards.

Harjit was relieved to see that Suhadna was still alive. She had tears in her eyes and was sat mere metres away from Raichand, with Veeraj nestled safely in her arms. However, they were not alone. Two of Raichand's guards were stood on either side of her with their swords drawn. But from the direction they were looking, their attention was on something else.

Harjit and Jai followed their gaze towards Baani, who was crying hysterically over the body of another person laying still upon on the cold stone floor. Jai instantly recognised the body of his sister. Her eyes were closed, and a trail of blood trickled down her face from the top of her head.

Jai could feel his blood starting to pulsate throughout his entire body. Suddenly, his heart felt as if it were about to explode, and his brain screamed at him to make sense of the image he was seeing before his eyes. There was no pain, no anguish, just a pure rage filling every cell in his body. It was the closest Jai had come to feeling an out of body experience. "RUHI!" screamed an uncontrollable Jai, at the top of his lungs.

Everyone except for Baani, immediately looked up at the balcony above to see where the ungodly cry had come from. Adrenaline once again started to surge throughout Jai's body, but this time his legs gave way like jelly. Jai dropped to his knees like a stone plunging in water.

No sooner had he fallen, a single bullet smashed into the stone column mere inches away from where Jai's head had just been. A furious Raichand had taken the single shot on his tamanchah (defensive pistol) and missed. "They're upstairs you idiots! Get them!" barked Raichand to his remaining men, as he stormed over to Suhadna and grabbed her by her hair.

The two guards standing beside Suhadna scrambled for the staircase, whilst Raichand began to drag her away from the main sitting area. The guards hadn't even made it to the first step when Kaka re-entered the courtyard from the main entrance, followed by a contingency of heavily armed soldiers dressed in black armor and dark green helmets. The sound of their footsteps now echoed throughout the halls of the haveli.

Only then did Harjit begin to realise the true horror of their situation. They were completely outnumbered and would have no chance fighting against heavily armed soldiers and all of Raichand's guards. Whatever Raichand wanted with his family, it was not death as they would all be laying dead beside Ruhi by now.

Harjit looked at Jai who was numb with shock and shook him as hard as he could. "Jai! We must leave now!" yelled Harjit, as he struggled to get his dazed friend to react.

The house guards were now beginning to ascend the blood-soaked staircase and Harjit knew that they were running out of time. The new soldiers stopped before Raichand, who shoved Suhadna over to them. "Here, take this," he said, referring to Suhadna with disgust.

Raichand then directed the new soldiers towards Ruhi and Baani. "And them too," he ordered. "But be careful, that one is still alive. She has already killed one of my guards," echoed Raichand's voice from below.

The old man's words seeped up into Jai's brain. As he processed the words, 'Still alive,' it was as if his whole body had just been struck by lightning. Blood surged around his muscles and Jai shot up. "Oi, fuck face! Get away from my sister!" he yelled, in a blinding rage.

But it was to no avail. Raichand continued to yell at his guards, who were now halfway up the staircase. Luckily for Harjit and Jai, they were on the opposite side of the hallway giving them a valuable opportunity to escape.

Harjit knew their time had run out and that they had to leave now. Before he could turn away, he moved towards the balcony one more time for a glimpse of his baby girl. But to his dismay, he was too late.

The soldiers had already gotten to her and had begun to carry her away as more of their reinforcements entered the courtyard. "Papa Ji!" came the terrified scream of Baani as she was mishandled by a scary looking soldier. The pain of hearing his daughter's voice crying out in terror stabbed at Harjit, directly into his heart.

But he knew his only chance at seeing his loved ones again was to retreat now, before they all suffered the same fate. Harjit looked over to Jai who was still transfixed on Ruhi's motionless body. Jai was trying his best to repress his emotions and ignore the voice in his head that screamed at him not to leave his sister behind. But he too knew the truth of the situation and the conflict within him was paralysing him.

"Jai…" Harjit pleaded in desperation. But he didn't need to finish his sentence as Jai turned to him and nodded, causing a teardrop to fall down his cheek and disappear into his beard. "Go," said Jai, choking out the word, but he didn't need to explain to Harjit as Jai could see the same pain in his eyes.

The pair bolted back down the hallway from which they had come. As they barreled into a dark bedroom at the end of the corridor, Jai hastily closed the door behind them just as Raichand's men had reached the top of the stairs. The guards hadn't seen which direction they had run in, so they spread out and began to search each of the rooms for their prey.

"Quick, back over the balcony, we only have a minute before they get here," said Jai in panicked voice. But Harjit was already one step ahead of him. They both climbed over the ledge and began their descent as quickly as they could. With only a few feet between them and the ground, Raichand's men burst into the room above them and began tossing the furniture aside looking for the duo.

Harjit and Jai reached the ground undetected and then ducked behind a row of bushes for cover. "We can't stay here, we're too exposed," whispered Jai, as he tried his best to keep his body hidden from sight. However, the bushes only gave them partial shelter from discovery and the soldiers were bound to find them if they remained where they were.

"To the stables, it is our only chance," whispered Harjit in return, as he cautiously poked his head above the hedge and scouted the path ahead.

"No, they'll expect that, we need to make a run for the forest, they'll never find us in the dark," insisted Jai.

But Harjit did not like the idea of walking into a forest at night, especially with no light or protection. "It is too dangerous brother Jai, if we take the horses, we can…"

"Check the stables!" came a voice shouting in the distance. The patrolling guards were getting closer to Harjit and Jai's location. Harjit stopped protesting and conceded to Jai's suggestion.

"The forest it is," he said, as they crept forward and made a dash for the tree line.

The fleeing pair passed through what looked like a dark wall of shrubbery. "That's far enough, we don't want to go any deeper," warned Harjit, as Jai was about to press on ahead without any real sense of direction. The light from the moon barely penetrated the thick cover of the forest, leaving them surrounded by a blanket of darkness and strange sounds from a forest very much alive.

"We must stick to the edge of the forest. Our best chance is to take refuge in the village. If we stay here, we will not make it through the night," warned Harjit. But Jai did not need to be convinced. Walking through a creepy forest at night was not something he wanted to do either.

"Where do you think they will take them?" asked Jai.

Harjit tried his best not to replay what he had just seen. "Later brother Jai, for now, it is *we* who must survive. We will find them again, I swear it," answered Harjit, with a resolve that neither he nor Jai knew he had.

The pair stuck to the edge of the forest, never venturing in too deep or coming too far out. It was not long before they came upon the outskirts of the village once again.

But from the moment they exited the forest, they both knew something was wrong. "Where the hell is everyone? This place was packed like an hour ago" commented Jai, as he scoped out the village for any signs of life.

But the streets were now virtually empty. Thankfully, there were still a few signs of life. There were lights coming from the houses and the smell of dinners cooking on their stoves wafted through the air. But all the villagers had closed their shops and doors early, as if they had locked themselves away for the night.

"Is it normally this dead in the evenings?" Jai asked skeptically.

"No. This is not normal. We must proceed with caution," replied Harjit.

"Proceed where? Where the hell are we going?" asked Jai, whilst trying his best to control the loudness of his voice.

"Daai Ji. She will help us," came the calm and measured response from Harjit.

"Seriously!? She totally sold us the fuck out. No... Yes... actually, we do need to see that traitor. She needs to answer for herself now!" ranted Jai.

Harjit tried his best to placate his friend. "Calm yourself brother Jai. You are right, we do need answers and you also need someone to tend to that wound. She is our only hope... for now."

Jai was starting to get annoyed with how logical Harjit was being, but he knew that he made sense. "Fine! Let's go," he said sulkily, as they marched forward into the village and towards Daai Ji's residence on the main street.

Jai couldn't help but think how eerie the whole village felt since they were last there. Other than a random stray dog crossing the street in front of them, Harjit and Jai arrived at Daai Ji's house without incident.

Even her house looked different at night, everything seemed far more foreboding, Jai thought to himself. But his companion was far less distracted by the environment around them. Harjit knocked on the door cautiously and they both waited anxiously for a reply.

After what felt like an eternity, they heard footsteps slowly approaching the door from the inside. "What do you want?" came the muffled voice of Daai Ji.

Taking care not to speak too loudly, his friend replied. "It is Harjit." They heard the sound of a bolt sliding back and Daai Ji's door creaked open a few inches. She looked at the duo and was clearly afraid.

"Go away, you must leave now," she said trying to control the fear in her voice.

"Daai Ji, please. You must let us in, we have no where else to go," replied Harjit.

The midwife looked away from the young father and began to close the door. "I am sorry, I cannot help you," she said, as she closed the door and began sliding the bolt back into its place.

"They took Veeraj and the girls!" replied a desperate Harjit.

The noise stopped and Daai Ji reopened the door and quickly ushered the pair into her courtyard, before bolting the door again. "Into my room," she instructed the men, as her eyes caught sight of Jai's bloody shoulder.

"I will get you some ointment," she added, as both Harjit and Jai complied with Daai Ji's instructions and entered her living quarters for the second time that day.

"I still don't trust her," whispered Jai to Harjit, as they both sat on the spare manji sahib in Daai Ji's room. "I don't think we should leave her by herself," he added, as she reappeared in the doorway with a jug in one hand and a bowl in the other. It was not clear whether she had heard Jai or not, but regardless, she began to tend to his wound.

"Sit still," she instructed Jai, as she undid his bloody sleeve and began cleaning his cut with some water and a towel. Harjit stood up and began to pace up and down the room, whilst Jai winced in pain as she tended to his wound.

"Daai Ji, why would Raichand betray us like this? Why did he take my family?" asked Harjit.

Before she could respond, Jai looked into Daai Ji's eyes and spoke first. "Did you know? Did you know what would happen to us?" he asked with a cold and deadly stare. It was too much for Daai Ji to take and she broke eye contact with Jai and looked away. "Well!?" Jai said, raising his voice.

"Brother Jai…" Harjit began, before Jai cut him off again.

"She knows something bro! She knew it was a trap and she sent us there anyway," said Jai, pulling back his arm away from Daai Ji who was fighting the urge to cry.

"No," she protested, as she placed the cloth down and stood up in an attempt to leave. But Harjit blocked her path.

"Daai Ji, please," he pleaded in a gentle and soft tone. Harjit could sense that she was afraid, and he owed her a chance to explain her actions. She looked at Harjit and then back to Jai.

Daai Ji could no longer hold back her emotion. Tears began to fill her eyes as she spoke. "I didn't know he was going to take Suhadna and the children too, I promise! I didn't know they were going to take any of you," she sobbed.

"Liar! I don't believe you for a fucking second. You were the one who sent us there. You knew soldiers would be waiting for us!" snapped Jai angrily.

"No, no, no, I don't know why, I promise you both," protested Daai Ji, as she tried to wipe her running tears away with her white chunni.

Harjit raised his hand towards Jai as if to calm him down and to give Daai Ji a chance to speak. "Daai Ji. Soldiers have taken Suhadna. They have taken my baby girl and they have taken my sons. They have taken brother Jai's sister too. Tell us what you *do* know," instructed Harjit, in a calm yet stern voice. Daai Ji hands were shaking, and she nodded in silence.

"Come, sit down," said Harjit, as he too, sat back down beside Jai.

The midwife did as commanded and sat down upon her manji sahib. She slowly looked up at Harjit and then to Jai. "A few days ago, Raichand summoned the whole town to the market. He had brought foreign soldiers with him. He commanded them to round up all the Sikh families and escort them back to his haveli. Anyone who resisted them was to be killed. You know we are just simple towns people. We do not have weapons to fight. When they started to round up the men, Bahadur Rai and his boys fought back. But they were no match for the soldiers, and they were killed on the spot. Raichand was furious. He warned us that anyone found to be harbouring or helping any of the Sikh's would join their fate and have their homes burnt down and their families killed. The Zamindar's men killed Bahadur's wife and children as an example to us all. They were just babies. They were children I had delivered with my own hands. Tell me Khalsa Ji, what should I have done? I am just an old woman who helps bring life into this world, I do not take life. This was Allah's will and his wrath. The Zamindar proclaimed one last decree before he left. Any future Sikh's that came into town were to be sent to him, up in the haveli. And anyone who dared to defy him, would pay with their life. I had no choice..."

The room was silent for a moment as Daai Ji's words sunk in. "So, you did know..." responded Jai. Daai Ji did not answer. "Well that at least explains the warm welcome we received from you when we stopped by earlier." Jai continued, "And you still sent us up there knowing it was trap. Why? What sort of monster are you? What else did you get out of it?"

Daai Ji's voice, heavy with emotion began to defend her position, "I didn't know they were going to take you all away..."

"Bullshit," replied Jai, cutting her off. "How did you not know? You just said they rounded up all the Sikh's and took them away. Why didn't you just warn us?" Daai Ji looked to Harjit for sympathy, but he stared back at her with a mix of disappointment and disgust that he hadn't experienced before, it was the feeling of betrayal.

"You sold us out," came the words from a hurt Harjit.

"No, betah! You don't understand, they said they would kill anyone who opposed them. They said they would burn our homes down. I had no choice!" Daai Ji insisted emotionally, but it was too late. Harjit was no longer listening to her excuses.

"You had a choice. You sold out people who looked up to you with dignity and respect. You chose to sell out people who loved and trusted you, to save yourself..." Harjit's voice began to trail off. The pain in his voice was too much for Daai Ji to hear and she began to cry again.

"I am sorry betah," she mumbled through her tears. "Just kill me now. Allah will never forgive me for what I have done." Daai Ji sobbed as she fell to her knees and pleaded at Harjit's feet for him to end her guilt.

Harjit ignored her pain. It did not matter to him whether she was genuinely repentant or not. All he could think about was Baani's voice, crying out to him in terror and the pain of betrayal within him started to turn into anger.

"Who are the soldiers?" he asked, through gritted teeth. Daai Ji shook her head as if to signal that she did not know. "Where are they taking them!?" he yelled as he grabbed her by each arm and shook her to reply.

"I don't know!" Daai Ji cried out, as she collapsed to the floor sobbing. Harjit let go of her and turned to Jai before moving to leave the room.

"Let's go, she is useless to us."

Jai stood up and checked his shoulder. For all of her betrayal, she had at least stitched his shoulder. "Wait," he said to Harjit, who was walking out to the courtyard. "She'll have a chance to show us just how sorry she is."

They both looked down at Daai Ji who had stopped crying and was now listening very intently to every word being spoken, as if her life depended on it.

Chapter 7

As the sun rose on a new day, the bright light of dawn began to fill Daai Ji's courtyard with light. Everything from the potted plants in the ground to the glass bottles on the shelves, began to light up with a golden glow. Jai stirred on the courtyard manji sahib as the light from the sky forced his eyelids open.

Once again, he found himself in the never-ending nightmare that was India. Dreams of hot crispy pizza suddenly began to fade away, only to be replaced by the cold hard reality that he was in. He was still in India. It was still 1753. His sister was still missing, and his shoulder hurt like… actually, it was surprisingly a lot better than it was last night.

Last night. New memories from the night before began flooding their way back into his brain. 'Ruhi.' Jai shot up in bed and took in his surroundings. He was in the courtyard, but there was no Harjit or Daai Ji. That's because they were in her living quarters.

Ah yes, he remembered everything now. Shortly after her breakdown, they had come up with a new plan. The guys needed answers and they were not getting what they needed from the midwife. They needed information from the source, they needed the Zamindar.

The details of Jai's plan were as clear to him as the morning. He couldn't have slept for more than a few hours, but it was enough. At least he still had a full belly from last night. Only God knew how his sister was. Jai tried his best to distract himself from thinking of her and where she could be. He tried his best not to think about whether she had been fed or whether her captors were making her starve like a slave. But at least she wasn't completely alone. That single thought offered him at least some comfort.

All that mattered now, was that they had a way forward and that it was time to kick their plan into action. Jai rose from his manji sahib and pulled his bed away from blocking the doorway to Daai Ji's quarters. This had been his backup plan just in case she had gotten 'cold feet,' and decided to make a run for it in the middle of the night.

He pushed open her bedroom door and fresh light crept into her room covering everything in its path. A cross-legged Harjit sat upon his bed with his eyes closed, whilst Daai Ji appeared to be fast asleep. Harjit was reciting the first daily prayer of the Sikh's, the Japji Sahib.

"Bro, its time," said Jai, not expecting a response as he knew Harjit was still a few minutes away from completing his prayers. Jai could hear the voice of his Dhaddhi Ji in his head. 'You should recite your Japji Sahib paat (prayer) every day Jaikaar.'

Even though she was lost to him in reality, she was still inside his head. Jai contemplated sitting down and joining Harjit for a moment, but then became distracted when Daai Ji sat up. He stared at her and then left the room as she put her slippers on and followed him out in silence.

Daai Ji walked past Jai and began to prepare breakfast for the three of them. Jai watched over her as she lit her stove and began to mix some flour for their methi paronteh (fenugreek dough bread) and morning chai. Harjit came out just as she had finished cooking.

"Now, it is time," he said, before taking a plate and devouring his breakfast. After the three of them had finished, they made their way out of the back of Daai Ji's property, and set off for the forest before her neighbors could see them.

The trio retraced the steps Harjit and Jai had taken the night before, until they had reached the grounds of the haveli. The grand house looked majestic in the morning light. It was a stark contrast to the horror which they had witnessed within its grounds, only hours before.

From their position, the trio could see the side of the haveli, the back entrance and the stables. "Good, the soldiers are gone. But by the looks of things, Raichand isn't taking any chances," Harjit said, as he pointed to the guards posted by the stables and the rear entrance of the house.

"Daai Ji, you are up. Are you sure you can do this?" Harjit asked the midwife. She nodded 'yes' without speaking.

"Now's the time to tell us if you're having second thoughts," probed Jai skeptically. But Daai Ji did her best to mask the emotion on her face.

"I will do my part. I will make amends," she replied, trying her best to keep the fear in her voice concealed. Jai looked at Harjit who nodded 'yes' to proceed with the plan.

It was a risk, but it was the only plan they had and both of them knew it. Daai Ji walked out of the forest, away from the men and headed towards the front of the house. It was not long before she was spotted by the guards and promptly escorted into the property.

They took her into the courtyard, where Raichand's nokar's were still busy cleaning the sticky blood from the floor and stairs, spilled from the night before. Daai Ji shuddered to think about what had actually happened there only hours earlier. She waited beside the guards for what felt like an eternity.

With every passing minute, she feared they would see the truth upon her face and execute her right there and then. "Subha Bakhair (Good Morning) Daai Ji! What good fortune do I have to be blessed by your presence this morning?" came the all to familiar voice of the Zamindar.

Raichand entered the courtyard from the ground floor. He was dressed in a far simpler kurta top and dhoti, compared to the outfit he wore the night before.

Daai Ji was taken back by his sudden appearance and failed to hide her shock well. "Ss..salaam Raichand Ji," she stuttered, before regaining her composure. "How are you today?" she asked.

Raichand smiled as he continued to walk towards his guest. Ignoring her question, he repeated his. "What can I do for you

Umra?" he asked, as he motioned her over to the seating area of his courtyard.

Daai Ji tried her best not to get flustered by the Zamindar's directness and sat down directly across from him. "I have news from the town Sahib Ji. The Khalsa boy and his friend came to my house yesterday evening, after the curfew. One of them was badly injured."

Raichand's demeanor changed and he now focused all of his attention upon his guest. "Go on..." he replied.

"Well, I had no choice but to stay with them for the evening. They would not let me leave. They forced me to mend the injured one's arm and then they made me feed and house them for the night. I was in fear for my life the whole time!" explained Daai Ji, as Raichand listened intently.

"If they would not let you go, how did you get here now?" enquired the Zamindar.

"When cooking their dinner, I mixed valerian root and opium into their sabji. They did not detect it. My concoction is a powerful tranquilizer that could keep even the largest of beasts incapacitated for hours. But your men must act now. They will awaken by noon and will know that I have escaped. You must help me, I beg of you," pleaded Daai Ji.

Raichand leaned forward in his chair. "Daai Ji... You did the right thing coming here. Do not worry yourself. My men will search your house and apprehend these fugitives at once." Raichand immediately turned his attention to his side table and rang his trusty gong. Four tired looking guards entered the courtyard and stood at their master's attention.

"Go to the Daai Ji's home and bring me Harjit Singh Khalsa and his accomplice now. They should be incapacitated, but take no chances. These men have already killed two of your colleagues. Take the perimeter guards too and report back to me immediately. And remember, I want them alive!" commanded Raichand, in sinister tone. He then turned his attention back to his guest.

"Ji Sahib!" came the response from the guards in unison, before they turned around and marched out of the courtyard, disappearing from sight.

"Thank you, Sahib Ji," remarked the midwife as she stood up to go. "I will take my leave now" she said, as she turned to face the main entrance. But the Zamindar was far from ready to let her go.

"Stop. I could not possibly allow you to leave now, it is not safe for you out there alone," said Raichand, with a false concern in his voice. "You must wait here until my men return, please... I insist." Raichand looked back at the seat from which Daai Ji had just risen up and she then understood that she had no choice but to stay.

Raichand stood up and walked slowly over to Daai Ji. But before he sat down, he turned to his servants. "Leave us!" he commanded. Startled by his abrupt order, the nokar's quickly dropped their towels and rags and ran from sight leaving Raichand and Daai Ji alone.

The Zamindar took the seat beside her and leaned uncomfortably close. "You were once a very beautiful woman…" he said, as he reached for her thigh and stroked it with his hand.

Daai Ji's heart began to pound, and she felt her blood rushing to her face. She was very conscious that she was completely alone and that Raichand was not a man who took 'no' as an answer to anything. A knot twisted in her stomach as she became increasingly terrified at the prospect of being assaulted by this monster of a man.

Daai Ji tried her best to hide her fear and looked the Zamindar in the eyes. "Raichand, I was a married woman! I am not yours, nor will I ever be!" she said, as sternly as she could muster.

But Raichand was undeterred. He preferred it when his prey put up a fight. "Right now, I am the closest thing you have to a husband," he said, as he tugged on her chunni making it fall from her head. Daai Ji stood up abruptly and moved to leave, but she could not get far as Raichand was still holding on to the other end of her clothes.

Daai Ji looked around the room for any sign of assistance or for anything she could use as a weapon, but she could not get away from him. "Help me!" she yelled out loud, but no voice answered her back, other than that of her attacker.

"No one is coming for you Umra. You are mine," insisted Raichand, as he too stood up and shoved Daai Ji hard to the ground. Daai Ji toppled over easily and clashed against the stone floor. Before she could even register what had just happened, Raichand began to straddle her.

"No, please stop!" she cried, as she mustered all of her will and strength to break free. But the more she struggled, the more Raichand seemed to enjoy himself. He laughed in her face. "I knew there was still some life left in you!" beamed Raichand in delight, as he pinned her arms to the floor.

Just as he reached down to untie his Dhoti, a wooden chair leg smashed against the back of his skull, knocking him unconscious in a single blow. The Zamindar slumped forward over Daai Ji, who was still struggling from beneath him. She felt a hand grab her arm and drag her out from beneath her attacker.

A handsome young Sikh man stood before her and offered her a hand to stand up. "Are you ok?" Jai asked the midwife. Daai Ji could not contain her emotion anymore and began to cry.

Jai looked down at Raichand slumped over and noticed that he was wearing a remarkably familiar looking gatra across his chest. Jai rolled Raichand over and saw that he had taken Ruhi's Kirpan. "You cheeky little shit! I'll take this," said Jai, as he pulled Piri and the gatra off the Zamindar's body and stood up to signal his accomplice.

Keeping watch by the main entrance, Harjit cautiously entered the courtyard too. Content that they were ok for the moment, Jai turned back to Daai Ji. "Relax…It's ok. You're ok now. Hey… look at me," said Jai, trying to stop her from crying and from drawing any more attention to them. Daai Ji looked up at Jai and started to calm down. "Listen, you did good. But now, we need to get out of here. You know the plan, follow the trail back to town and stay out of sight for a few days."

"What about him?" Daai Ji asked, as she wiped the tears from her eyes and stared down at an unconscious Raichand.

"Do not worry about him, you will never see him again," interrupted Harjit, who had since moved over to Jai.

"Go now!" ordered Harjit, as he leant down to bind Raichand's hands. Daai Ji looked at the pair who had saved her from being violated and uttered a final blessing. "Barak allahu fik (may god bless you)," before leaving the haveli forever.

Both Harjit and Jai knew that time was not on their side. They only had a small window in which to escape with the Zamindar. "Here, take this, you're going to need it," said Jai, as he passed Piri to his new friend. Whilst Harjit had noticed the exquisite Kirpan's before, it was only now that he could see just how beautiful the Jade sculpted handle really was. With no more time to lose, he graciously accepted the weapon and quickly fastened the gatra across his torso.

Jai knelt down and began to lift the Zamindar's body onto his shoulders with some help from his friend. Jai wobbled a little as he straightened up, but he managed to balance the 'would be rapist' across his back. The duo then made their way outside and headed straight towards the unprotected stables as planned.

Once inside the stables, Harjit prepared two horses as quickly as possible, whilst Jai loaded Raichand over the back of Billo. Within minutes, the pair were ready to depart. They led their horses out of the back of the stables and once again they entered into the dense forest.

Jai kept looking around for any sign of pursuit, but thankfully, there was none. To both of their surprise, their plan had actually worked. For the first time since he had arrived in 1753, Jai felt a glimmer of hope for the future.

The pair continued to lead their mare's deep into the forest. After thirty minutes of walking and avoiding low branches, the forest began to thin out, allowing them an opportunity to ride unobstructed. But just as Jai was building up the courage to ride his horse, Raichand began to stir and so Harjit signalled them to stop.

"This place will do" he said, as he tied Billo's reins to a nearby tree and instructed Jai to follow suit with his black horse. Jai looked up at the beast and was a little apprehensive at getting so close to such a majestic animal. "Don't worry, she will not bite," Harjit joked, as he saw Jai's hesitation. After Jai had successfully secured his horse, the pair turned their attention back to the matter at hand, Raichand.

Harjit dragged the semi-unconscious Zamindar, down from Billo and he dropped to forest floor with a deep thud and loud moan. "Shut it," Jai remarked, as he moved to assist Harjit with dragging the prisoner to a large tree away from the horses. They sat Raichand up against the thick base of a Rosewood tree and bound him to it by tying some rope across his shoulders and waist and leaving his hands tied behind his back.

Raichand could barely feel the blood circulating in his hands as he came too. His head throbbed from the strike to the back of his skull. It took him a moment to realise where he was and who the people standing before him were. Raichand chuckled to himself when he recognised Harjit and Jai.

"You two?" he said with genuine surprise. "Untie me now and I will consider letting you both live," he remarked calmly, as if he were instructing the nokar's in his own home.

Now it was Jai's time to be surprised. "Can you believe the balls on this guy?" he said to Harjit, who ignored his prisoner's remark. Jai was both amused and impressed with Raichand's self-confidence, but Harjit was not in the mood to engage in a pointless conversation the Zamindar.

"Where are our families Raichand? Where are my wife and children?" Harjit asked in an unnerving disposition.

"Hmm… let me think. Oh yes, that quaint little wife of yours and those vermin you call children. Now, what was it that I did with them?" Raichand taunted playfully. "Oh yes, now I remember. I sold them to a whore house for one rupee a piece. Even that was a fate too good for them if you ask me. But it is still far better than the one you shall both suffer for this insolence. Release me now, at once!" commanded Raichand, as he became increasingly agitated.

"Holy shit bags. You are seriously one crazy motherfucker!" said Jai in disbelief. "Answer the man's questions. Tell us where my sister and his family are, or we are seriously going to fuck you up."

Raichand laughed at Jai's threat. "You two are just boys pretending to be men. I can smell the fear on you from here. You are afraid. You are both cowards. But most importantly, you will both be dead very soon and I shall enjoy watching you beg and suffer for every last minute of your pathetic lives, just like your women…"

Raichand's speech was interrupted by Harjit's fist striking him in the face. Harjit was about to pummel Raichand once more when Jai pulled him back. "Bro, wait! Relax! We need him to be able to talk. We're just going to have to 'Jack Bauer' this shit," said Jai, as he reached down and picked up some fallen tree branches. "Here, use this or you're going to mess up your hand."

Jai handed Harjit a log at least a metre in length. Harjit's fist was throbbing from the punch as it had been many years since he had last struck anyone. But he understood what Jai was getting at. It was much more sensible to beat Raichand with logs rather than to use their fists. Raichand spat the warm blood from his mouth into the dirt. "You hit like a woman," he laughed, whilst smiling at Harjit.

Harjit looked at the improvised weapon in his hands and brought it down hard over Raichand's legs that were spread out open across the ground. There was a cracking sound as the wood hit his left thigh, but it wasn't clear whether it was his bone or the log that had broken. Raichand briefly cried out in pain, before regaining his composure. He was determined not to show any weakness, even though he was now sweating profusely. Raichand forced a smile to continue tormenting his captor's.

'Fuck. This is too slow. We don't have time for this,' Jai said to himself as he dropped his own log to the floor and reached down for his Kirpan. Miri was still tied to Jai's gatra which he now wore openly above his white kurta top. When he unsheathed the graceful blade, he held it in front of himself for all to see.

Raichand's smile quickly faded from his face when his eyes fell upon the beautiful gunmetal coloured blade. "Last chance… Where is my sister?" Jai asked in an ominous tone.

Raichand chuckled a nervous laugh before replying. "Did you check my bed?"

Jai did not wait for Harjit's input. He simply knelt down in front of the Zamindar and grabbed the prisoner's right foot. Raichand began to kick his leg's and tried his best to wriggle free.

"No! No! Stop!" panicked Raichand, as he looked to Harjit for assistance. Harjit too knelt down and put his weight on Raichand's left leg, immobilising him completely.

Holding Miri firm in his hand and without any anger, fear or regret, Jai pressed his blade down hard upon Raichand's big toe, severing it from his foot in one simple fluidic motion. The toe fell to the floor causing Raichand to scream out in pain.

Jai could not hear his cry, as his only focus was on the severed appendage laying on the ground besides Raichand's bleeding foot.

Harjit used a cloth from his pocket to gag Raichand, who now withered in pain as Jai released his foot.

Jai had never so much as hurt a fly before today, yet here he now knelt, having severed the toe of another human being. As Jai stared at the separated limb, he realised that he didn't feel any remorse. In fact, he didn't really feel anything at all.

It was as if it wasn't even him who had done it. Jai suddenly thought back to the stables and replayed his first fight with the soldier. Harjit had killed his attacker and saved his life back then, whilst Jai had done nothing. This moment had been Jai's first true act of violence against another person and yet it felt scarily right.

Jai felt Harjit's hand on his arm. "Brother Jai…" he asked with concern, as Jai seemed to have spaced out for a moment. Jai snapped back to reality and looked down at Miri who had tasted blood for the first time in years. Every cell in his body now seemed to be attuned with its surroundings.

Jai felt a sense of inner calm and a serenity that had always seemed to escape him. For his whole life, peace had always been just out of reach, yet here in this moment and in this place, he felt an overwhelming wave of focus and clarity.

Jai nodded to Harjit to signal that he was ok. But in reality, he was far better than ok. He had never felt more alive in his entire life. Jai turned to Raichand who was still trying to manage the pain of losing a limb and pulled the rag from his mouth.

"My sister," Jai said calmly.

"She's dead! She's fucking dead just like you bastards!" yelled Raichand, before Jai stuffed the cloth back into his mouth and went to grab the other foot with Harjit's assistance. Jai gave Raichand a quick glance before repeating the process and relieved him of his other big toe. Raichand muffled his way through an agonising scream, as his second open wound gushed fresh blood onto the forest floor.

"You can let go of his leg," Jai told Harjit quietly, as he stood up. Harjit stared at Jai for a moment not quite recognising the person before him. But he complied and stood up in silence. They both watched Raichand writhe in pain and muffle curses at them. Jai held Miri by his side and spoke to Raichand in an eerily calm voice.

"You have eight more toes. Then… I will take your fingers and your hands."

Jai squatted from where he stood so that he could be eye level with his prisoner. Raichand stopped wriggling and was now listening very intently to his captor's words, almost as if his life depended on it.

Jai looked at the Zamindar directly into his eyes and spoke very slowly and deliberately, so that there could be no misunderstanding. "I will take you apart, piece by piece, until there is nothing left of you for the scavengers to find. Now, tell me Raichand. Am I lying?" Jai continued to stare into the landowner's eyes until the prisoner could not take it anymore.

Raichand shook his head in submission and broke eye contact. He had to look away for he had just seen a darkness in Jai, that he knew he could not beat.

"My sister," Jai repeated calmly. Raichand looked up at Harjit and signaled to him that he was ready to speak. Harjit removed the bloody rag and dropped it on the floor. Raichand took in some deep breaths as he struggled to manage the pain surging through his feet.

"The governor's men took them," he spluttered out. Jai looked over to Harjit to see if that meant anything to him. By the expression on his face, it could not have been good news.

"Where?" demanded Harjit, as he seemed greatly disturbed by the Zamindar's words. Raichand looked up at Harjit and spluttered out two more words.

"Lahore fort." Harjit looked up, as if he had just had the wind knocked out of him. He turned to Jai and instead of an expression of anger on his face, Jai could see that his friend was afraid.

"Lahore fort? What does that mean? Why would the governor want our families?" Jai asked them both.

"I thought they were only rumours," replied a dazed Harjit.

"What!?" demanded Jai, who was becoming increasingly agitated. Raichand noticed this and answered before Jai decided to take another toe.

"The governor has declared that all Sikhs are to be detained and transported to him in Lahore at the great fort. Last week, I received news that his soldiers would be visiting our town next.

Any man, woman or child who follows the word of Gobind and Nanak, is to be captured and prepared for transport. Anyone who resists them is to be eliminated."

"Bullshit. Those soldiers last night answered to you," replied Jai. "What did you get out of it, you sick fuck?" Jai asked with disgust. Raichand considered lying for a moment, but then looked down at his feet and then up to Miri, who was still by his captor's side.

"The governor has offered ten rupees for every Sikh that is delivered to him alive." Raichand replied, as he looked away.

"But why? What does he want with them?" questioned Harjit.

"I do not know!" replied a panicked Raichand. "My orders were simple. I am to help co-ordinate with his men and send every Sikh to the capital. I do not know what he is doing with them, I swear it!"

"And my son, Ajay? I found his horse in your stables. What did you do with him?" Harjit said, not really wanting to hear the answer out loud.

"The governors soldiers took him away with the Grewal family two days ago," replied a nervous Raichand. Harjit felt his heart sink deep into his chest as the rage within him began to burn and consume him once more, just like the night before. He reached down for Piri and unsheathed Ruhi's majestic blade, before pressing it up against Raichand's belly.

The Zamindar started to panic. "I have told you all that I know! He shouted in desperation. But Harjit did not believe him. The husband and father leaned closer to Raichand.

"Why does Ahmed Shah want the Sikhs? We are no threat to him," asked Harjit, still holding the blade against the cotton fabric covering Raichand's gut.

Raichand paused and wondered if this was a trick question. "Ahmed Shah is not the Governor of Lahore. This command is from his proxy, Muin ul Mulk," stuttered Raichand in pain, as he looked at their blank faces for any sign of recognition. "We know him as Mir Mannu! He is the Subedar of Lahore! He controls all of the Punjab for Ahmed Shah Durrani. Durrani went back to Afghanistan and left Mir in charge," Raichand added, hoping that they had heard at least one of those names. Jai looked over at Harjit blankly, who now looked even more worried than before.

"The 'Butcher' has my family!" Roared Harjit. "Where in the fort!?" he yelled, as he pressed the blade hard enough to cut the fabric and draw blood.

Raichand panted in fear at the thought of being gutted alive. "I do not know! I have never even seen his face. How could I? I have not left Sidhwan in years!" he replied with a mixture of fear and anger in his voice. Harjit looked up at Jai and nodded as if to signal that he believed Raichand.

"Which road did they take to Lahore? Can we still catch up with them?" Jai asked Raichand urgently. Raichand started to panic as he had run out of answers. "I don't know! I just oversee

Sidhwan and collect his taxes! They could have taken any of five different paths to Lahore, for all I know," protested Raichand.

Jai looked at Harjit and they both knew that Raichand was not going to be of any more value to them. "We need to leave now if we are gonna have any chance of rescuing them before they get to Lahore bro," said Jai, as he wiped his blade clean and returned it to its metal sheath.

Harjit glanced at Raichand before replying to Jai. "*If* we knew the road they were taking, then we might have stood a chance. But even then, it would have only been the two of us, against at least twenty of them. If we are to have any hope of rescuing our women and my children, we will need help. We cannot free them alone brother Jai."

"Fine. What do you suggest?" asked Jai.

"We will ride to Jagraon and we will find my brother, Harpal. He can lead us to the Dal Khalsa. We need to tell them about what has happened here and about Tehara," replied Harjit.

"The Dal Khalsa? Who are they?" Jai asked skeptically.

"They are the Sikh army and they fight for truth, honour and justice for all. They will help us," said Harjit, with a distant certainty in his voice.

"That's great, but what makes you so sure they will help *us* bro?"

Harjit wiped a burdened look from his face before replying to Jai's question. "Because my brother is one of them."

Jai could tell from Harjit's expression that he did not wish to discuss the matter any further.

As they began to walk back to their horses Jai paused. "Wait, what should we do this piece of shit?" he said, looking back at Raichand, who was still bleeding from his wounds.

Harjit looked down at Piri in his hand and walked back over to their prisoner. He lifted the Zamindar's shirt and before Raichand could protest, Harjit sliced open the Zamindar's belly from left to right with almost medical precision.

Raichand's intestines spilled out from their natural home into his lap, as he screamed out in agony and begged for mercy. Harjit then picked up the dirty rag still laying on the floor and stuffed it back into Raichand's mouth in order to silence his wailing. As Harjit stood up and walked over to Jai, he glanced back one last time. "He belongs to the forest now."

Jai looked back at the dying prisoner and for the briefest of moments, he felt a pang of horror overcome him for what they had just done to another human being.

But as the moment passed, Jai turned his attention back to the horses. "C'est le vie bitch," he said out loud, as he walked away from the dying prisoner and proceeded to join his friend in their quest to liberate their loved ones.

The pair mounted their mare's and began their journey out of the forest, towards the town of Jagraon. As they rode away, muffled screams echoed out from behind them as the forest feasted on its new bounty.

Chapter 8

A cool breeze blew over her face and flowed through her free-flowing hair, as Ruhi Kaur flew high above the cotton like clouds, and across a cobalt-blue sky. She was free like an eagle soaring high above the earth, gazing down upon the lord's vast creation down below.

'Everything seems so small from up here,' she thought to herself, as she swooped lower through the clouds. As she passed through wispy pockets of air, Ruhi emerged from other side and noticed that the colour of the sky had begun to change. It had started to turn pink and then slowly red, as the once fluffy white clouds became darker and heavier. A giant black cloud loomed in the distance spewing out lightning and rain relentlessly, as it moved closer to her.

The temperature began to drop, and the gales increased, as Ruhi struggled to maintain her flight through the foreboding atmosphere. Dark heavy clouds now surrounded her, and lightning flashed across a blood red sky, followed instantly by the roar of deafening thunder.

She was now in the eye of the storm, battling ferocious gales that caused her to drop to the earth like a stone. Ruhi could feel herself falling faster and faster until finally, she slammed into the depths of the dark earth below with a violent thud.

'Ow…my head,' Ruhi said to herself, as she was jolted awake. With her eyes still closed, she instinctively reached for the back of her head and felt the new bump that had formed, from where she had been struck. "Ouchy," she said out loud, as she struggled to open her eyes.

Every muscle in her body seemed to ache and whatever surface she was lying on, felt as hard as hell. She could feel the presence of other bodies around her, pressed up against her arms and legs. Wherever she was, it was a little too cozy for her liking.

Ruhi willed her eyes to open and slowly, the darkness surrounding her began to filter into her brain. She figured she was on some kind of cart, from the rocking motion of the surface beneath her. But her arms and legs felt so heavy. "Hey, slowly…" came a familiar voice, but Ruhi could barely make out the persons face due to the absence of light.

At first, Ruhi's limbs resisted her command to raise her body up, but she forced them to obey and the world around her began to swirl. "I am pretty sure this is what a concussion feels like," she said out loud. But when she looked to her right, she did not recognise the face of the lady sat beside her.

New smells and sounds from the environment around her began to overwhelm Ruhi's senses. She could smell the aroma of stale body odour and fresh vomit mixed within the air. It was almost enough to make her retch herself. But the sounds of women and children sobbing and crying around her, distracted her from following through.

"It's ok, we're here," came the voice again. Ruhi was relieved to see Suhadna sat by her legs, with baby Veeraj still in her arms and with Baani's head asleep on her lap. Suddenly, everything around her became clearer. She was in a cart similar to Harjit and Suhadna's, yet this one was far bigger and filled with strange women and children that she had never seen before.

Ruhi looked behind herself, only to be confronted with a grid of iron bars that wrapped themselves around the entire carriage. That is when she realised that she and the others, were all prisoners.

Ruhi looked around for any space to move, but there was none. The woman to her right had spread out into the space Ruhi had just vacated by sitting up. "What happened?" Ruhi asked Suhadna. But she could barely make out her companion's face in the darkness of the night. The only light coming into the carriage, came from the moon above and was occasionally masked by a passing cloud.

"Raichand sold us out," replied Suhadna.

"What do you mean?" Ruhi asked, as she struggled to remember the events of last night. "The last thing I remember was a knock at the door… it was that creepy housekeeper and some guards. They tried to take the children… I told them to stop… we both did."

Ruhi looked at Suhadna who sat in silence as everything else came back to her all at once. "They had swords and I thought they were going to hurt Baani… I didn't mean too…" Ruhi said slowly, as she remembered drawing her Kirpan and facing off with one of the guards. "He swung at me first. I don't know why though. I didn't mean to cut him so deeply." Ruhi's voice trailed off as she realised, she had killed one of the guards in her confrontation with them.

"The last thing I remember was reaching for Baani when…" Ruhi struggled to finish her sentence, but then Suhadna filled in the blanks.

"Raichand struck you from behind with his pistol. You didn't see it coming. Neither of us did. His men dragged you down the stairs and we were all handed over to these mercenaries."

"Mercenaries? All of us? They got Jai and Harjit too!?" Ruhi asked loudly.

"Shush! Quietly," Suhadna replied quickly, as she looked outside the carriage for any sign of the guards riding around them. "I don't know. I don't know if they managed to get away. I didn't see them with the other men." Suhadna pointed to the rear of the carriage where several iron chains dangled from the top of the metal cage and fell out of sight.

Ruhi shifted her weight forward as much as she could, to get a clearer view from the rear of the cart. Tied to the metal chains were three columns of Sikh men and boys, being forced to walk behind the carriage like slaves. Soldiers rode beside the columns and intermittently whipped and yelled at the men to keep pace with the carriage.

Ruhi gasped at the sight and the reality of her situation finally began to sink in. She was a prisoner in 1753 and she was being carted off to an unknown location by a group of savages. She desperately looked around for any means of escape and then instinctively reached down for her Kirpan.

The moment she realised it was gone, Ruhi felt a wave of panic and despair overtake her. 'You're going to die here in the past, you're going to die as a prisoner in the past!' Her mind kept racing with thoughts of her demise, because deep inside her heart she recognised the soldiers by their uniforms. She had known who they really were from the moment she first saw them. There were not mercenaries. The were Mughal soldiers.

Whilst Ruhi wasn't exactly well versed in all of Sikh history, she knew the one consistent force in the Punjab that had been trying to eliminate the Sikh's for centuries, was the Mughal empire. They had tortured and butchered the Sikh's for hundreds of years and whilst she couldn't exactly be sure it was them, she felt it in her heart.

"We have to get out of here," she said to Suhadna, but before she could respond, another voice beside them spoke out.

"There is no escaping this." Ruhi looked up at the stranger who was sat on her right-hand side. The stranger continued to speak. "They have soldiers and mercenaries searching every town and village for Sikhs up to fifty miles away from here. Where would you go? Nowhere is safe for us now. Not anymore..." said the woman, as she stared at Ruhi with a soulless expression.

"Silence in there!" came the shrill voice of a guard from outside the cage. He had ridden up to the edge of the cart where Ruhi was sat and addressed their general direction. "Anymore more noise from this carriage and I will cut out all of your tongue's!"

The rider did not wait for a response and galloped off ahead. Ruhi followed his path with her eyes and that is when she saw the true reality of their situation. They were not the only carriage. They were merely part of a convoy that included at least two more packed carriages, with dozens of men and boys being dragged behind them.

Ruhi closed her eyes and prayed to her Guru Ji. 'Please tell me this is all just a bad dream.' Ruhi kept her eyes closed, as she could no longer bare to take in any more reality. "This can't be real, this can't be real," she started to repeat to herself quietly. Suhadna balanced Veeraj in one arm and then wrapped her other arm around Ruhi and whispered in her ear. "Guru Ji is with us always. We will be ok."

Whilst the words helped, Ruhi could not stop a tear or two from falling from her eyes. She took in a deep breath and nodded to Suhadna to let her know that she had understood. Ruhi wiped her tears away and did a quick look for any more guards before whispering back to Suhadna. "Where are they taking us?"

"I don't know," replied Suhadna cautiously. Ruhi saw a fear in Suhadna's eyes that matched her own and the two ladies sat together and awaited their fate with the rest of convoy.

As the hours passed by, the sun began to rise on a new day. Warm hues of pink and gold lit up the sky, filling the blank canvass with an array of colour. Ruhi stared up at the fading moon as the vile world around her began to slowly fill with light. Dawn was still one of her favourite times of day, despite her current reality.

She tried her best to recite her Japji Sahib paat from her memory, but something was stopping her from seeing all of the words within her mind. She needed clarity and focus.

Ruhi racked her mind until she remembered a time when she would sit by the river with her Dhaddha Ji and Dhaddhi Ji, and practice reciting naam Simran (meditation). Ruhi began to recite the word 'Waheguru,' in her heart and in her mind and within seconds, she began to feel better. With every breath, the name of God began to help her centre herself and focus on the here and now, as opposed to her uncertain future.

Ruhi closed her eyes and continued to repeat the word 'Waheguru,' within. The sounds from the convoy around her started to drown out, as did the pain from sitting on the hard wooden floor of the carriage. Ruhi could feel the outside world around her fading away. It was almost as if she were floating, just like in her dream. When suddenly, the carriage jolted to a stop, and she was back to where she had started. Except this time, her heart wasn't pounding with anxiety.

Ruhi looked up at Suhadna who was trying her best to feed Veeraj, who was clearly hungry. Baani was awake too, along with the rest of the carriage. Everyone seemed to be on edge as no one knew why they had stopped. They could hear the sound of some men shouting from up ahead, but no sooner had the convoy stopped, it started trudging forward again but this time, the scenery around them began to change. Houses and stone buildings started to fill the countryside around them.

Hindu and Muslim families began to pass the convoy in carts of their own, as the prisoners passed through ransacked towns and villages. Ruhi could see burnt down houses and buildings similar to those in Tehara. Everyone in the carriage now understood what a burnt down house meant. Strangers continued to pass the convoy by in silence, as nobody dared to speak to the prisoners in fear of being made to join them.

As the number of people around the carriages began to grow, so did the height and number of the buildings around them. The prisoners did not know it then, but they had finally reached one of the many entrances to Lahore, the Akbari gate.

The convoy proceeded to pass though the heavily defended gate to the city, as crowds of people began to gather around the carriages. They scuttled out from the busy streets and crowded neighbourhoods, just to catch a glimpse of the new Sikh prisoners, being escorted to Lahore's most infamous jail.

The city was a spectacle that outshone Sidhwan on every level. Beautifully hand sculpted buildings up to three stories high were scattered across both sides of the packed-out streets. Giant arches and walkways that were hundreds of years old, intertwined with a network of paths and walkways that were packed with stalls and street merchants from all walks of life.

The overwhelming noise and smells the city generated, was unlike anything the Sikh prisoners from the countryside had ever experienced before. Some people in the crowd began to throw rotten meat and vegetables at the carriages, as they wobbled past them on the uneven, muddy roads.

The deeper into the city they travelled, the more hostile the crowds became. Vegetables were replaced with pellets and rocks, which began to rain down upon the convoy striking defenseless prisoners as they were paraded through the streets.

Ruhi picked up Baani and held her close to her body, as to shield her from any incoming missiles. Men, women, and children of all ages shouted curses at the Sikh's, as they approached Lahore's mighty fort.

The size and scale of the walled fortress surprised even Ruhi. Tall crimson and grey-coloured walls soared all around the giant compound as far as her eyes could see.

"Where are we?" Ruhi asked Suhadna, as they took in the grand sight before them. Suhadna shook her head as she did not know for certain, but then a voice spoke out from behind them. It was the lady sitting to the right of Ruhi again.

Ruhi hadn't noticed it before, but the stranger had beautiful green eyes and she spoke with a hint of defiance in her voice. "We are in Lahore, and this is Ahmed Shah Durrani's fort. The Afghan's have us now," said the lady, as she looked away.

Ruhi did not know what to do with that information, other than to squeeze onto Baani a little tighter.

The guards patrolling the convoy began to circle the carriages in greater numbers. They did not want to risk losing any of their precious bounty to an angry crowd. Finally, the carriages were ushered through a giant-sized archway, that served as an entrance to their new prison. The size of the compound within, was on par with the great wall that secluded it from the outside.

Ruhi and Suhadna had found themselves imprisoned in a giant square like courtyard, surrounded by walls at least twenty feet high on every side. Each wall had a grand archway built into it, that served as an entrance and exit, in and out of the great courtyard.

At each of these points were a dozen guards. Some patrolled the prison from the top of the archways and others around the wall itself. All of the guards were armed with spears, but those on top of the walls were also equipped with bows and arrows.

Ruhi's carriage was the last to enter the great square through the southern gate. It was only then that she saw the true number of prisoners around her. Almost a hundred Sikh men and boys, ranging from the ages of ten to eighty, lay collapsed upon the muddy floor, still bound by the chains that had dragged them there. All of them were exhausted from their long journey and by the looks of them, many hadn't eaten or drunk any water for days.

Dozens of more guards began to file into the courtyard. They had come to process the male prisoners first. The men and boys were unchained from the carriages and marched through the northern gate, one group at a time. Within fifteen minutes, all the men and boys had been cleared from the great square.

It was an immensely efficient process, one that Ruhi could tell had been performed many times before. The guards then turned their attention towards the carriages. All of the women and children were herded into the centre of the courtyard, where they were made to sit in large rows in complete silence.

The prison guards then proceeded to inspect them all for any signs of illness or disease. Anyone who appeared to be too old or sick, was dragged from their row to the front of the group and then marched through the northern gate, to accompany the men.

Ruhi was sat in the third row from the front with Baani in her lap. Whilst she was grateful to have Suhadna and Veeraj next to her, they dared not speak to one another, in fear of being separated. A young girl from behind them started to protest, as her sick mother was dragged to front of the group. The girl did not want to be separated from her parent, but the guards continued to drag her mother away.

The leader of the guards, walked over to the little girl and slapped her hard across the face, dropping her to the ground like a sack of potatoes. The other ladies around her gasped in protest as they went to her aid, but they were soon silenced as he turned his attention towards them. "Silence!" the leader bellowed out.

"You are all now property of the great and benevolent Governor of Lahore. The honourable Subedar, Mir Mannu!"

The ladies all quietened down as the prison leader's words echoed around the square. "I am Amir Jahangir, the Subedar's warden. And I am master of this prison. Within these walls, my commands are second only to that of the Subedar's. On this dirt, my guards and I execute *his* will."

Jahangir had given this same speech every day for the last two years, and yet it still gave him immense pleasure to see the shock and fear sink in the eyes of his new inmates. The Amir cut an imposing figure for a Mughal guard. He wore the traditional green kurta top and matching dhoti uniform. Yet his clothes were clean and unstained compared to those of his subordinates. Jahangir proudly wore his large bushy beard, trimmed moustache and small matching green turban. From a distance, he could have almost been mistaken for a Sikh.

Ruhi could tell that this was a man who took pride in his own appearance. She observed him closely as he slowly circled his new prisoners and continued the speech he had given a hundred times before.

"The Subedar was appointed by the almighty himself. It is he who now decides who lives and who dies here on this earth. Anyone who does not comply with an order from me or my guards, shall suffer a pain unlike any they have ever seen or felt before."

A gong rang in the distance that seemed to interrupt the Amir's speech. But Jahangir was not annoyed. On the contrary, he seemed excited. The Amir's smile sent a chill down Ruhi's spine.

"Subhan Allah! (Praise Allah) he said, in an almost joyous tone. "We have an unexpected visitor. You vermin are indeed blessed. The Subedar himself has come to see you!"

The large doors of the western gate opened before them and out walked a lean turbaned man. He was dressed in an ivory robe, made up of the finest silk's imported from the farthest reaches of the Mughal empire. He was escorted by a contingency of personal servants and guards, all ready to obey their master's command, at the drop of a word.

Small precious gems hemmed within seams of his dress like robes, glistened against the sunlight. But nothing was as extravagant as the weapon he had hoisted to his hip, bound by a red sash. The Subedar had a long thin sabre attached to his waist with a shiny metal sheath encrusted with rubies and diamonds.

Everything about his wardrobe from the peacock feathers in his gold turban, to his bright red silk sandals, had been designed to attract the attention of others and to promote a vision of power, wealth, and status.

Mir Mannu strode towards his Amir, whilst the new prisoners looked on with a reserved fascination. That is when Ruhi saw his face properly for the first time. His dark brown hair and black beard had been trimmed short as if to disguise the strands of white that now threatened to show through.

But it was his narrow eyes and sharp nose that grabbed Ruhi's attention the most. She felt a pang of anxiety return as she saw a sternness upon his face and an emptiness in eyes. Mir tapped

Jahangir on the shoulder as if welcoming an old friend and then forced a smile as he gazed upon the faces of his new inmates below.

"Welcome ladies! Thank you for coming to Lahore. We are all humbled here by your presence," said the Subedar, as he placed his hand on his chest as a gesture of his sincerity.

"Let us go, haramzada (bastard)!" shouted a woman from the back. The Amir glanced over to his men, who immediately proceeded to plough their way through the prisoners, until they dragged a woman in her mid-forties up to her feet and held her up by her throat.

One of the guards then drew his Pesh Kabz and pressed it against her neck. The other Sikh ladies around her started to protest, but everyone stopped when a single voice spoke out above the commotion.

"Now, now, there is no need for all of this 'excitement,' on such a beautiful morning," announced Mir loudly, as he addressed his guards and the crowd at the same time.

"You ladies are my guests! But as any good host, I do have some house rules that my friend Jahangir here, will explain to you all. I am simply here to give you the opportunity of a lifetime."

The crowd listened intently as the guard continued to press his cool blade against the woman's throat.

"You are all like my children. Except that you have all been very lost. Not every person is as fortunate as I have been. I was shown the light at a very young age and now it is my honour and duty, to spread that light throughout the darkness that covers these troubled lands. That light is the beauty of Allah. Let his love wash over you all. Let his light into your hearts and minds, and your souls shall be washed clean. It is my duty as your father to show you the righteous path. Sometimes, children need love and sometimes children need hard work and discipline. You will find all three of these virtues within these walls. Accept the light. Accept the will and love of Allah in your hearts and you shall be set free, I give you my word as your father." Mir smiled down upon the faces in the crowd, as he seemed to glow with serenity.

The Sikh ladies stared back at Mir with looks of contempt and confusion. Ruhi glanced at Suhadna with a look of concern and had that same look reflected back at her. Ruhi knew they were in more trouble than she had first thought. 'This guy is bat shit crazy and we're all screwed,' she thought to herself.

Mir continued talking as he ignored the harsh looks he was receiving back. "Any of you who accept Islam before me and renounce the false prophet Gobind, shall be free to leave here now."

Mir once again scanned the faces of the women and children before him for any signs of acknowledgement or movement from within the group. But only silence greeted him back, until a single voice replied.

"Bole so nihal!" (Shout aloud in ecstasy) came the cry from the woman who was stood up with a blade pressed against her throat.

"Sat Sri Akal!" (True is the great timeless one) came the immediate and synchronised reply from all of the women and children within the group. The women had given Mir their answer. They had answered him with the Sikh Jaikara (war cry).

Mir smirked to himself, as the standing woman once again cried out. "Bole so nihal!" and was once again answered in unison with, "Sat Sri Akal!"

Mir simply looked at his Amir, who then immediately signalled his guards holding the girl. They sliced open her throat, allowing arterial blood to spew freely from her neck and cover the women and children who were sat around them. There was no third Jaikara, as gasps and cries of protest started to erupt from within the crowd of prisoners.

"SILENCE! Or you will ALL join her now!" The Amir roared out in fury. Jahangir's voice echoed around the courtyard, bringing the silence he desired along with it. The crowd turned their attention back to Mir and Jahangir, as their soldiers circled all of the remaining prisoners with their spears lowered, ready to strike.

"Hard work and discipline it is," Mir said softly, with a hint of disappointment, as he once again tapped Jahangir on his shoulder and then turned to leave. But before he took a step, Mir paused and leaned closer to his Amir, who was stood at attention.

Mir whispered something indistinguishable into his subordinates' ear and then proceeded to depart along with his own contingency of servants and guards who followed his every step.

Jahangir smiled to himself as he waited for Mir to leave the courtyard. He then issued his next set of commands. "The Subedar is a far kinder and generous man than I am. Anyone who tries that shit again will join your little friend over there. Is that understood?" he yelled at the prisoners, who dared not answer him back.

"Every bloody time," Jahangir muttered to himself, in disbelief at the crowd's insolent behaviour. The Amir then summoned his next in command, who began to single out several young women from within the crowd. "You and you, to the front! Jahangir ordered.

The girls did not even have a chance to stand, before his guards barged through the crowd and began to drag them to the front. The Amir continued to scan the rows and his eyes fell upon Ruhi for the first time. "And you!" he said, pointing directly to her.

Ruhi looked at Suhadna who started to panic. "No!" she protested. But then Ruhi shook her head at Suhadna, signaling her not to resist. Ruhi did not want to lose her only friend over something neither of them could control.

Baani clung on to Ruhi's leg as she began to stand up and Ruhi looked down at the little girl. "It's ok, I'll be back soon, I promise." Another woman grabbed Baani for Suhadna and calmed her down before she could make a scene. Ruhi then walked up to the front, to join the other four girls who had been selected by the Amir.

The remaining prisoners were then commanded to follow the other guards through the eastern gate, whilst Ruhi and the four other women stayed behind with the Amir and several guards.

She did not want to think about why they had been singled out, but she had an inkling. The other four girls just happened to be the prettiest amongst the group. So whatever the reason was, it probably wasn't good.

Ruhi felt her anxiety building up in her stomach again, so she began to recite, 'Waheguru, Waheguru, Waheguru...' to herself. The Amir stared at each of them before turning to his guards and issuing them with a command. Ruhi and the four other girls were then marched through the western gate, deep into the heart of the prison.

As she followed the prisoners in front of her, Ruhi could not help but feel afraid of what lay inside the walls before her. She thought about Suhadna and her children and her Dhaddha and Dhaddhi Ji. And then about her brother Jai, who was still out there somewhere.

And for the briefest of moments, she didn't feel so alone anymore. "Jai," Ruhi whispered to herself, as she took a deep breath and marched forwards through the dark archway.

Chapter 9

A horse trotted though a field with its unexperienced rider holding on to it for dear life. The path to Jagraon had not been as simple as Jai had hoped it would be. Harjit had recommended that they stay off the main roads, to avoid any patrols that could be searching for them.

But what Harjit had not told him, was that riding through forests, fields and jungle terrain was not going to be easy, especially in the soaring heat.

"Bro, tell me we're stopping soon, my ass is killing me! No one ever told me riding a horse could be so painful. I ain't gonna be able to sit or walk for a week!" said Jai, as he rubbed his thighs and behind, whilst struggling to maintain his balance on the horse. "I am calling you Chittar (ass) from now on," Jai said to his horse.

Harjit tried his best not to laugh at his strange friend. He looked down at Billo and slowed to a stop. "What do you think girl? Could you do with a rest?" The horse began to graze on the grass below and Harjit had his answer. "You are right brother Jai. The horses need a rest, and we could do with a water break too. There is a stream not far from here. We will rest the horses there briefly and then take the main trail to Jagraon."

"Wait, didn't you say trails were dangerous?" Jai asked, whilst still trying to bring Chittar to a stop.

"We have no choice brother Jai. The Shuruti trail is the only way to enter Jagraon from the north. If we go around the stream, we will lose a day. And the longer we are out here, the more chance there is that we could be discovered," reasoned Harjit.

"Hell, you ain't gonna get no argument from me. Lead the way bro!" replied Jai enthusiastically, as the pair regained their pace and headed towards to the cool waters. After a few minutes, the duo came across some overgrown trees and bushes beside the stream. 'It was the perfect spot,' Harjit thought to himself, as the shrubbery gave them some natural cover.

The horses quenched their thirst whilst Jai took the opportunity to stretch his legs. He had never been so glad to see running water in his whole life. A strong current meant the water would be fresh enough to drink, which was a relief for them both. After tending to their horses' thirst, the men secured them to some pear trees nearby, allowing them plenty of time to eat the fallen fruit.

Jai could not wait any longer and dunked his whole head into the refreshing stream, soaking his turban and hair too. "Oh wow, you totally have to try this! I needed that dip so badly," said Jai as he turned to Harjit, who was now feasting on some fruit of his own.

He passed some pears to Jai who took immediately took a giant bite. The sweetness took him by surprise, as the pear was unlike any other fruit he had tried before. Harjit saw his expression and laughed.

"It's the soil. Punjab has always had some of the richest soil in all of India," he said with a hint of pride. And for a moment, both of them almost forgot what had brought them there to that point. They had almost forgotten how they were betrayed and how their loved ones were taken away from them. Almost.

A small silence fell between them, but it was Jai who broke it first. "Do you think we went too far back there?" he asked Harjit, without making any eye contact. Harjit continued to chew the bite in his mouth whilst he contemplated his answer. Jai could tell that this topic had also been weighing upon Harjit's mind, but finally he replied.

"I do not know. But if I had to… I would do it again." Jai knew the same was true for him. Thinking about whether their actions were right or wrong was a luxury for another time. Time was something they both knew they did not have. His sister and Harjit's family had been carted away to Lahore, to face only God knew what.

"Back in the forest, when Raichand mentioned that guy… Mir Mannu. You kind of freaked out a little and called him the 'Butcher.' This is probably a stupid question, but why? Why are you afraid of that name?" Jai asked in all seriousness. Harjit threw the core of his pear towards the horses and looked uncomfortable as he wrestled with what to say next.

"Several years ago, when I used to live in Sidhwan. Our neighbour Teja Singh Thakkar decided he wanted to see Amritsar before he died. He wanted to take his whole family with him. His wife, two son's and his daughter in-laws. I had grown up with his boys, so he asked us if we wanted to come too. But Baani was just a baby and we couldn't leave the farm for a week. They left just before the Puranmashi (night of the full moon) and stopped for the night at the fort in Ram Rauni. Puranmashi came and went, but they never returned. We later found out that the fort had been attacked by the Mughal's and that they had left no survivors. That fort would have housed over five hundred men, women, and children that night. Sidhwan never felt like home for me after that, so we moved out on our own shortly after. It was Mir Mannu who led those soldiers at Ram Rauni that night. It was he who ordered the slaughter of them all, just because they were Sikh. So it is a name I will never forget."

"Well fuck me..." said Jai, as he looked down at the floor in despair. "This is the prick who has Ruhi, Suhadna and the kids? Oh bro, I have heard about these Mughal's before, and they are fucking barbarians. I'll admit, my Sikh history and knowledge is pretty shit, but I at least know that these are the fuckers who butchered our Guru's and their families. We have to get our girls and kids back man. I ain't letting my sister get fucked over by some Mughals in the 18th century, not on my watch!" said Jai getting all riled up.

Harjit smiled at Jai's newfound enthusiasm. Whilst he didn't understand all of his friend's words, he got the gist. "You are right brother Jai; we must proceed with haste."

162

"Well, what are we waiting for? Let's go! You remember where your brother lives right?" Jai asked, as he stood up abruptly and began to dust himself off. That is when the pain hit him again. "Aagghh! My ass, seriously man! How can you ride these things!?" he asked, as he tried to self-massage his buttock muscles.

"Patience brother Jai, patience," said Harjit, as he too stood up and stretched, before preparing the horses for the next stage of their journey.

Luckily for them, the remainder of their journey to Jagraon passed without incident. Jai was finally getting the hang of riding Chittar in relative comfort, whilst Harjit's thoughts began dwell on seeing his brother again for the first time in five years.

As they approached the outskirts of Jagraon, their trail began to snake left and right through elevated woodlands. The thick curtain of trees acted like a natural barrier, completely obscuring the town on the other side. As they reached the last curve in the road, the whole town of Jagraon came into focus for them. Almost a quarter of a mile away in front of them, stood a town almost identical in size to Sidhwan Bet.

But that is where the similarities ended. Where Sidhwan was a busy farming town, Jagraon resembled more of a warzone. Plumes of black smoke billowed off the buildings, as heavily armed soldiers on horseback clashed with the locals using their swords and spears. It was a picture of complete and utter chaos. Harjit and Jai had inadvertently stumbled upon a Mughal raid.

Both of them were speechless. Yet neither of them could take their eyes away from the mayhem unfolding before them. Distant screams of people being stabbed and burnt, was not what either of them had expected as they turned that last corner.

"Seriously? What the... I can't take this shit no more," Jai blurted out first. But even Harjit was struggling to process the carnage before them. "What do we do?" panicked Jai, as the horses became startled at sound of people screaming in the distance.

"I... I do not know..." stuttered Harjit, as he finally managed to tear his eyes away from the commotion in front of them. Jai could see that this was one situation too much for the young farmer. But Jai was strangely content too, as he once again felt on equal footing with his new friend.

Ever since Sidhwan, Jai had always felt one step behind Harjit, having to solely rely upon his guidance and knowledge. It was not a comfortable position for him to have been in and he hadn't even realised how much it had bothered him, until that very moment.

"It's OK. We can handle this," said Jai, trying to reassure himself, as much as his friend. "Either we stay and fight or we run and hide. Those are literally our only two options."

Whilst Jai juggled with the reins in an attempt to calm Chittar down, Harjit seemed to come back to the present moment. "We only have Kirpan's. They are no match for bows and arrows and spears and swords!" exclaimed Harjit.

"You are right. Then let us get some of our own." Harjit was puzzled with Jai's response.

"Look, I don't wanna die and I know our families are counting on us. But I am sick and tired of these motherfuckers burning and kidnapping innocent people. You know we can't run or hide from this. I know I'd never be able to live with myself if we walked away right now," said Jai, as he looked at his friend.

"Ok... What do you have in mind?" asked Harjit. Jai looked across their field of vision for any kind of an advantage. Jagraon was flanked by forests on either side and all that stood between them and the town, was open farmland.

"Look over there, to the left," pointed Jai, as he spotted three empty carriages just outside of the town, parked behind one another in the middle of a field. "It looks like no one is guarding those carriages other than the drivers. Three carriages probably means three drivers', right? I reckon we could take them and then pick off the others from a distance. At the very least, we could slow them down. What do you reckon?"

Harjit looked at the carriages and then back to Jai. "I think we have a plan brother Jai. Let's ride!"

Jai nodded to his friend and then tapped his heel into Chittar's side, causing her to launch forward towards the transport wagons, followed closely by Harjit and Billo. As they rode downhill into the open field, the sound of iron clashing and people screaming grew louder.

The duo did their best to approach the wagons from the rear, as to mask their arrival. When they were within ten metres of the last wagon, the duo dismounted their horses and withdrew their

Kirpan's. Even though his heart was pounding in his chest, Jai knew that this was their only option.

As he held the lapis blue handle tight in his right hand, Jai felt a moment of gratitude towards his Dhaddhi Ji. Even though she was missing, he felt like she was with him now. The duo stood together at the back of the last carriage with their weapons drawn, ready to charge the first driver.

Harjit could sense that Jai was nervous. This was unlike the previous situation back at the stables or even in the forest with Raichand. This time, they were moving forward with an intent to kill. "This is the right thing to do brother Jai," reassured Harjit. Jai appreciated his words of reassurance, but he didn't need them as Jai's mind was made up.

"It's ok bro. I will do what I have to do. At least we have the element of surprise, right?" said Jai, taking in deep breaths. He quickly glanced around one last time, before continuing. "Ok. Let's try and take this first one quietly. You take the left side and I'll take the right. First who stabs him wins?" Jai joked. He could just hear his sisters voice of disapproval, but then remembered why he was there.

Harjit looked at his friend and smiled. "This one is mine," he said playfully, before turning around and heading up the left side of the carriage. Not wanting to be outdone, Jai too darted down the right side of the carriage in a bid to get to the driver first.

As Jai moved closer to his target, he could hear the sound of two voices having a conversation. 'So much for one driver,' Jai thought to himself. But no sooner had he completed that thought, the sound of the conversation stopped and was replaced with the sound of a struggle.

Jai approached the driver's bench from the right, only to find a soldier sitting above him, facing an ongoing situation that had developed to the left. The soldier reached for his sword, as Harjit attacked the driver on the left-hand side of the carriage. The young father held his opponent down with his left arm and proceeded to stab him multiple times with Piri.

Jai used Harjit's attack as a diversion to climb up on to the drivers bench unnoticed. With his back towards Jai, the soldier attempted to slide down the left-hand side of the carriage in a bid to help the driver. The soldier was so preoccupied with Harjit's attack, that he did not notice Jai standing directly behind him.

For Jai, it was now or never. Using the element of surprise, Jai raised his arm up and thrust Miri downwards. The blade struck the unwitting soldier between his shoulder and neck, cutting diagonally into his torso at least five inches before getting stuck.

The soldier dropped his sword in an attempt to clutch his neck, but it was too late. Before he could cry out or make any other sound, Jai pulled the blade out and stabbed the soldier in the back of his neck. The soldiers neck tore wide open splattering warm blood across Jai's face, yet he did not relent. Jai continued to hack away at the disarmed soldier until there was no movement left at all.

Content that the soldier was dead. Jai looked across to Harjit who was too busy relieving the driver of his weapons, to notice what had just happened. Jai looked down at the decimated carcass before him and wiped the dripping blood from his face. He hadn't planned on being so savage. It just came to him.

Yet despite having just taken his first human life, Jai was only focused on the next task ahead. There was no voice of remorse from within him, telling him to stop, or consciousness telling him to find another way. Jai simply pushed the remains of his deceased target over the edge of the carriage and picked up the dead man's Talwar.

Holding his new weapon up in the air, Jai turned to Harjit. "Hey, look what I got..." he whispered to his friend.

Harjit noticed Jai's blood-soaked beard and top before seeing the metre long sword in his hand. Harjit held up a sword of his own before showing off the new bow on his shoulder and the quiver full of arrows now tied to his waist.

Armed with their new weapons, the duo looked ahead to their next target. "Same plan?" asked Jai.

Harjit looked back at the bodies of the butchered driver and soldier and nodded before replying coldly. "Same plan."

The duo proceeded to takedown the next carriage. But with every step forward, the screams of the villagers dying and people being burned alive increased. The distressing noise only gave Harjit and Jai a greater sense of urgency. Once again, they rushed forward towards the drivers of the second carriage.

This time, a young man of no more than eighteen years in age, was sat alone on the driver's bench. He was waiting for the return of his platoon along with a new batch of Sikh prisoners. By the time he had heard Harjit's footsteps approaching from the left, it was already too late for him to react.

The young driver felt the cold hard steel of Jai's new blade pierce through his back, until the tip of his sword protruded from the driver's chest. In an attempt to cry out, the boy simply spluttered out blood all over himself, before Harjit slit his throat like an assassin.

The young lad slumped forward and once again, Harjit and Jai had taken a life in a harrowingly efficient manner. Without pausing to rest or to acknowledge their latest kill, the pair swarmed to the front of the last carriage only to find it empty.

Even through the smoke and mayhem up ahead, Harjit and Jai could see dozens of heavily armed Mughal soldiers on horseback, continuing to plough their way through the townsfolk. Some soldiers trampled down people with their horses, whilst others continued to maim the men with their arrows, spears and fire.

The women and children were being separated and taken to what looked like a marketplace in the centre of the town. Harjit turned to his newly ordained fellow warrior. "Brother Jai, even with these weapons, we are no match for a platoon of soldiers. I do not fear death, but I also do not wish to die in vain. At least not until I have had the chance to hold my children and wife in my arms once more."

Despite his recent blood lust, Jai understood Harjit's intent. It served no purpose for them to die in a hopeless charge, yet he could not bring himself to just stand by and watch. "I know bro. But there must be something else we can do," Jai replied in desperation.

But before Harjit could respond, two riders from up ahead spotted the duo and began to gallop directly towards them at full speed. Unfortunately, their enthusiasm to clear the final carriage had left them exposed. There was now nothing between them and the fighting in town.

Harjit and Jai knew they barely had a minute before the riders would be upon them. Harjit dropped his sword and reached for the bow on his shoulder. "We could make a run for it?" Jai said, with a hint of panic in his voice. But even he knew they would not be able to make it back to their horses in time.

With no other options left to them, Jai held his new sword up high in front of himself. It was the only thing he could think to do. He hadn't even learnt how to wield a sword properly, let alone fight a trained soldier, charging at him on horseback. 'You idiot Jai, how could you have been so stupid?' he thought to himself.

His little sister was counting on him and now he was going to die in the stupidest of ways. "I don't want to die, at least not like this." Jai said out loud. But his friend was too busy loading an arrow on to his bow to pay attention.

Harjit tried his best to stop his arm from shaking, as the riders narrowed the distance between them at an alarming rate. Taking a deep breath, he drew back his bow, took aim and released the arrow. The single missile cut through the air with a sharp whistle and flew straight past its target, to both Harjit and Jai's dismay.

Harjit shot Jai a look of panic before he fumbled around for another arrow. But it was too late. Their attackers were almost upon them and had begun to lower their spears with the intent of skewering their opponents.

In that moment, Harjit and Jai knew they stood no chance. As Jai tightened the grip on his sword, a new whistling sound pierced through the air between to the two opposing forces.

The two attacking Mughal soldiers dropped from their horses and crashed into the ground in a spectacular fashion. It was as if they had been struck by a wrecking ball. The crunch of flesh and bone smashing into the ground at high speed was so loud that even Billo and Chittar heard it.

Jai and Harjit jumped out of the way, as the rider-less horses charged straight past them. The duo then hurried to regain their footing and scanned the horizon for any sign of the shooter. But there was none. If it hadn't been for the giant arrows sticking out from the dead riders, Jai would have sworn it was a miracle.

But before they could celebrate their lucky escape, the sound of a horn blowing, vibrated through the air. It was coming from the edge of the forest to their right.

Uniformed soldiers on horseback began to appear from the forest armed with an array of weaponry, from bows and arrows, to metre long Talwar's. But they were not the same as the soldiers from the village. Many of these new soldiers were dressed in the vibrant colours of the Khalsa and they outnumbered the Mughal attackers by at least five to one.

With their saffron coloured turbans and deep blue chola's (robes), the new warriors shone to Harjit and Jai like a beacon of light.

"Bole so nihal!" came the Jaikara, which was answered by over a hundred voices in unison.

"Sat Sri Akal!" they yelled, as they poured out of the forest and charged into the town. The squadron of Khalsa warriors seemed to wash over the attacking Mughal's like a tsunami devouring everything in its path.

They were relentless as they systematically chopped and slashed their way through every last opponent, leaving only a wake of mutilated bodies and limbs behind them.

The engagement was all over within a matter of minutes. Where there had once been chaos, there was now a harrowed silence. Harjit and Jai looked at each other as they were both beyond astounded. "Er…you saw all that too, right?" Jai asked skeptically.

"Yes, brother Jai. That just happened. We should meet with their leaders," responded an equally shocked Harjit. Jai nodded in agreement. Without speaking another word, the duo retrieved their horses and rode into the centre of town to great their new saviours.

As the pair entered the town, the true cost of the battle became clearer. The entrance to Jagraon was littered with the bodies and limbs of the dead.

Khalsa soldiers were freeing Sikh prisoners from their chains, whilst others helped to extinguish the fires with what little water they had. Seeing dead bodies on the floor was starting to become the norm for Jai. But what worried him now, was how little it was affecting him.

Just the thought of seeing a disfigured corpse would have been enough to make him vomit twenty-four hours ago, yet here he now sat having contributed to the body count himself. He pressed the wound on his shoulder for a moment and felt grateful to know that he could still feel pain. He was not completely numb, not just yet.

The pair continued riding through the town whilst looking for any sign of the Khalsa leaders. Harjit scouted their different faces as he passed them by in hope of finding his brother. He was surprised to see that so many of the cavalry were just regular Sikh men. Some were just boys as young as ten and some were as old as seventy.

Eventually, they came across a group of Khalsa warriors gathered within the remains of the market square. A dozen Sikh warriors were stood around a tall, powerful man with leathery brown skin and a bright long white beard. They were all listening intently to his every word.

The man wore a commanding white turban, adorned with a single Chakram (circular blade) to protect his head and to serve as a weapon. But that was not the only piece of functional weaponry that he wore. Covering his deep blue chola was a silver-plated armored vest, that matched the Khanda (double edged sword) resting by his side.

His intimidating sword was accompanied by a pair of smaller Kirpan's that were tucked into his dark green belt. Whilst his armour and weapons were impressive, it was the unmistakable aura around him that first drew Harjit and Jai's attention.

Despite his older age, Nawab Kapur Singh Virk seemed to radiate a mixture of strength and serenity. He spoke in a calm yet authoritative voice that held the attention of all those around him.

"Round up any supplies you can find and load them onto the empty carriages. Burn the dead and prepare the wounded for transport. I want us all out of here within the hour. That is all," commanded the leader of the Khalsa soldiers.

"Ji Hukam!" the warriors chimed in unison, as the majority of them turned and walked away to perform their duties.

That is when Harjit and Jai saw the Nawab clearly for the first time. He had a scar across his left eye and from the damage to his armour, it was clear to them that he had seen plenty of conflict in his life. Kapur had been busy talking to his subordinates when he noticed the strangers staring at him.

"Waheguru Ji Ka Khalsa, Waheguru Ji Ki Fateh!" (The Khalsa belongs to God, Victory belongs to God) spoke Harjit loudly, as

174

he addressed the leader of the Khalsa squadron. Kapur stopped his conversation with his fellow warriors and walked over towards Harjit and Jai.

His piercing brown eyes appeared to study their appearance and that is when he noticed the unique Kirpan's hanging near their waists. Kapur pressed his palms together and repeated the same greeting back to them. "Waheguru Ji Ka Khalsa, Waheguru Ji Ki Fateh," he said, as he bowed his head slightly to them as a sign of humility and respect.

"You are the men from the hill," Kapur stated, as he turned and offered them a place in the shade, beside the other warriors in the market.

Harjit and Jai obliged and were relieved to be sheltered from the burning sun, if only for a few minutes. As they took their place beside the remaining soldiers, one of the warriors spoke up. "Why are you here?" she asked, with a hint of mistrust in her voice.

Jai was taken back as he did not expect to find a woman in the circle of soldiers. But standing to the right of the Nawab, was a girl no older than Jai. Yet, she wore the traditional saffron and blue garbs of a Khalsa warrior, along with the swords and a shield of a fighter. Jai was mesmerised by her eyes from the second he looked into them and was speechless for the second time that day. Harjit realised that he had lost his friend for a moment and nudged him back to reality before answering her question.

"My name is Harjit Pehn Ji, and this is my friend Jai. We have come to find my brother Harpal Singh Khalsa and to request your help," he said, now looking at the Nawab.

"Yesterday, Mughals soldiers raided and attacked our villages and took our people, including my wife and children and his sister. They have been taken to Lahore fort and we need your help to get them back before it is too late," stated Harjit, with a sense of urgency.

The Khalsa warriors remained silent as if waiting for their commander to reply. He looked upon Harjit and Jai with a sorrow in his eyes. "Then I am afraid you are too late. If they have been taken to Lahore fort, then there is nothing that we can do for them. I am sorry young warriors, but your families are gone. Help yourselves to any provisions and supplies, but we move out within the hour." Kapur turned his attention back to his soldiers as if the conversation was over. But for Harjit and Jai, it was far from done.

"What? Are you serious? That's it? Too bad, too late? I thought you guys were supposed to be the Khalsa, the good guys. What the hell sort of answer is that?" retorted Jai, as he started to get upset. Harjit held him by the arm as if to restrain him from saying or doing anything further that he might regret.

"Please Sahib Ji, you are our only hope. These prisoners are all alone. The Mughal's are taking every Sikh man, woman and child they can find. Nowhere is safe for our people," pleaded Harjit, as he tried to get through to the commander.

"I know son. Trust me. The last time the Mughal's tried to eradicate the Sikh's, we rode into Lahore with over five hundred men. But even that was not enough to stop their tyranny. This period of time we are living through, these burdens we are all bearing, are all the Guru Ji's hukam. It is his will, and we are just trying our best to save as many lives as we can. That is why we are here today. We are trying to reach as many towns and villages before the Subedar's men sweep through the whole country and annihilate us all. For every soldier I would send to Lahore, that is one less person out here fighting the Mughal's. That is one less life saved from their barbarity. For those who have been captured already, it is too late my sons." Kapur looked away as he felt a sense of defeat.

"No! Don't you get it? If you don't stop the 'Butcher' now, he'll never stop coming for you. I don't know what exactly what went wrong last time when you guys attacked Lahore, but this time it will be different. This time, we won't stop until we take the fucker's head. Don't you understand? Yes, people may die out here, but that is not a guarantee. The people captured so far will die for a certainty, unless *we* act now. You are just dealing with the symptom's here. The only way to stop a disease is to cut it out from the root. If this Mir Mannu prick is the root of all of this, then we need to remove him from this earth. I don't know about hukam and the Guru's will. All I know is that my baby sister is going to die in the hands of some evil bastard, unless we go there and stop him once and for all. If it isn't the duty of a Sikh to stand up to all kinds of evil, then I don't know what is!" Jai's heartfelt words took the Nawab and his soldiers by surprise. They stood in silence as they weighed and contemplated his argument.

After a moment, Kapur looked at Jai and smiled. "You talk with passion and from the heart my boy. I admire that. But my duty is to these people first, I must…"

"Nawab Ji!" came the call from two soldiers, as they ran into the marketplace and interrupted their commander. "Forgive us Nawab Ji. Our scouts report Mughal reinforcements from the east. They will be here in less than thirty minutes," reported the taller of the two soldiers.

Without hesitation, Kapur issued new orders to his soldiers. "Round up everyone and give the order to leave, now! Back to the camp!" commanded the Nawab, with absolute authority. But before he turned to leave, Kapur looked at Harjit and Jai. "You too. We will finish this discussion back at camp." And with that final word, the Nawab and his Khalsa warriors dispersed immediately, rushing to complete the evacuation of all the Sikh's from the town.

The Khalsa soldiers focused on loading as much food and weaponry into the three empty carriages as possible. As soon as the carriages were full, they were driven out of the town and into the forest.

The rest of the townspeople aided the Sikh survivors by giving them whatever provisions they could carry, and they too disappeared into the woods after the carriages.

Not wanting to be left behind to face an incoming Mughal hoard, Harjit and Jai also decided to accompany their new friends to their secret base camp. The duo wasted no time in mounting their faithful mare's and hastily joined the convoy leaving town.

Within fifteen minutes, the evacuation had been completed and the surviving Sikhs who had been destined for slavery or death, had now begun their new lives as refugees. Harjit and Jai stayed together as they followed the other riders through a maze of uneven paths and thick shrubbery.

After an hour or so of dodging protruding branches, thorny bushes and crossing streams, the terrain seemed to flatten out and open up. It was only then that Jai started to take in his surroundings.

He looked up at the great Banyan trees that surrounded him and stared in wonder, as the golden light of the sun filtered through the branches. The light illuminated the world below in an array of different shades of green and brown. The whole forest seemed to resonate with life all around him and for a moment, Jai almost forgot that he was in India.

'Maybe this place isn't so... son of bitch!' Jai said to himself, as he slapped the side of his neck. "God damn mosquitos! I should have known. I hate this bloody place!" he said out loud, as he attempted to swat away the blood sucking bugs. A few townsfolk looked at him strangely and began to distance themselves from the raving man on a horse.

Harjit saw Jai battling the bugs and closed the gap between them. "Here, rub this onto your skin. It will help keep them away," said Harjit, as he handed Jai an ointment from his saddle, for which he was incredibly grateful for.

"Do you think these guys will help us?" Jai asked, as he applied the ointment with one hand and balanced on Chittar with the other.

"I hope so," replied Harjit. There really wasn't anything either of them could say further on the matter, as they were now both dependent on the kindness of strangers. Neither Harjit nor Jai liked being in such a vulnerable position, but they had no choice for now. Excitement up ahead distracted them both from their morbid train of thoughts.

Jai looked up and was relieved to see that they had finally reached their destination. A few hundred feet in front of them, lay a blue lake that stretched on as far as the eye could see. Hundreds of tents lined up between them and the edge of the water.

As they looked from left to right and in the space between the giant trees, they saw an army of makeshift homes that had been constructed using wood, rope and large sheets of cloth sown together.

It was as if they had entered a tribal village within the forest. Sikh civilians began to emerge from their temporary homes and began to take in the new supplies and aid the refugees from Jagraon. It was a remarkable sight to behold. A fully functional village constructed from the resources of the forest.

Jai looked at Harjit. "Did you know about any of this?" he asked in amazement. Harjit shook his head. "I had no idea brother Jai," said the young farmer, as they continued on a path that led them straight through, to the heart of the encampment.

Their path took them to four giant marquees that had been constructed in the very centre of the camp. Each one of them held a special purpose and served the community of refugees that had been forced into hiding. From the amazing aroma of fresh dhal cooking nearby, Jai could tell that one of the tents was definitely a langar (communal) kitchen.

He was amazed how simple civilians had managed to create a series of structures that could easily accommodate over four hundred people each. The other three marquees each served a different purpose.

The smallest of the three acted as the headquarters of the camp, where the Khalsa panth (committee), would meet and take any appropriate actions for the group. The remaining two marquees also served equally important yet different roles for their community.

One had been made to serve as a temporary Gurdwara (house of God), allowing the inhabitants a quiet place to gather and pray together, whilst the final tent was by far the most interesting to Jai.

That is where the weapons were being constructed and where the civilians were being taught how to fight and defend themselves. Both Harjit and Jai, couldn't help but be impressed by the simplicity and efficiency of the Sikh base camp.

The sound of people practicing Kirtan (hymns) could be heard in the background, whilst others trained with swords and steel. "Where do we go first? I have to admit, I am starving mate!" said Jai, excited at the prospect of having a hot and nourishing meal.

"We should tend to the horses first. I believe the horse pen is by the lake," said Harjit, as he pointed to a large enclosure that had been cordoned off from the rest of the woods. With access to fresh water, it was the perfect place for the horses to rest, feed and replenish their energy. Clearly, a lot of care and thought had gone into their wellbeing.

Jai followed Harjit's lead, and they headed straight for the horse pen first. He was relieved to dismount Chittar for the last time that day. "Thank you, girl. You may have killed my ass, but I'm pretty sure you saved my life too, so we're even," Jai joked with his horse, as he led her into the horse pen along with Harjit and Billo.

Content that the horses were ok, Harjit and Jai strolled back to the center of the camp. On the way, they passed some new refugees who were being shown how to build tents of their own. Others worked on sowing new clothes or tended to the wounded. Every person seemed to have a purpose or task that contributed towards the collective.

Even the children were busy learning how to read and write and how to defend themselves. As they passed the training tent, Jai spotted the female warrior from Jagraon inside, and he stopped dead in his tracks. She was busy coordinating the new weaponry they had salvaged from Jagraon, yet Jai could not take his eyes off her.

There was a strength and simplicity to her unmistakable beauty, that he had never seen in a woman before. She was truly one of a kind. "Brother Jai, this way…" came Harjit's voice, snapping him back to reality once again. Jai looked at Harjit in embarrassment. He had spoken to dozens of girls before now, yet he had never been infatuated with one like this before.

"Sorry! My bad bro. Where were we…" he said, trying to recompose himself. Harjit looked to see what Jai had been staring at, but the girl had since moved on.

"Do not worry brother Jai, I am sure we will have plenty of time to pick out new weapons, but first we must finish our discussion with the Nawab."

"Yes, totally. Let's go," said Jai, not wanting to draw any more attention to himself. The duo proceeded to the camp's headquarters and entered into the smallest of the four marquees. Of all the tents, this was the only one with a purpose-built seating area.

Rows of benches made up of fallen tree trunks and Indian bamboo, had been arranged in a large semi-circle, similar to that of a Greek auditorium. On the floor at the very centre, lay a maroon-coloured rug big enough to accommodate over thirty people.

This was the seating area for the Khalsa panth. They sat on the floor as a gesture of humility, whilst the people they served could sit above and around them and listen to their discussions. It was a reminder of the panth's primary purpose, to serve the others.

Harjit and Jai entered the tent and made their way to the rug, where the Nawab was sat alongside other the members of the Khalsa panth. Dozens of other Khalsa warriors were sat around the small group of baptised Sikhs, who were deep in conversation.

As they approached the center, a lady also entered the tent from the other side. After having finished her business in the training tent, Ikamroop took her place beside her father, the Nawab.

From the moment she entered, Jai could feel his heart starting to beat faster. 'Stop it!' he said to himself. 'This ain't the time, you idiot. Focus Jai, focus!'

Harjit noticed his friend had become a little distracted and then followed his line of sight to Ikamroop. He then understood what had distracted his friend. Harjit coughed discreetly to bring Jai's attention back to matter at hand. The duo then removed their shoes and sat down on the rug opposite the Nawab and the others.

The panth greeted their guests in the same manner as before. "Waheguru Ji Ka Khalsa, Waheguru Ji Ki Fateh!" to which Jai and Harjit promptly repeated back to them. Jai observed that the Nawab looked slightly more tired than before. It was as if he was carrying the weight of the world upon his shoulders.

"I have informed our brothers and sisters here of our discussion and of your request," began Kapur. "Are you certain that they were taken to Lahore? The governor also has a stronghold in Sirhind," asked the Nawab.

Harjit and Jai exchanged a quick glance as they thought back to Raichand's confession in the forest. "Yes, Nawab Ji. We are certain. By my estimate, they would have reached the fort by now," replied Harjit.

"What makes you so sure you they are still alive?" asked Ikamroop. Both Harjit and Jai were taken back by the warrior's directness, but this time it was Jai who replied first.

"They are still alive. The Mughal's would have killed them back in Sidhwan if they wanted them dead. I don't know why they were taken. But as long as there is a chance, Harjit and I will do whatever it takes to get them back. With or without your help… preferably with though," Jai added quickly.

Ikamroop looked at her father, who took a deep breath before he spoke. "I cannot order any warriors to accompany you to Lahore. There are over thirty thousand Mughal soldiers and mercenaries roaming all of the Punjab right now. They are looking for us. Not even our Hindu and Muslim neighbors are safe from the Subedar's forces. With every day that passes, another town or village falls, and another drop of blood is spilt. Even we cannot remain here. We are short on food and supplies and it is only a matter of time before they discover this camp," said Kapur, with a sadness in voice that he could not disguise.

One of the Khalsa warriors, a serious looking man in his forties spoke next. "These people need the Khalsa to protect and watch over them. Without our presence, they would be defenseless," the warrior added.

Kapur looked at his friend Surjit and nodded gently in agreement. Whilst Harjit and Jai could empathise with the panth, they were still determined to find a way to rescue their loved ones.

"Look, we get it. What you guys have done here is amazing and you're right. It probably is only a matter of time until they find you here too. But that is why this needs to end now. We need to send a message to this Mannu prick, once and for all. That no matter how many of us they try to chop and burn. We will never give in. We will fight them down to the very last man, woman, and child. Now, my brother Harjit and I are going to Lahore, and we will find his family and my sister, and we will make those fuckers pay. And yes, we may die in the attempt, but at least we will have lived and died as Sikhs." Jai could feel a pain building up within his chest again.

He forced himself to stop talking before he let anymore emotion spill out of him. He had said all that he could think to say, and he would not plead or beg. If he needed to go to Lahore alone, then so be it.

Jai's words seemed to have placed a blanket of silence upon the group as everyone looked to the Nawab for his response. Kapur closed his eyes whilst the group waited patiently. Harjit turned to his friend and placed his hand on his shoulder, signalling to him that it was over. But Jai did not need to be told to leave. As pair rose to their feet, Kapur Singh Virk opened his eyes and spoke.

"Surjit. Take the camp west to Lakhi jungle. There you will find Jassa Singh Ahluwalia. He will take you all in. I am going to Lahore fort to pay the Governor one last visit. My only regret is that I should have gone back sooner. As I said before, I will not command anyone to Lahore. Anyone who wishes to join us, will do so of their own accord."

Harjit and Jai stood there in silence as the Nawab's words sunk in. Before either of them could speak, all of the other Sikh warriors around them volunteered to join the mission to Lahore, including Ikamroop. Kapur smiled at their enthusiasm.

"I had no doubt that all of you would want to come too. But if this mission is to succeed, we will need keep our numbers small. We have attacked the fort in great numbers once before and failed. This time, we will slip in unnoticed. I will take ten of you with me. Any more and we risk drawing too much attention to ourselves. We will need to travel fast and light, if we are to have any hope of freeing our people from the 'Butcher'. The rest of you will remain behind to aid Surjit. The greater risk will be to the people travelling to Lakhi. Surjit will need your bravery and strength to protect those already in our care."

"Ji Hukam!" came the unified response from the Khalsa warriors around them. Surjit stood up and took his leave, along with the majority of the Khalsa warriors. Only ten stayed behind as per the Nawab's command, including Ikamroop.

When he first heard the number ten, Harjit's first reaction was one of disappointment. But then he came to accept the Nawab's logic. A total of thirteen fighters was still better than two, he reasoned to himself.

"Thank you, Sahib Ji. We are truly grateful to you all..." Harjit began before Jai cut him off. "Yes, thank you! You guys are awesome. So how are we gonna get our people back and kill these scum bags once and for all? I take it you have a plan? We should probably make a plan though, right?" rambled Jai.

"Breath brother Jai, breath," interrupted Harjit, who seemed to be the only one left who could calm his friend down.

Kapur looked at the odd duo before him and smiled. He had indeed thought of a plan that would require them to act swiftly and bravely. "Do not worry young warriors. Before this mission is over, you will have both had more than your fill of blood," said the Nawab, as he proceeded to explain his plan to the duo and the Khalsa volunteers.

Harjit and Jai listened intently, as Kapur showed them the path they were going to take through the jungles and hills and the positions they would take once they entered into the city.

After the briefing had concluded, Kapur introduced each of the ten new soldiers to Harjit and Jai, including his daughter Ikamroop. Jai tried his best to solely focus on the task ahead, despite feeling himself being drawn towards her. But not even a beautiful lady could distract him from a nagging feeling, eating away at him from within.

After the introductions had been completed, the new rescue squad proceeded to the langar marquee, to share a meal together.

They joined rows of people who were sat on the floor, busy consuming their humble yet nutritious meal of dhal and rice together. Sewadar's (volunteers) including the Nawab, helped to distribute the food to all of the newcomers, including Harjit and Jai.

The warm meal was a welcome change for the pair, who had barely eaten all day. But even with their full bellies and a solid plan in place, Jai's pang of anxiety still remained. He turned to his friend and pointed to the lake.

"Hey bro, I'm just gonna get some air. I'll be down by the lake if you need me," Jai informed Harjit, as he left the langar area and went for a solitary walk. Harjit understood the need for some time alone and went into the Gurdwara tent to pray and to meditate.

Seeing the lake, Jai could not help but think about his grandmother and sister. Even the tranquility of watching the water ripple away, gave Jai no relief from the pain building within him. He sat on the floor alone and stared out across the great blue expanse, thinking only of how he had let his loved ones down. That is when the sound of footsteps behind him broke his concentration. It was the Nawab.

Without asking permission, Kapur sat down beside him and took out a mala (prayer beads) and began to stare out at the water too. "Ah, the end to another beautiful day," said Kapur, as Jai looked around to see who he was talking too, but they were alone.

"I guess..." replied Jai. "If you don't mind... I'd rather be alone," he said, hoping that the Nawab would get the hint and leave him be. But the Nawab remained seated and continued to watch the birds skim the water, looking for their next meal.

"I sense much fear in you son. Why is it so important to you that you rescue your sister?" Kapur asked calmly, as he continued to move the mala between his fingers and stare out into the distance.

Jai could just sense a 'talk' coming along and began to grow impatient. "Look, no disrespect, but I have known lots of 'religious' people in my life. They all used to tell me to go to the Gurdwara. Read Paat or to do Kirtan, but none of them ever changed who *they* were. They were all happy to preach to me and to everyone else about what I should do and how I should act. But they never practiced what they preached. Those same people secretly drank alcohol and ate meat and slagged off others behind their backs. I've even seen so called religious people go home and abuse their spouses and treat each other like shit and that is when I realised it was all bullshit. It's all just a front. A way to control people. If religion really worked then they wouldn't all act like assholes to one another behind closed doors. But my sister... Ru... was different. She *is* different. She always believed that God was inside of us. That God *was* us ultimately. She believes that we can be better. She believes in love and kindness, and I really want to believe in all that stuff too, just like she does, but... I can't. It might be too late for me, but I'll be damned to hell before I let anything happen to her. She's not like me. She's not broken inside. She didn't deserve to be taken. It should have been me...

190

Jai didn't realise that he had tears falling down his cheeks until his sight began to blur. He wiped his eyes and felt ashamed of sharing his anger and truth with a complete stranger.

"Son, it is not about her or them. It is about you and your journey, your faith. No one can tell you what to believe. All you can do is listen to your heart. If there is one truth I have learnt in this life, it is that the Guru is within each and every living creature within this universe. Waheguru is all of life and existence, past, present and future. That unlimited power of the universe is within you too. It is a light that binds us all together. Your sister *is* right, we are all connected. From all the people around us, to all the animals living above the land and to all the creatures within the sea, we all belong to the one. Even our perceived enemies in Lahore do. Each lifeform is sacred, and we are all bound by the will and hukam of the Guru. I do not know about religion, but our duty as Sikhs is a simple one. Live by his hukam. Live by the command of God as laid out in the Guru Granth Sahib and open your heart to love. Paat (prayer), Seva (selfless service) and Simran (meditation), these are gifts given to us by our Guru. But they all need love to work. Everything in Sikhi centers around love. Without love, there is no Sikhi. Find the Guru within you and you will always be victorious."

"But how? How can you love someone you hate? These Mughal's bastards are pure evil. Are you telling me, I'm meant to 'love' them too? I'm sorry, but that ain't happening. I just want to kill every last one of them!" replied a frustrated Jai. He hated nothing more than being lectured too and none of this is what he wanted to hear right now.

"There is a difference between justice and revenge. The five thieves (lust, anger, greed, attachment, and egotism), all have their place too. Without anger in the heat of battle, you are likely to fall at your enemy's blade. But you must learn to live *with* them and respect their power. Only by connecting to the light within, will you learn to harness their control over you," said Kapur, as he saw the confusion and impatience growing in Jai's eyes.

The Nawab smiled at Jai. "We are bound to fight for justice and if that means taking the life of someone who has killed another, then so be it. Sikh's must stand up for themselves and for the innocent. It is the reason the Khalsa exists."

Kapur stopped there as he sensed that Jai needed some time alone to think about what he had said. As he stood to up to leave, the Nawab stretched out his hand. "You can start here, it is never too late," he said, as he handed Jai his Mala and left.

Jai looked down at the wooden beads in his hand and for a moment he felt an urge to throw them into the lake. But the more he stared at them, the less angry he began to feel. If anything, he just felt exhausted. With only a few hours left before they set off for Lahore, Jai decided it would be best if he got some rest.

As Jai rose to his feet, he brushed off the dirt from his blood-stained clothes and stuffed the Mala into his pajama pocket.

"Oh, there you are brother Jai. Come, we have been given a place to rest," came a familiar voice. Jai smiled at seeing his friend and walked over to join him. As he got closer, Jai could tell that something was wrong, from the expression on Harjit's face.

"What's up bro? You look…different," enquired Jai. Whatever it was, Jai could see that it was a difficult topic for Harjit to discuss. He seemed to struggle to find the words to explain.

"My… my brother Harpal was killed in the attack earlier today," replied Harjit, despondently.

"Oh shit, I'm sorry to hear that bro. Were you guys close?"

"Once. Many years ago. We stopped talking over something small. I can barely remember now what it was. I suppose I lost my brother back then. But a part of me always believed that we would be close again. I suppose it is too late for that now," said Harjit, with a sadness in his voice that Jai knew only too well.

Whilst Jai knew all the cliché lines he could offer Harjit, none of them felt like they could have made a difference in that moment.

"Well, for what it's worth, you're the closest thing to a brother I've ever had," said Jai, as he looked away awkwardly. Harjit felt overwhelmed by the gesture and nodded his head in appreciation of the sentiment. Jai understood the acknowledgement and they proceeded to walk towards the new tent that had been built for them, in silence.

Whilst it was literally a few sheets on the ground, covered by a tarp that was being held up by bamboo, it was enough to provide them with shelter from the open sky for a few hours.

Harjit took the space to the left and Jai took the empty space to the right, and within minutes Harjit was fast asleep. As Jai lay down, he reached inside his pocket and retrieved the Mala. He stared at it for a moment and thought about the Nawab's words. Holding it tight in his hand, Jai closed his eyes and he too drifted off to sleep.

Chapter 10

The great wooden doors of the western gate slammed shut, causing a resounding echo, as Jahangir and the guards marched Ruhi and the other four prisoners down a long and narrow corridor. To Ruhi's surprise, the corridor did not lead onto another building or courtyard, as she had anticipated.

Instead, the corridor opened up into a trench. There were now tall red brick walls on either side of her and a clear blue sky above her head. None of the girls had any idea where they were being taken, yet they were all equally afraid.

"Right!" barked Jahangir, from behind them. The procession of prisoners seemed to have arrived at a dead end, but in reality there were two staircases on either side of them built into the walls. The guards ushered them up the right-hand side staircase and led them to the surface above.

It was only then that Ruhi began to understand where she really was. As her head rose above the surface, the first thing that hit her was the dust and then the noise.

There before her, was an open space greater in size than four football fields combined together. But the vast expanse was far from empty. There were dozens of giant trees scattered across the horizon, giving their shade to large groups of people spread out far across the land.

But Ruhi could instantly tell something was wrong. These were not just any people; they were Sikh women and children being made to toil away in the burning sun.

Before she could take in anymore, Jahangir shoved Ruhi from behind, almost causing her to topple over. "Move it! To the court!" he bellowed, as he pointed ahead towards a towering structure that sat directly to the right of the great expanse. It looked as if someone had just stuck two completely different buildings together, to form a giant behemoth.

The left side of the structure was the people's court, and its beauty was unmistakable. At over two hundred feet long, thirty feet high and seventy feet wide, the rectangular block cast an imposing shadow across the vast land below. It's three outward facing sides were each made up of a series of grand archways that were supported by one of forty red pillars, that propped up the entire structure.

The raised paved floor of the court extended almost one hundred feet outwards from the block into the expanse. It was a true testament to Persian architecture. In a stark contrast, the right side of the great structure was just a plain stone coloured building that was over three storeys high, and in no way a match for the court in terms of its extravagance.

But Ruhi was now far too distracted by the commotion around her to care about where she was being led. All of the Sikh women and children across the multiple fields, seemed to be working in some kind of twisted production line. But it was too dusty and chaotic to clearly see what was going on.

Ruhi and the four girls marched on, as the sound of whips tearing into the backs of slaves cut through the air, followed closely by cries of pain from the innocent. Yet the sound of torment was almost masked by a melody that seemed to float above the misery surrounding them. It was the chanting of a single word being repeated all around them, 'Waheguru, Waheguru, Waheguru…'

Hearing the name of the lord spoken in such a godforsaken place, struck a chord in Ruhi's heart. She too began to chant the name of God, further inciting Jahangir's wrath. Just as he was about to strike her across the back of the head, he paused, as he remembered the Subedar's orders. Instead, the Amir clasped his hand around her arm and dragged her away from the great expanse and towards the rear of the superstructure.

As Ruhi was escorted to the rear entrance along with the others, she couldn't help but notice how the ivory coloured building resembled Raichand's haveli. Ruhi could see that each level of the building also has it own open archways and decorated balconies.

The higher she looked, the more intricate the carvings and the architecture became. Her group was hoarded into a large open-air chamber on the ground floor, which was largely empty, except for a single desk and a chair in its centre. Running across the length of the far wall, was a long wooden water trough, that looked very much out of place.

The ladies were taken to the trough and ordered to clean themselves with the cloudy water. Ruhi exchanged a look of apprehension with the prisoner standing next to her. It was the girl from the carriage with green eyes. Her fellow prisoner scooped up some water first and cleaned her face and Ruhi followed her lead as the guards stood by and watched all of them closely.

"Enough!" sighed Jahangir, as he pulled out his chair and sat at his desk. "What are they still doing here? Take them upstairs now," said the Amir impatiently, as he tended to some papers on his desk. The guards immediately grabbed each of the girls and forced them through a doorway and up a staircase, that led them up to the second floor.

But the layout of this level was completely different to the ground floor. There were no separate rooms or corridors this time. The entire floor was just one open chamber. Tall, chiseled pillars reached up to a painted ceiling, whilst sunlight flooded in from large window-like archways on the south, east and west sides of the building.

Silk cushions and padded seats lined the entire room. It struck Ruhi as more of a royal lounge than a room belonging to a court. There were tables covered with food and wine and exotic fruits from all over Asia. Paintings adorned the walls and delicate oil lamps stood on standby, for when the light of day faded. On the northern wall furthest from them, were five wide doorways, leading out to what looked like a balcony.

The guards wasted no time and dragged the girls into the centre of the chamber, where there were multiple sets of iron shackles anchored to the floor waiting for them. The guards started with the youngest of the girls and began to chain each of them by their hands and feet.

"No way! That is not happening," said Ruhi in defiance, as a guard reached for her wrist.

"Silence!" he ordered, as he struck her hard across the face with the back of his hand. Ruhi's bottom lip split open, and she could taste the warmth of her blood in her mouth.

"Speak again and I will really show you who the master is here," said the guard, as he took her hands and shackled them to the chains on the floor. Once the five prisoners had been secured, the guards left the chamber via the same staircase, leaving the prisoners alone.

Two of the girls who were no older than fourteen or fifteen began to cry. With her cheek still burning, Ruhi looked around before whispering to them. "Don't worry, whatever happens we stick together, ok?" The green-eyed lady looked at Ruhi and was about to speak, when they heard voices coming from the balcony outside.

In the central doorway, a man appeared and entered the chamber. He was quickly followed by an entourage of servants and guards. Mir Mannu looked at his new presents waiting for him in the centre of the room and made his way slowly over to them. He walked as a man without a care in the world, savouring each and every moment.

Even from twenty feet away, he could feel their fear and anticipation building with every step he took forward towards them. It made him feel powerful and excited as they began to realise that their lives were in his hands.

"Greetings, once again ladies. I trust you have all been well cared for," said the Subedar playfully, as he walked by each of them purposefully and examined them closely. It was as if he were picking his favourite dessert from a tray. None of the girls knew whether to speak or not, as the memory of the guard striking Ruhi was still fresh in their minds.

Mir noticed the blood trickling down from Ruhi's lip and seemed genuinely concerned with her wellbeing. "Who did this to you? It is a crime to strike such a beautiful flower," he said gently, as he looked her in the eyes and moved closer towards her. Mir raised his hand in an attempt to wipe the blood from her face with his thumb.

Ruhi saw Mir's hand coming closer and did not react at first. But as soon as his skin touched her face, she struck like a viper and bit down hard on his thumb.

Mir screamed out in pain, causing his guards to run from their positions towards their master. But Ruhi was determined. She clamped her teeth down as hard as she could and yanked back her head as violently as she could manage. The thumb separated from his hand and Mir recoiled to the floor in agony. Blood poured down Ruhi's face, as she spat the thumb out of her mouth and onto the floor.

The craziness of what she had done hadn't even registered with her, as the attack had been based purely on instinct. As Mir bowed over in pain, his guards stormed towards Ruhi with their spears lowered, ready to skewer her. It was in that moment, she realised what she had just done.

Her final thoughts were of shock and surprise, as the nearest guard pulled back his spear and lunged forward to strike her down.

"STOP!" cried out Mir in pain, as he fought to control his senses.

The guard froze mid-attack, with his blade only inches away from tearing her flesh apart. Mir stood up clutching his hand and smiled wildly to himself, as blood squirted out from his wound. He pressed down hard on his new stub to stop the bleeding and was now sweating profusely.

"I did not see that coming!" he said loudly, and slightly out of breath, as he breathed deeply through the pain. To the shock of all those around him, Mir began to laugh at himself.

Within a split second, his face changed. "Don't just stand there, get me the doctor!" he yelled at the nearest guard, who immediately bolted for the stairs. Mir's other servants now swarmed around him and tried their best to tend to his wound, as he stood there with dark red blood stains all over his expensive clothes. "That was *my* mistake and not one I will be making again," he said, still trying to manage his breathing.

Ruhi stood there chained, with the taste of his blood in her mouth and stared down at the severed thumb on the floor. She was still in shock and disbelief at what she had done. She didn't know the words to say. Nothing about what had just happened made any sense to her. More servants along with a well-dressed attendant ran up the stairs and towards the Subedar.

Out of nowhere, someone had pulled up a chair and sat him down in it, as the physician tended to his thumb. "Come, I need to take you to my study," said the healer.

"NO!" roared Mir in pain. "Fix it here!" he commanded, in a deadly serious tone that was in complete contrast to his laughing from only seconds earlier.

The physician looked worried and nodded immediately to demonstrate his compliance. He knew better than to argue with the Subedar.

A guard handed the physician Mir's severed thumb. It was all purple and red and chewed up. "There is no re-attaching this, we must clean and cauterise the wound immediately. Bring me a hot iron and the green ointment from my study, immediately," ordered the physician, to the nearest servant. The servant bolted away as the physician gave Mir some opium for the pain.

The drugs flooded his system with ecstasy and within seconds, Mir's throbbing pain began to float away like a cloud. The Subedar took a deep breath, as he looked past the doctor at Ruhi

Kaur still standing there in shock. She looked as if she had just devoured a lion raw.

Mir was impressed. He stood up cautiously and walked closer to her, but this time, he kept his limbs out of her reach. "You… You are a challenge," he said to Ruhi, as he smiled in admiration of her bravery or stupidity. He couldn't quite decide which it was, but she fascinated him, nevertheless.

"Come, I wish to show you something," he said, as he turned and slowly walked over to the doorway from which he had come. "Bring her!" Mir commanded his guards. Keeping their weapons drawn, the guards pulled her by her chains and led her onto the balcony.

'This is it. They're going to throw me out of a window or something. What the hell was that Ruhi!?' she asked herself.

But the guards simply tied her to edge of the balcony, several feet away from the Subedar and left. "Welcome to the 'Diwan e Aam' (the people's court)," said Mir, as he took pleasure in observing the shock and awe on Ruhi's face. Ruhi looked out at the great expanse before her and was completely subdued by the true scale of Mir's operation.

There were not just a few large groups of women and children working, there were hundreds of them. From teenage girls to old women who had survived the journey, all of them sat in segregated fields, grinding grain into flour using Chakki's (stone mills). But these didn't just look like normal stone mills, the grinding stones were almost a metre across in diameter and over forty kilograms in weight.

Not even the little ones had been spared. Children as young as three were pushing carts of flour toward the central granary and were returning with carts loaded with grain, in what looked like an endless cycle.

Guards patrolled the perimeter and whipped those who worked too slowly or had fallen behind. Ruhi looked at the end field towards the right and saw dozens of women tied to the ground, with heavy boulders sat upon their bodies, crushing them into the dirt.

Ruhi did not know if this was truly a nightmare or whether she was hallucinating it all. None of it made any sense. She could not comprehend the motivation behind such cruelty. She turned to Mir and asked one question only. "Why?"

Mir simply smiled at her, but before he could reply, the physician interrupted them. "Forgive me my lord, but we must do this now." Mir's servant had returned with a hot poker and the healing ointment and stood beside the physician, ready to assist.

Whilst he seemed annoyed for a second, Mir waved them over to proceed, without breaking eye contact with Ruhi. "Tell me young one, what is your name?" Ruhi considered lying for a moment, but she could think of no advantage in concealing the truth.

"Ruhi Kaur," she replied, in the steadiest voice she could muster. Her courage seemed to be returning to her. "Why have you done this to us? What do you want with us?" she asked, feeling a streak of anger building up from inside her body again.

But the physician interrupted them again, as he needed the Subedar's attention. The physician braced Mir for some extreme pain, before he pressed the bright orange iron rod against his stub, sealing his wound once and for all. Mir gritted his teeth and groaned in pain as his skin burned and sizzled to a close.

It was all over within seconds and the physician applied his ointments and bandaged the wound as quickly as he could. Once he was done, Mir stood up and examined the healer's work. Content with the treatment, he dismissed his servants and turned his attention back to Ruhi.

"Why? The 'why' has driven humanity to accomplish great feats. The quest for 'why' is the quest for knowledge and reason, and in that, I can see now that we are both alike. But I have a 'why' of my own for you first. I want to understand why you and all of those people out there, still continue to cling to the belief that Nanak and Gobind were some kind of divine saviours of mankind, when they were nothing more than charlatans. The likes of Nanak and Gobind were nothing more than conjurers of magic. So then why is it, that you are all willing to die for these false prophets?"

Ruhi looked at the Subedar in disbelief, as he continued to keep a healthy distance between them. She paused for a moment before replying to his queries.

"Seriously? Why? It's simple. Guru Nanak was the light of the Universe in human form. He taught us that God is in every living creature, within all of creation, including those with the darkest of souls. His light was passed on through nine more Guru's who all added their knowledge, wisdom and love and made it available for all of humanity, not just us. Our Guru lives within the heart of each and every person and their name is the Guru Granth Sahib Ji. So you can slander our Guru's all that you want, but you cannot change the truth. 'Ek-Onkar' means there is only one God, and it is the same God for all. Those people you are torturing down there, are your mothers and sisters just as much as they are mine. And for the way you have treated all of them, you will be punished. You *deserve* to be punished. I can spot a coward from a mile away and you Mannu, are just a pathetic nobody. God's justice will be delivered to you one day, I swear it. Whether it's by my hand or another Sikh, you will get what is coming to you."

Ruhi did not know what had overcome her, but she felt better for having spoken the truth from her heart. To Mir's credit, he did listen to Ruhi respectfully. But her words did not have the impact she had hoped for. Instead, Mir smiled back at her, before enjoying the view from his balcony.

"You Sikh's are consistent; I will give you that. But I would be lying if I said I was not disappointed. I was hoping that you would have had more of an open mind than your predecessors. But we shall see just how long that 'will' of yours lasts. There has only ever been one prophet and his name was Mohammed (peace be upon him). He was God's only messenger and the only words of truth that exist in this world are that of the holy Qu'ran. The sooner you and your people realise this truth, the sooner your suffering shall end. There is only one way out of my servitude. Renounce your false prophets and accept Islam as the true religion for all of humanity, and you shall all be set free. I give you my word."

Ruhi could not tell if Mir was just an Islamic extremist or truly crazy, but either way she knew she was better off down there in the working fields, than on a balcony with a psycho.

"No thank you. But I will take my leave now. Can you show me the way out of this place? Oh, and the whole 'evil vibe' thing you have going on back there with the décor and chains, is very last century," said Ruhi, as she channeled her brother's flair for sarcasm.

Mir's disposition changed when he realised that his prisoner had resorted to mocking him. "How disappointing. Perhaps a few days of discipline and hard work will change your mind... GUARDS!" yelled the Subedar.

His guards who were positioned by the doorway, ran to his side and awaited their next command. "See to it that Miss Kaur here, is put to work with the new arrivals. I would like her to enjoy our full hospitality."

"Ji Hukam!" chimed the guards in unison, before they turned their attention to Ruhi.

But the guard nearest to Mir stood his ground for a moment, "What about the others my lord?" he asked the Subedar. Mir paused as he seemed to have completely forgotten about the other four girls he had chained to the floor in his chamber.

"Oh yes, give them to Jahangir. You men may share them *after* you have seen to your duties. I have found the one I was looking for," said Mir, as he smiled at Ruhi once more, before looking down at his injured hand. The guards proceeded to follow their orders and unshackle Ruhi from the balcony.

"No!" protested Ruhi. "You can't do that, they're just girls. Please! They haven't done anything to you!" she yelled. Mir sat down on his throne like chair and ignored her pleas for mercy.

The Subedar looked out in pride at his production line of kafir's, as they toiled away in the burning heat. Ruhi continued to yell and protest as she was dragged back into Subedar's chamber and straight past the four other girls, still shackled to the floor.

"Didi!" called out the youngest of the girls, as they watched the guards drag their companion away. Ruhi tried her best to struggle against the men who had bound her hands and feet, yet she was no match for them.

"I'm sorry!" she called out, as she was dragged outside and dumped unceremoniously into the dusty working fields, along with the other new prisoners that had been brought in earlier that today.

The new prisoners had been fenced off from the others like cattle. As the guards undid Ruhi's shackles, they kicked her to the ground and closed the gate to the 'pen' behind them. Lying in the dirt, covered by dust and overcome with guilt, Ruhi tried her best not to cry.

She couldn't help but think about the four other girls she had left behind and what fate awaited them. Just the thought of multiple dirty and sweaty guards forcing themselves on the young girls was too much for her to bare.

With an aching jaw and a bruised leg from the guard's kick, Ruhi tried her best to regain her composure. She looked around her enclosure for a familiar face, but she did not recognise anyone. Even though she was surrounded by other women and children, she had never felt so alone in her life.

"Didi?" came a familiar voice. Ruhi spun around, desperately looking to match a face to the voice. Then her eyes fell upon Suhadna, Veeraj and Baani and a wave of relief washed over her, causing her eyes to fill with tears.

By some miracle, they were all still together and had just been hidden from view by another group of ladies who were standing nearby. Ruhi had never been so happy to see anyone in her entire life. She rushed over to them and embraced Suhadna and the children tightly.

Ruhi was comforted to see that they were all still ok. Especially little Veeraj. "What happened to you? Are you ok? What happened to your lip? Did they hurt you?" asked Suhadna, as she bombarded Ruhi with questions. She too had been deeply concerned for the welfare of her new friend.

"I'm ok," replied Ruhi, in an attempt to calm her friend down. Ruhi touched her lip and realised she must have looked a bloody mess. "I'm ok, honestly. It's just a cut. Here, let me hold him, you must be exhausted," offered Ruhi to Suhadna, who had been cradling her newborn this whole time.

Suhadna still looked worried but obliged and placed the little man into Ruhi's arms, whilst Baani cuddled up to her too. For a moment, Ruhi felt as if she could have been anywhere else. She looked down at Veeraj's little face and closed her eyes for a second, as she took in the moment. 'Thank you, Guru Ji,' she said to herself, as she gently rocked Veeraj in her arms.

The peace however, was not destined to last. Just as Ruhi was filling Suhadna in on her experience with the Subedar, new guards entered their enclosure and began to transport the prisoners to their new workstations. Ruhi handed Veeraj back to Suhadna and held on to Baani's hand, whilst they anxiously waited for their turn.

One by one, everyone was led out of the holding pen and made to walk through the vast fields of workers. The prisoners who had been slaving away since the break of dawn looked exhausted. Ruhi couldn't decide which was worse, seeing the massive scale of the incarceration from the balcony above, or witnessing it close up.

Everywhere she looked, there were rows of women of all ages struggling to grind grain, using the giant stone mills that had been made especially for them. Small, starving children wandered in between them, looking to collect grounded flour or to deliver more grain.

As they proceeded past a dome shaped granary in the centre of the fields, Ruhi looked up at the great court that loomed over them all and shook her head at the thought of that twisted tyrant sitting up there, taking great pleasure in their collective pain.

Ruhi's thoughts were rudely interrupted when a guard pulled her and Baani aside. He pointed them towards a stone mill with only one other lady sitting at the helm. "Go!" he shouted at them. Ruhi knew better than to argue with a guard as her lip still throbbed. She quickly signalled to Suhadna that Baani was safe with her and then proceeded to walk over to her new workstation, with Baani in tow.

Sitting over the grinding stone, was a woman in her mid-thirties. Although, she looked as if she had been turning the wheel for years. Her back was arched, and she had torn pieces of cloth wrapped around her hands. She was clearly worn out from spinning the large grindstone all by herself.

"Here, take this handle," she ordered Ruhi, whilst she looked around nervously for any guards. The lady then handed Baani some grain. "Here Beti, drop these pieces of grain into the middle here, slowly," she said, pointing to the centre of the grinding stone.

Both Ruhi and Baani complied with their new orders and began to assist the lady with her work. Ruhi pushed and pulled the wooden handle in a clockwise motion causing fresh flour to spill out from the sides and into a gutter designed to collect the produce. The grindstone was impossibly heavy.

"I am Sushil. Don't look at the guards, just keep turning that handle until they say stop," said the lady.

"When will that be?" Ruhi replied cautiously, as she attempted to settle into a steady rhythm of turning the handle, whilst Sushil collected the flour.

"Tonight," came the reply. Ruhi feared that was going to be the response, but at least the children were still with them. Ruhi looked behind her and saw that Suhadna had been placed only three mills away. She had somehow managed to carry Veeraj in her Chunni whilst pushing the handle of her own grinding wheel.

It was backbreaking work, especially in the heat. Ruhi did not have to ask, because it was clear there was no food or water for them.

Before Ruhi could ask another question, Sushil spoke again. "Forty kilograms of grain a day. That is how much we need to grind. Any less, and we will *all* spend the remainder of our lives in that last field," warned Sushil, as she pointed to the field furthest to the right.

But Ruhi did not need to look up to know which field that was. Ruhi looked at Baani who was trying her best to drop handfuls of grain into the mill, from the cart. "It's ok sweetheart, we will get out of here. I promise." Ruhi tried her best to give Baani a smile, even though deep down in her heart, she feared for them all.

Chapter 11

"Brother Jai, wake up, it is time to go…" said Harjit, as he shook Jai by the arm. Despite having been in the deepest of sleeps, Jai opened his eyes. He felt as if the earth had swallowed him whole.

As his eyes adjusted to the darkness surrounding him, Jai instantly knew where he was and why he was awoken. "Thank you, I needed that," he said out loud, as he sat up and took in his surroundings.

"What time is it?" Jai asked Harjit, who gave him a puzzled look in return.

"It is nighttime…" his friend replied, as if that were a strange question to ask, but Harjit quickly dismissed the thought, as they both had much to do.

"Come, they will be waiting for us," said Harjit, as he helped Jai up by the hand. After finding their footwear, the duo made their way out of their tent and breathed in the warm evening air.

The lake across from them looked even more beautiful at night than it did during the day, Jai thought to himself, as he watched the moonlight ripple across the water. With no more time left to enjoy their surroundings, the duo proceeded down the pathway that led back towards the centre of the camp.

Small fires and oil lamps aided the moonlight in illuminating the camp all around them. In every direction they looked, the camp seemed to be thriving with life. People were enjoying langar, whilst others sat in groups listening to stories being told from their elders. The people here were not just surviving, they were thriving.

Jai could almost see himself being a part of a community like this. It felt nice to see other people who looked like him for a change. Growing up in the UK had been difficult for the young man, especially since the loss of his father. He had always felt lost between two worlds.

On one hand, his Sikh heritage and culture was of great importance to him and his family, especially his grandparents. Yet on the other hand, the freedom to express himself and to live as he wanted to, also came from his western upbringing. A part of him yearned to live on his own terms, without rules and responsibilities and without religion. But something was holding him back from committing to one side or the other.

The more he looked around and watched the Sikh's from the past, the more Jai was reminded that he didn't truly belong there either. Shaking the thoughts from his mind, he attempted to focus on something else.

"They've done a pretty good job here," he commented, as they approached the four giant marquees.

"Yes. I think Suhadna and the children would have liked it here too..." replied Harjit, whilst trying to disguise the sadness in his voice. Jai instantly felt bad for not asking how his friend was doing. He was not the only one who had lost somebody.

"Hey…how are you holding up? I'm not like, the best with words, but I'm here if wanna talk about anything," offered Jai uncomfortably. Harjit smiled to himself at seeing Jai's embarrassment in discussing this topic.

"Thank you, brother Jai, but the only thing that will make me feel better, will be seeing my family again. Between now and then, we have much to do," replied Harjit as he led them into the armory marquee.

The armory was far busier than either of them had anticipated. On the right-hand side, villagers new and old were busy carving bows and arrows, from bamboo cane. Whilst at the far end of the tent, a group of elderly men were busy making armour and shields to compliment the racks of swords, spears, and maces, that were lined up in rows against the left-hand side of the marquee.

"Wow! This place is crazy. Now I know how Neo felt!" joked Jai, as his friend stood there equally shocked. Even though Harjit did not understand the reference, he too was impressed by the efficient set up of the armory.

"Over here," came the voice of the Nawab, as he noticed Harjit and Jai's arrival and called them over to join him in the centre of the tent, along with the other Khalsa volunteers. The Sikh warriors had already assembled and were in the process of selecting their weaponry, when Harjit and Jai joined them.

"I hope you two managed to get some rest. The real work begins now," said Kapur, as he led them over to a table covered in a variety of weapons.

"Yes sir, it was more than sufficient," replied Harjit.

The Nawab looked at the both of them again, as if he were sizing them up. That is when he noticed Harjit and Jai's matching Kirpan's again.

"May I?" requested Kapur, as he asked to see Harjit's Kirpan. Harjit obliged and handed the weapon to the Nawab.

"It belongs to brother Jai's sister, Ruhi Kaur," informed Harjit, as the Nawab stared at the weapon in his hands.

Kapur seemed to recognise the weapon from the eagle carved into its elegant jade handle. He bowed to it, before he withdrew the blade and examined its beauty in the flickering light. The blade reflected the light emanating from the cackling fire beside them.

"When did you come upon this son?" the Nawab asked Jai.

Jai was puzzled by Kapur's fascination with the Kirpan, but answered him all the same. "They were a gift from our grandparents," he replied.

Kapur seemed to understand something in that moment, but then kept it to himself. He then placed the blade back into its sheath and handed the Kirpan back to Harjit.

"Make sure this gets back to its owner," he added calmly, before turning his attention back to the table. "These Shastar are at your disposal. Take what you need and meet me in the Diwan when you are done. I would like to obtain the Guru's blessings before we depart. Ikamroop will help you if you need any assistance."

Jai turned around at the sound of her name being mentioned and quickly scanned the tent for the female warrior. And there she was, on the other side of the marquee loading a quiver full of arrows. She was dressed differently from the last time he had seen her. This time, she was dressed in a black suit and no longer wore a turban upon her head. Instead, she had her hair tied back in a bun and wore strange overalls, over her suit.

In fact, as he looked closer at the other members of the rescue squad, all of them had changed into strange civilian looking clothes too. Noticing that he had lost Jai's attention, Kapur raised his voice. "That reminds me, you will also need a change of clothes."

Jai spun back around, slightly embarrassed that he had been caught looking at the Nawab's daughter. But Kapur continued. "We will travel to Lahore as Sufi saints in case we come across any patrols. I do not want to draw any unnecessary attention to ourselves on our way to the fort."

And with those final words, the Nawab left Harjit and Jai standing beside the weapons and proceeded to the Gurdwara marquee.

The duo were a little overwhelmed by the assortment of swords, spears and shields before them. Harjit picked up a curved Talwar with a handguard from the table and held it up in front of him. "What do you think?" he asked Jai.

"That is pretty bad ass! I wish we had found something like that when we went for those carriages!" Not wanting to be outdone, Jai scanned the table for an equally impressive sword. There were so many different shapes and sizes of blades available to him, he didn't know where to start.

Just as he was about to reach for a thick and wide Tegha sword, the voice of a stranger interrupted him.

"Not that one. You are likely to get yourself and others killed," said Ikamroop, as she stood behind the both of them observing their behaviour.

"Wow, you're like a ninja or something. I thought you were on the other side of the tent," Jai said in surprise, as he was slightly embarrassed to be caught off guard by the young warrior. Ikamroop ignored his response and went directly to a weapon that was stored on top of an adjacent rack.

She unsheathed a double edged Khanda sword, similar to the Nawab's in size. At almost a metre in length, the straight sword was vastly different to every other blade on the table. Its edges were serrated and near the very top, there was a five-inch slit in the middle of the blade.

"Here, try this. It is the Naag Jeev (snake tongue) Khanda, designed to be wielded with strength and precision. Can you handle it?" she asked Jai directly, as she offered the weapon to him.

Jai could not help but smile at the lady before him, as he reached out to accept the sword. From the second he wrapped his fingers around the cold iron handle, he knew that this was the weapon for him.

Despite its hefty appearance, it sat perfectly balanced in his hand. Jai held the sword out before him and practiced cutting it through the air. He even surprised himself at how easily he was able to command the weapon with grace and precision.

"She's perfect," he said looking directly at Ikamroop. The young warrior was taken back by Jai's comment and looked away towards Harjit, who had suddenly become very interested in the structure of the ceiling.

"Thank you Ikamroop," Jai continued, "I think you just saved my life."

It was rare for the young warrior to be at a loss for words. Jai's smoldering stare had broken her concentration and her train of thought, yet she returned his gaze and looked into his big brown eyes. It was a mistake. For she momentarily found herself being drawn towards his handsome face, just as he was being drawn towards her.

Ikamroop forced herself to look away, as she reminded herself not to be controlled by her base instincts. She was better than that. She was now a Sikh soldier, first and foremost and her only duty was to the Khalsa. Ikamroop regained her composure and once again looked at Harjit, before continuing with her orders.

"Now that you have your weapons, Nihal Singh will provide you with a change of clothes. Get your outfits and report to the langar hall when you are done. You will both be allocated with food provisions for the journey and then we will assemble in the Gurdwara Diwan, before heading out to the horse pen. Any questions?" asked Ikamroop, as she looked from Harjit to Jai, but this time without making any eye contact with him.

"Understood Pehn Ji," replied Harjit promptly, to her relief. Ikamroop nodded in acknowledgment and then marched away from the both of them.

"Did you see that?" Jai asked his friend, with the biggest grin on his face.

"I could see you losing focus on why we are here," Harjit replied, as he looked over to Nihal Singh who was ready and waiting for them with their change of clothes.

"She felt it too, I could tell," Jai whispered excitedly to his friend.

Harjit shook his head with disapproval and started walking over to the armory master. "What? You telling me you didn't see that? I think I'm in love," said Jai chasing after his friend.

"I think we need to get changed and go rescue our families," replied Harjit, as he tried to re-focus his friend on the seriousness of task at hand. Jai's eyes dimmed, and the spell of infatuation seemed to disappear from his mind. "Fuck. Yes. You're right. I'm sorry. To Lahore and to take care of that sadistic prick once and for all!" he said with rising enthusiasm.

Harjit nodded in relief, at finally having his friend back. This distraction with Ikamroop was beginning to worry him a little, yet he pushed the thought out of his mind and focused on the matter at hand. All of them needed to stay focused on the task ahead if their families were to have any chance of survival.

Jai seemed to understand this without being told and changed into his outfit as quickly as he could. They were now dressed in matching black and maroon Sufi robes, with white Persian style turbans. When the both of them were ready, they met up with the Nawab and the others inside the Diwan.

Kapur conducted an Ardas for their upcoming mission, which concluded with them all bowing down to the Guru Granth Sahib Ji, who was sat on a raised platform in the center of the Diwan. Even Jai found some comfort in seeking the blessing of the lord, before undertaking the next part of their journey.

They all left the Diwan together and headed for the horse pen. Harjit ensured that Jai maintained a healthy distance from Ikamroop, so that neither of them would become distracted from the mission ahead. Once all the warriors had loaded up their weapons and supplies, they mounted their fresh horses and awaited the Nawab's next command.

Jai started to feel a hint of remorse at his childishness back in the tent. He didn't know what had overcome him. There had been dozens of crushes in his past, yet none of them had affected him like this before. He looked over to Harjit, who was listening out for the Nawab's next command and maneuvered Chittar next to Billo, so that only Harjit could hear him speak.

"Psst. Hey… I'm sorry about earlier. I…" began Jai, before Harjit cut him off.

"No brother Jai, it is I who is sorry. Normally, I would be overjoyed for the both of you. But you know as well as I do, what is at stake here…" Harjit did not need to say anything further, as Jai fully understood the repercussions of their failure.

The duo were finally ready to rescue their loved ones. Both of them knew, that they would do whatever it took to see their families again. The Nawab passed them by and mounted his white horse. Jai was impressed at how easily a man in his mid-fifties could mount a horse.

Kapur circled around the twelve other warriors and inspected his squad one last time. Satisfied that they were all ready to go, he rode his beautiful stead up to the head of the pack and issued a mighty Jaikara. "Bole so Nihal!" he shouted at the top of his voice.

"Sat Sri Akal!" the group roared back to him in unison. Recognising his master's command, Kapur's horse bolted ahead out of the horse pen and into the dark cover of the forest, followed by Harjit, Jai, Ikamroop and the other nine Khalsa warriors.

Whilst Jai's journey to Lahore had only just begun, ninety miles east of their location, his little sister was facing a great challenge of her own. Despite taking turns with Sushil, Ruhi's hands had become blistered from gripping the wooden handle of her stone mill.

Between her aching back and blistering hands, the last ten hours had been agony. 'I should have totally joined a gym earlier,' Ruhi thought to herself, as she tried to distract her mind from the pain coursing throughout her body.

Little Baani lay on the floor next Ruhi, covered in a sprinkling of white flour dust. With each rotation of the stone mill a little more dust fell on top of the sleeping child. She had lasted almost four hours before she collapsed with exhaustion.

Mercifully, the guards had decided to leave her alone. As long as the daily quota of grain was met, they didn't seem to care who made it.

The prison guards were far more interested in which of the new prisoners would cry out first. The sound of a bull whip striking new flesh indicated to the others who had won. Random screams from the new prisoners sent a chill down Ruhi's spine, despite the oppressive heat radiating from a fading sun.

A horn sounding out across the great expanse signalled the end of the workday. The prisoners groaned a collective sigh of relief, as they could finally stop turning the Chakki for the day.

Ruhi helped Sushil collect the last bits of flour from the edges of the mill, and they scooped them into a wooden cart that sat beside them. Sushil then looked at Ruhi and indicated that it was her turn to deposit the flour in the granary.

But Ruhi did not mind that part of the job, because she could at least stretch out her legs and back. It was her third and final run of the day and just like before, she followed a procession of prisoners who were already on their way to deposit their flour.

Ruhi waited patiently in the line for her turn. When it was finally time to enter the granary, Ruhi stated her mill number, and the guards made her wait by the cart as they weighed the flour before her. She watched anxiously as the giant scales tipped in her favour.

Content with her deposit, the guards allowed Ruhi to stack her empty cart along with the others and return back to her workstation. As she turned to leave, another lady who was having her flour weighed, was told that her deposit was underweight and that she had failed to meet the daily quota.

Two guards immediately seized the woman as she began to panic and cry. She pleaded with them to let her go, but her cries for mercy fell upon deaf ears. The guards dragged her by her arms, across the dusty floor and out of the granary. Ruhi instantly realised where they were headed. They were taking her to the end field.

"No!" Ruhi protested instinctively, as she watched them drag the woman away. But some of the other prisoners intervened and stopped Ruhi before she could get herself into trouble.

"Don't. You will only end up with her," they warned, as they promptly returned to their carts for processing. But Ruhi could not let the matter go. She followed the guards, as they continued to drag the woman kicking and screaming.

By now, the Sun had long set, allowing the cool white light of the moon to shine down upon them from the great black abyss from above. Despite the moonlight, the guards had lit an array of fire pits and torches to illuminate the great expanse around them.

The fields could have almost been considered beautiful, if it weren't for the fact they were facilitating slavery, torture, and death. But Ruhi did not need a fire to show her the horrors in the end field. She could hear the cries of pain from the women who were already there, being slowly crushed to death.

The guards entered the end field and threw their prisoner to the ground. One of them went for her feet, whilst the other went for her hands. Between the two of them, they pinned the woman to the floor despite her efforts to fight them off. For a moment, Ruhi feared they may try to rape her, but what she witnessed next, was just as bad if not worse.

Ruhi watched two different guards stumble over to the woman, with a boulder in their arms that they could barely carry between the two of them. The woman continued to cry and plead with the guards for mercy, but they ignored her as the boulder carrying men positioned themselves over her body.

Without warning, they dropped the rock onto the woman's waist. There was a crunching sound as the boulder crushed her pelvis and pinned her to the floor. The woman could not even scream out in pain, as she was overwhelmed in agony. Her upper body began to convulse, and she started to choke on her own blood.

A group of men, women, and children, cheered from outside the field, as the bolder crushed the defenseless prisoner. Ruhi looked up and saw a large crowd of people who had come to see this daily ritual take place. They were all stood safe upon the raised patio of the people's court.

Ruhi now understood the true purpose of that courtyard. It was an observation deck, for the public to witness and enjoy the torture of all those who opposed Islam.

The guards holding the dying prisoner by her hands and feet, let her go and started arguing with the guards who had dropped the boulder. They were meant to have placed the rock upon the prisoner slowly, to ensure that death took the maximum amount of time possible.

The two guards who had dragged the woman from the granary, went to pick up another boulder to demonstrate. This time, they slowly and carefully lowered the rock onto the woman's chest. This way, her rib cage would be crushed slowly when they added more rocks on top of it tomorrow. The other set of guards acknowledged their mistake and left the woman to die, as they returned to their duties.

Ruhi stood at the edge of the field and watched the boulders slowly rob the woman off her last breath. As the light faded from the woman's eyes, Ruhi finally understood what fate awaited her, should she resist them any further.

Whilst Ruhi was grateful that the woman's suffering was over, the same could not be said for the dozens of other women who were laying nearby, with large stones slowly crushing them to death.

Many cried out from the pain, whilst others had no more tears to cry. Ruhi had never witnessed such barbarity, in all of her twenty-two years. Unable to stare at the women's suffering any longer, Ruhi turned back and headed straight for her workstation. The last thing she wanted, was to end up there with them.

As Ruhi passed the other stone mills, she looked for Suhadna at her station and was worried to see that she was no longer there. Ruhi rushed back to her own stone mill and was relieved to see that Sushil had stayed with Baani, who was now awake and very upset.

Ruhi immediately knelt down beside the crying little girl and scooped her up into her arms. "Oh sweetheart, what's wrong?" Ruhi asked, trying to cheer her up. But Baani did not reply, she simply clung on to Ruhi for comfort and Ruhi gave her a reassuring hug in return.

"She thought you had left her behind," Sushil said flatly.

"Baby girl, I wouldn't leave you like that. I promise. I'll look after you, ok?" reassured Ruhi. Baani nodded without breaking her hug and they both felt a little bit better.

"What happens now? Ruhi asked Sushil, who was now laying on the floor by their Chakki, completely worn out.

"We eat, sleep and repeat at dawn," she replied with zero enthusiasm.

"What? Right here?" Ruhi asked puzzled. Sushil shot Ruhi a look that indicated that she was in no mood to talk or worse, to get into trouble for talking.

"No. Just sit down and be quiet. They will take us soon princess," said Sushil, as she rolled over and faced away from Ruhi. Ruhi didn't take it personally. If she had been here for months like Sushil, then she probably wouldn't want to get too close to anyone either.

Ruhi did not have to wait long for her answers. All of the prisoners were marched out row by row up the main staircase of the Diwan e Aam, and to the very center of its courtyard. There in middle of the great patio, amongst its forty towering pillars, was an entrance built into the floor.

It was the opening to a staircase that led deep underground towards a grand basement, that had been built directly beneath the people's court. Members of the public, but more importantly the Subedar himself, were able to watch the prisoners being escorted to and from their underground prison on a daily basis.

Ruhi and Baani followed the other prisoners, as they were led down the staircase and through a corridor towards an archway. The archway was the entrance to a massive underground hall that was big enough to accommodate hundreds of inmates.

'Ah, so this is the prison,' Ruhi said to herself, as she was herded into the large hall. The first thing that struck her was the smell. The stink of raw sewage and a variety of other vile odours all struck Baani and her at the same time.

Ruhi tried her best not to vomit on the spot. As she fought her tummy's instinct to retch all over the floor, her eyes slowly adjusted to distinct lack of light.

Despite a few dozen oil lamps attached the black walls around them, visibility in the hall was terrible. All Ruhi knew for certain, was that she was not alone anymore. There was a sea of people in front of her for at least a hundred feet. It was difficult for her to get a sense of just how many people there were in total or just how far the hall extended.

The air was stuffy and stale making it difficult for Ruhi to adapt her breathing. She held on to Baani's hand for reassurance and to make sure that they did not get separated in the crowd of women and children.

Thankfully, there seemed to be some order to the chaos before her. Each of the rows that had entered the hall, had to pass by a food station that had been set up along the left-hand side wall. As the rows before them gathered their food and found a place to sit, Ruhi was able to better take in her surroundings.

As she looked around, Ruhi thought the hall resembled more of a medieval dungeon than a prison. The far-right corner had been designated as the toilet. In reality, it was just a series of wooden buckets that were being emptied into a large open cart, once the prisoners had completed their 'business'. That is where the main smell was coming from.

Unfortunately, the basement was also their kitchen and bedroom. Even though the ceiling was at least twenty feet high, the hall was barely a quarter of the size of the great expanse outside. Still, it was large enough to house the five hundred or so prisoners that would be sleeping there that evening.

As they waited for their lump of bread the size of her fist, Ruhi observed the other prisoners, whilst scanning the hall for Suhadna and Veeraj. Everyone looked so broken and worn out. Children were too hungry and tired to cry, and their mothers were too drained to comfort them. Some tended to the wounds of the slaves who were unfortunate enough to have felt the lash of the guards. Yet despite their low morale, they had endured.

"Hands!" yelled the guard in front of her, breaking Ruhi's concentration. Ruhi held out her hands obediently as the guard dumped a doughy lump of bread into her blistered palms and looked to the next prisoner.

Ruhi stood her ground and lifted Baani up to the guard's attention. Annoyedly, the guard gave her another lump of bread for the little girl, before ordering them to move on.

Not wanting to test his patience, Ruhi and Baani took their food and ate it immediately. Despite its lumpy and bland flavour, it felt amazing to have food in their bellies after such a terrible day. The duo continued to follow the other prisoners to the communal water trough located on the wall furthest from the entrance.

People were washing their hands and faces in the water, as well as drinking it. Ruhi peered over the edge and saw that the water was even dirtier here, than in the trough from Jahangir's office. But as their only source of water, Ruhi and Baani had no choice but to drink from it.

Following the other prisoners lead, Ruhi dunked her head into the trough and drunk deeply, whilst she tried her best not to think about what she had just swallowed. Baani copied her and instantly looked better, like a flower perking up in the sunlight.

Baani pointed to Ruhi's chin, which was still covered in dry blood and reminded her to wash it away. With their rumbling bellies full of water, it was time to find somewhere to sleep. Ruhi continued to scour the hallway for any signs of Suhadna and Veeraj, but it was too dark and too crowded to find them.

After a few minutes of searching, Ruhi decided it was best if they just slept wherever they could. She found a space on the cold stone floor, as far away from the toilet as possible. It was an area just big enough to accommodate her and Baani, as there were people scattered all around them.

As Ruhi lay down, Baani curled up beside her and wrapped her arms around Ruhi's waist, squeezing her tight. The hug provided them both with some much-needed comfort.

Every muscle and bone in Ruhi's body seemed to ache, especially the ones in her back. "Well, at least sleeping on the floor is good for your spine. Right little one?" she said to Baani, who did not really understand what she meant.

"Didi, where is my Mama?" Baani asked in response. Despite it being one of the first times she had spoken all day, Ruhi did not have an answer for the little girl.

"Don't worry sweetie, we'll find her. Everything will be ok. Ok?" Baani fell silent again.

Not knowing what else to do, Ruhi looked to her right to the woman closest to them, but the woman turned away to avoid eye contact.

With Baani's arms still wrapped around her, Ruhi tried her best to close her eyes and to get some sleep. After a few minutes, the noise in the hall started to die down, as the last of the women and children finished their sparse supper and found a space to lay down for the night.

As usual, there was no gossiping or chatting or getting to know one another. As for many of the women, this was far from their first night and most had nothing left to say.

One woman started the final prayer of the day, the Kirtan Sohila (song of praise) paat, and the whole basement of women and children joined her, as they all recited the prayer in unison.

Hearing the words of her Guru spoken aloud, soothed Ruhi's aching body and heart, finally allowing her to fall asleep. Those who remained awake, softly repeated the words, "Satnam (truth is his name), Waheguru (wonderful lord)," until a silence eventually fell upon all of the prisoners within the dark hall.

Chapter 12

Billo and Chittar rode strong and true, through the dark forests and open fields. They navigated across hills and streams, through jungles and over rivers, never slowing down and never giving up on their riders. They galloped throughout the night as if their lives depended on it. It was as if they had known the true purpose of their mission and journey all along.

Their strength and grace spurred on the other horses behind them and together, the herd sped their Khalsa riders onwards, towards the city of Lahore.

Harjit and Jai rode with a fire burning in their hearts, driving them past the point of obsession. For they knew the longer it took them to get to Lahore, the less chance they would have at ever seeing their loved ones again. The black starry sky masked their presence over the Punjabi countryside, like a blanket in the night.

As the dawn of a new day grew ever closer, the small Khalsa taskforce finally reached their destination, the Shahdara forest. Situated just north of the ancient city, the woodlands provided them with ample cover from the elements and shielded them from any eyes that may have been upon them.

The Khalsa warriors wasted no time in setting up their temporary base camp near the banks of the river Ravi. Their first order of duty was to provide their faithful horses with fresh flowing water and plenty of well-deserved rest.

Jai dismounted his mare and stroked her mane in appreciation of her service to him. He never thought it was possible to travel such a great distance with a horse before.

The Khalsa taskforce spent the next few minutes adjusting their disguises and arming themselves with their weaponry. Their Sufi cloaks were perfect for concealing their swords and shields. Jai picked up his Naag Jeev Khanda and glanced over to Ikamroop, who was busy arming herself with weapons of her own.

As the only woman in the group, Ikamroop had to adapt her disguise. Instead of wearing the black and maroon cloak of a Sufi scholar, she unveiled a large black chunni and wrapped it around her head and face, in order to disguise her identity completely. Only her eyes remained visible, but now she would be able to pass through the city as a local Muslim woman.

Jai watched Ikamroop transform into a shadow of the woman he had met earlier. He had never meant to endanger her and the others. But nevertheless, he was glad that she and the other warriors were there to help him and Harjit, liberate the prisoners.

"Brother Jai are you ready?" enquired Harjit, as he passed Billo's reins over to Mohan. Someone needed to stay behind and protect the horses and the camp and the Nawab had selected a young warrior called Mohan.

"I'm ready bro. Let's do this," replied Jai, as he focused his thoughts on the task ahead. Following his friend's lead, Jai handed

Chittar's reins over to the young warrior, who reassured him that she would be well taken care of.

The duo headed over to the other Khalsa warriors, who were waiting patiently for the Nawab to begin his final briefing. With a maroon cloak covering his battle armour and the giant Khanda strapped to his back, Nawab Kapur Singh Virk, entered the Khalsa circle and looked at each and every one of the Sikh warriors standing before him.

Despite the monumental task before them, memories of a similar gathering from many years ago, began to flash before his eyes. Kapur tried his best to dismiss them from his mind yet, they still continued to haunt him even after all this time.

The last time he had travelled to Lahore to free the Sikhs from the 'Butcher's' grasp, many of his fellow warriors died. But worst still, they had also failed in their attempt to locate and kill the Subedar. Kapur reminded himself of his Guru Ji's hukam and took a deep breath before pressing forward, as he had always done.

"With Guru Ji's blessings, we have arrived here quicker than I expected. But that only works to our advantage. We shall now enter the city before the Fajr (Islamic morning prayer) begins. Once we are within the city walls, we will split up into three groups and head to our assigned gates. Each team is to scout guard numbers and positions at their gate, and then report back to the Shahi Akhara (wrestling grounds) within the hour. But most importantly, we must find out where the Subedar is. You all know what is at stake here. If we do this properly, we can end the

Subedar's tyranny once and for all. Any questions?" asked the Nawab, as he looked into the eyes of the people who had volunteered to risk their lives for freedom.

"Then we go with God. Waheguru Ji Ka Khalsa, Waheguru Ji Ki Fateh," said the Nawab, as everyone repeated the rallying cry of the Khalsa back to him. The Nawab then turned around and led the Khalsa unit out of the forest and into the great city, leaving Mohan and their horses behind.

The break of dawn was but minutes away, when the Khalsa warriors penetrated the outer perimeter wall in their Sufi disguises. As the Imam's called to the people of Lahore to attend their morning prayers, many of the local inhabitants left the warmth of their beds and made their way through the city streets, towards their nearest Masjid (Mosque).

The Sufi disguises helped the Khalsa warriors blend in perfectly, just as they had hoped. As they passed by the empty markets and bazaars, the warriors split up into three teams as planned. Despite Harjit's initial reservations, he and Jai were paired with the Nawab and Ikamroop and their primary target was the Alamgiri Gate, located at the west side of the great fort.

The team wasted no time in passing through narrow alleys and city streets in an attempt to reach the Alamgiri Gate as quickly as possible. Jai was taken back by the sheer scale and beauty of Lahore's magnificent fort, as they moved through the shadows of its domineering walls. Never in his life had he imagined that he would have the opportunity to visit such a majestic place, let alone infiltrate it.

As they approached the main street leading towards the western gate, Jai had to slow down to fully take in the two-giant ivory-coloured towers, that stood before them. At over a hundred feet high, the two heavily armoured towers watched over a large archway, over thirty feet high and twenty feet wide.

To their collective surprise, the large wooden doors of the Alamgiri Gate were wide open, and members of the public seemed to pass through the doorway unobstructed. The four of them paused and exchanged looks of confusion as they considered the direct approach. It was a risky opportunity, but not one they could afford to miss.

Seizing their chance, the team pressed forward and attempted to blend in with a group of locals heading straight through the open gate. Jai kept his head down and his eyes forward, as he focused on the Nawab's last command. 'No talking, no stopping, and no eye contact'.

Despite the feeling of a thousand eyes upon them, the four Sikh's passed though the Alamgiri gate without incident. They found themselves facing a multitude of interconnected parks, pathways and buildings of all different shapes and sizes, spread out in every direction.

"What the hell? This place is bloody massive! How the hell are we gonna find them in less than an hour?" whispered Jai to Harjit, with a sense of urgency in his voice. But his friend was equally overwhelmed by the choices available to them. The duo looked to their mighty leader for guidance.

Luckily for them, Kapur looked unfazed by the layout before them and signaled to his team to keep pace with the locals in front of them. All of the people seemed to be headed east in the same direction. Jai glanced behind them and to his surprise, there were even more people behind them, than there were in front.

Something was clearly happening in the fort that morning and whatever it was, they all had a feeling it wasn't going to be good.

Once again Harjit, Jai, Ikamroop and Kapur blended in with the crowd around them, and they continued their journey through the grounds of the fort. They passed by landscaped gardens and affluent structures that had stood for hundreds of years. The open spaces and well-maintained grounds were a stark contrast to the dirty and cramped streets outside the great walls of the fort.

Surprisingly to the four disguised warriors, their crowd passed by the Masjid too. 'Well, wherever we're all headed it ain't to pray,' Jai said to himself. Ikamroop noticed that even her father had started to look concerned. But they did not have to wait much longer for their destination to be revealed to them.

The crowd stopped in the middle of a large field, just outside the horse stables. As soon as the Nawab realised where they were, he pushed his way through the ever-increasing crowd and headed straight to the front.

Harjit, Jai and Ikamroop stuck with him until suddenly, they were all forced to an abrupt stop. A wooden fence prohibited them all, from moving any further forward. That is when Kapur realised his worst fears. Even though it has been almost twenty years since he was last there, history was about to repeat itself.

Outside the horse stables on the other side of the wooden barrier, were hundreds of Sikh men and boys. They were all sat in long rows, bound to one another by heavy iron chains. All of them had been stripped down to their Kachera's (undergarments) and bore the fresh marks of a bull whip upon their bloody and torn up backs.

The crowd of locals began to clap and cheer as a group of guards emerged from the stables. They walked straight past the sea of prisoners as if they weren't even there and headed directly for a large wooden platform that had been constructed in the very centre of the field.

The platform almost resembled that of a concert stage. It was at least five feet high and wide enough to accommodate a hundred people. It's most unusual feature however, was the row of cushioned chairs that had been placed along its right side, facing inwards.

The chairs were directed to a large wooden block that sat dead in the center of the stage all by itself. The solid piece of wood was stained red and black, with the dried blood of its many previous occupants.

Harjit scanned the faces of the men and boys, desperately looking for the face of his son. Jai looked at his friend and could see that he was getting upset. "Do you see him?" whispered Jai.

But Harjit could not speak. He could barely take in a breath, as his gaze moved rapidly from one prisoner to another. Harjit instinctively began to reach for his concealed Talwar, when he felt a strong hand on his arm stopping him from reaching for his weapon.

"Please, don't," pleaded Jai, desperate for them not to break their cover. Not just yet. Harjit turned from the prisoners and looked at Jai with tears in eyes. His son was not amongst them. The realisation that Ajay had most probably been executed several days ago hit his father hard. Jai felt Harjit's arm go limp, as the light within him seemed to fade away.

Harjit lowered his gaze to the floor, as if his whole world had just come crashing down. Jai could not imagine the pain of losing a child, but he understood the pain of losing a loved one. He leaned in close to Harjit, so that only his friend could hear his words.

"We will make them pay. I promise you that. We're not done yet. Suhadna needs you. Baani and Veeraj need you."

Harjit wiped the tears from his eyes. His friend was right. This was not the time to mourn. This was the time to act. Harjit nodded to his friend and they both looked to their leader for guidance, as to what to do next.

But the Nawab seemed to be battling demons of his own. His eyes were fixed on the worn-down chopping block. Kapur knew all too well what was about to happen to the men and boys in front of him and he could not bring himself to witness it all over again.

The last of the guards carried a Tarangalah (large axe) to the stage, which excited the crowd as they waited in anticipation of the first execution. The team looked on helplessly, as the executioner stood in position beside the chopping block. Any move they made, would mean revealing who they were and that would mean the end of Ruhi, Suhadna and the children forever.

Then the moment Kapur's team had been dreading, finally arrived. The guards dragged the first of the Sikh prisoners to the chopping block and tied his head down to it, using a leather strap. The prisoner was a boy no older than nineteen years in age. His body was covered in scars and his hands and feet were still bound. Yet he did not struggle or fight, much to disappointment of the people who had come to watch him die.

But the executioner did not make his move, as he seemed to be waiting for someone. Jai did not have to look far to spot who it was. A flamboyant man dressed in a bright yellow and blue Jama coat, made up of the finest Persian silks, entered the field on his white horse. Once again, he was surrounded by an entourage of servants and guards, but this time he was not alone.

More servants followed behind him, carrying an excessively decorated palanquin. They gently sat the passenger vehicle down upon the ground and helped its heavily pregnant occupant out.

Mughalani Begum joined her husband Mir Mannu, as the couple took their places on the cushioned sofa chairs, that had been prepared especially for them. Their stage thrones gave them the best view of the executioner's block and of the crowd.

The crowd cheered when they saw the Subedar and his exquisitely beautiful wife. She was dressed in a diamond encrusted purple lehengar, that contrasted elegantly with her dove white skin. Fine gold jewelry and pearl necklaces adorned her slender neck, quaint wrists, and dainty ankles. Despite a matching chunni partially concealing her face, she was unmistakably a spectacle of beauty.

Mir raised his hands to silence the crowd and that is when Jai noticed that his right hand was injured. 'Ha, I hope that hurt bitch,' Jai said to himself, as he waited impatiently alongside the other members of his team for the Subedar to speak.

"Welcome my friends on this glorious new day," said Mir, as he addressed the crowd first. "As normal, we shall give the kafir's an opportunity to renounce their false prophets and accept the love of Allah within their hearts." Mir turned his attention to the four hundred Sikh men and boys chained before him.

"Any prisoner who wishes to embrace the truth, speak now and you shall be set free and reborn," bellowed Mir, as he scanned the faces of his prisoners and awaited a response.

Mir was met with silence as the prisoners stared up at him with indifference. The restless public had quietened down in anticipation, until a single voice called out from within the crowd of prisoners. "Go fuck a pig Mannu!"

That was not what Jai, or the others had expected to hear. Jai tried his best not to laugh as everyone looked to the Subedar, who was clearly not impressed by the act of insolence.

Mir turned to his wife and swallowed his anger. "Well, at least it is original. I was expecting…" but before Mir could finish his sentence, the boy on the block shouted, "Bole so Nihal!" and three hundred and ninety-nine voices answered him back in unison. "Sat Sri Akal!"

Mir closed his eyes and forced a smile, but inside he was furious. He returned to his chair and then waved his injured hand for to the executioner to proceed. The guard immediately raised up his axe up and swung it down hard upon the cutting block.

The executioners strike had been impressively swift and accurate. The boy's head separated from his body and bounced off the wooden platform, before a guard collected it and threw into an empty cart standing nearby. The crowd clapped and cheered as the boy's body was dragged away and thrown into a separate cart, whilst two different guards prepared the next prisoner for the block.

But this time, the executioner did not have to wait. He simply chopped off the next head and waited for the next prisoner to be brought to him. It was clear to anyone watching, that the guards were very well versed in their duties.

Mir sat back in his chair and stared intently, as fresh blood continued to spill upon the deck of the stage. Every head that was severed added more blood to a puddle that had begun to form at the base of the block. Mir watched as the puddle became bigger and bigger until finally, it started to spill over the side of the platform and into the dirt below.

He watched the blood go from a trickle to a stream, until finally, it flowed over the edge like a waterfall. It was in that moment that Mir realised that it did not matter whether one head fell or a thousand. Another one would be born to take its place eventually.

Something was missing here, and it had been gnawing at him for days and weeks, if not years. It was their spirit. No matter what he had tried, no matter how he had their bones crushed or skin peeled, none of them ever saw the truth. None of them ever accepted Islam into their hearts. He seemed to be dealing with a level of fundamentalism, that he simply did not understand.

What was it about this Sikh god that made these people so willing to die for it? Are human beings so weak that they are willing to accept any lie as the truth? What is it that he needed to do, to stop this plague from affecting his own children one day?

Even his father and brothers and emperors before him, had not managed to stop the Sikhs. But he would not fail like they had. He would not burden his unborn children with the same duty and responsibility of fighting this poison. He would do, what they all could not.

He was going to wipe out Sikhi once and for all. But just killing them would not be enough. He wanted to break their spirits first. He needed too. So that no matter how many more Sikh's came after them, they would know that deep down, Sikhi was nothing compared to the righteous truth of Islam. This was now his sacred duty from Allah, bestowed only upon him. This was his Jihad now.

Mir looked across to the love of his life and then at the innocent soul growing within her belly and smiled. He now felt a clarity and a sense of purpose that had almost eluded him his entire life. The Subedar now knew exactly what needed to be done. With no more time to waste, Mir stood up and summoned the commander of his guards. Today was the day, he would fulfil his destiny, once and for all.

Jahangir rode to the horse stables as commanded and reported to his master. "How may I serve you great Subedar Ji?" said the Amir, as he knelt before his governor. Mir looked down at his burly commander and smiled. "Old friend, I have been truly blessed. Almighty Allah has shown me the answer to our problem. He has given me the cure. Now listen carefully..."

Jahangir listened intently as Mir explained the instructions of his plan step by step. "You and your men are to begin at once," commanded the Subedar, as he dismissed his commander and summoned his horse.

"Ji Hukam my lord!" replied Jahangir, as he instantly turned around and mounted his own horse. Without waiting for any further commands, Jahangir rode back to the Diwan e Aam, with his contingency of men.

As Mir mounted his own horse, he turned to his wife. "Come my love, you are going to want to see this too." And with those words, he too rode back to the people's court, in anticipation of the day ahead.

The Nawab watched Mir leave abruptly and knew that they had to follow him now, if they were to have any chance of stopping him once and for all. Kapur pushed his way back through the crowd, towards the main path followed closely by Harjit, Jai and Ikamroop. But by the time they got clear of the local people, Mir and his guards had already disappeared from sight.

"We can still follow the Palanquin," Jai recommended discreetly, as he pointed towards Mughalani, who was being slowly helped into her vehicle. Kapur considered their options and agreed to Jai's suggestion.

"Ok, you two follow the wife. Roop and I will see if we can trace Mir's path. But we must still meet up with the others within the hour, no matter what. Understood?" whispered the Nawab. Harjit and Jai nodded in acknowledgment and the team proceeded to split in two.

Only a quarter of a mile away, deep underground, Ruhi Kaur opened her eyes for the first time that day. As the light entered into her eyes, her brain struggled to process the images around her. She did not recognise the black stone walls of the basement, or the flickering light from the oil lamps dancing on the ceiling above.

Panic began to set in, causing Ruhi to sit up abruptly. Little Baani, who was still asleep beside her began to stir, causing reality to come back to her slowly, piece by piece.

Suddenly, she felt every muscle in her body aching with stiffness. Sleeping on a rock-hard surface hadn't done her body any favours. 'I miss my bed,' Ruhi said to herself, as she tried her best to block out her reality.

She sat there for a moment in a daze with her eyes closed, trying to picture her bedroom back home snuggled up with a warm blanket, whilst laying in her cozy bed. She also missed the feeling of sleeping in on a lazy Sunday morning. What she wouldn't give for that feeling right now.

But then Ruhi opened her eyes properly and the full horror of her reality came flooding back to her, as if a gate had been opened in her mind. 'How on earth did I get here? How is any of this even possible? Why me God? Why?' she asked herself, as her senses struggled to adjust to her environment.

At least when she was asleep, she didn't have to tolerate that smell. Ruhi fought the urge to retch again and then looked around. Many of the women and children were already awake and were helping one another get ready for the day ahead.

Some were bandaging new wounds, whilst others massaged sore legs and backs. 'Even in this hell hole, there are still some glimpses of humanity,' Ruhi thought to herself.

That is when Baani woke up. "Mama," she cried out, as she instantly realised where she was. Although Baani rarely spoke, her few words had a profound impact upon Ruhi.

"It's ok sweetheart, we'll find her. She must be around here somewhere," said Ruhi, as she tried to reassure the little girl. Baani sat up and hugged Ruhi for comfort. They were both grateful that they at least had each other.

Ruhi looked down at her hands that were now covered in large white blisters. She closed her eyes at the thought of the pain she would experience when they eventually burst. But her thoughts were interrupted by the sound of the basement doors opening from afar. They let in a sorely needed breeze of air, that made it slightly more bearable to breath.

Several guards entered the hall and sounded the morning work horn. It signalled that it was time to start the day all over again. Ruhi quickly rushed Baani over to the toilet section, where they both reluctantly used the facilities, along with dozens of other women and children. They quickly stopped at the trough, where Ruhi encouraged Baani to drink as much water as she could, as they wouldn't be back there again until nightfall.

Ruhi and Baani were as ready as they were ever going to be for the day ahead. They joined the queue of women being led back up to the work fields outside. Ruhi kept an eye out for Suhadna, as she was beginning to worry about her new friend and baby Veeraj.

Once they had climbed up the last few steps into the centre of the people's court, it took Ruhi a moment for her eyes to adjust to the brightness of the world outside.

'Everything looks so peaceful,' she thought to herself, as she looked out at the great expanse and drew in some much-needed breaths of fresh air. It was just such a relief to not be in the dungeon below anymore.

Ruhi held Baani's hand, as they were led to the edge of the patio and instructed to sit in a row alongside the other prisoners. Ruhi looked around, but she wasn't the only one who was confused.

Everyone had expected to be taken to the stone mills and to be put to work, but not today. Something was different about this morning. As the guards continued to seat the prisoners in long rows that resembled a school assembly, Baani spotted a familiar face coming up from the stairs, out of the basement.

"Mama!" Baani cried out. It was her mother, and she was still holding her baby brother in her arms. Suhadna turned and spotted her daughter and friend and was so relieved, that she almost began crying.

Suhadna was made to sit on the opposite side of the patio, but she was just relieved to know that her daughter was safe.

Ruhi calmed Baani down, as she did not want either of them to suffer the wrath of the guards today. Her lip along with every other part of her body still ached. Once the guards had completed their task, they lined up along the pillars and awaited their next command.

But the guards did not have to wait long, as the Amir entered the Diwan e Aam, and stood before all the prisoners like a headmaster addressing his students.

"The honourable and great Subedar himself, Mir Mannu, has blessed you all today with his presence. Behold and gaze upon greatness." Jahangir turned and faced the balcony that hovered above them all and waited patiently for his master to appear.

Mir walked through the central doorway, as if on cue and took his seat at the centre of the stage. His wife and the other servants took their place by his side, until the balcony was full of spectators. Nobody wanted to miss what the Subedar had in store for the prisoners today.

Mir did not waste any time with pleasantries. He stood up in front of his chair and addressed the crowd below.

"My children today is indeed a blessed day. Almighty Allah himself has bestowed upon me a vision. He has shown me, that you have all been plagued with a sickness. Your hearts and your minds have been corrupted by false prophets who have led you astray. But there is good news. There is a cure for this ailment. It is the word of Allah," said the Subedar, as he looked up at the ceiling and then back down at faces of the bewildered women and children before him.

"I have tried to teach you about his light through love and patience and through hard work and discipline. But sometimes love and patience and hard work are not enough. Sometimes we have to lose the things we love the most, in order for us to grow and to see the light. So this is my gift to you all, my children. I am setting you free from the bonds that are holding you back. Show me you have seen his light and I give you my word, you shall be set free." Mir paused and then signalled to Jahangir to proceed before he took his seat.

"Guards!" Yelled the Amir.

Dozens of guards swarmed across the patio floor and began snatching the children away from their mothers. The women started to scream and yell as they tried to fight back, but it was futile. They were defenseless. The guards struck any mother who refused to hand over her child, with the butt of their spears.

It became a scene of absolute chaos.

Mothers held onto their babies for dear life as the guards clubbed and stabbed any woman who resisted. They had been instructed not to kill any off the mothers, but flesh wounds were acceptable.

Children and babies screamed in terror as they were torn away from the arms of their mothers and sisters, who did not stop resisting until they laid bloody upon the floor.

But the carnage had only just begun.

The guards started to kill the children right before their mother's eyes. Babies were flung into the air and skewered on the end of spears, as guards threw them to one another for sport. Some of the guards did not bother with the spears and just preferred to cut the children's throat, before dumping their lifeless bodies onto the ground.

Two guards swarmed towards Suhadna and tried to pull Veeraj out from her arms. Suhadna tried her best to get to her feet and scramble away from them, but before she could even rise to a knee, one of the guards thrust their spear into her thigh.

The spear hit her leg with such force, that it went straight through her leg and into the patio, pinning her to the floor. The other guard ripped Veeraj out of her arms as she screamed out in agony and pleaded with them to stop. "Please, I beg you, spare my baby!" she cried out.

But the guard acted as if he hadn't heard a word. He violently flipped Veeraj upside down and held his naked body by his legs. Veeraj cried at being so roughly handled and separated from his mother. Suhadna grabbed the spear with all of her might and tried her best to pull it out from her leg, but it was of no use.

Before she could do anything further, the guard took out his dagger and thrust it into her son's stomach. Suhadna screamed out in horror as she saw her baby boy being gutted alive. The guard slowly cut Veeraj downward, opening up his entire chest until he stopped crying and wriggling in agony. He then dropped Veeraj's lifeless body to the floor, cracking open his skull, as he walked away leaving the newborn to be collected by his broken mother.

Ruhi could not believe the sight before her eyes. She instinctively grabbed Baani, as the guards continued to pull children away from their mother's left and right. Ruhi looked behind her, but she was surrounded by guards. There was no way out. A guard spotted Baani and went to grab her by the arm.

Baani screamed at the top of her lungs in terror. "Didi!" Ruhi managed to stand up and then launched herself at the guard, who had his hand clamped around Baani's arm. The guard was caught off balance by the ferocity of Ruhi's attack and fell backwards, as she barged into to him with all of her strength.

The guard hit the floor and dropped his dagger which Ruhi promptly picked up, as she pinned him to the ground. Lifting her arm in the air, Ruhi stabbed the guard in his neck as many times as she could. Arterial blood sprayed across the ground and across Ruhi's face, as she immobilised him.

Ruhi then reached out for Baani, who was crying hysterically on the ground beside the body of the dead guard. But just as Ruhi grabbed Baani's hand, the wooden shaft of a spear smacked Ruhi across the back of her head, dropping her to the stone floor like a rag doll.

Ruhi felt the world around her spin as her body took the impact of several more strikes, across her arms and back. Jolts of pain seared throughout her body, keeping her conscious long enough to see two guards pin down the little girl beside her.

Ruhi's vision began to blur, as she tried her best to sit up. But she could not move. Her body did not respond to her command to move. As her eyelids opened and closed, Ruhi could hear Baani's terrified screams, as the guards laughed and held her down by her throat. Ruhi tried her best to speak, but no voice came out. She watched hopelessly as the guards pushed their thin Pesh-Kabz blades, into the little girl's chest.

Baani's body began to convulse in pain, and she started to choke on her own blood. Ruhi watched in silence as they chopped Baani limb from limb, until her small heart could not take anymore. When they let go of her throat, they started to remove her head and that is when Ruhi finally lost consciousness. Baani's tears fell into the puddles of blood around her, but there was no one left to watch them fall.

The massacre had only lasted moments, but within that time, a lifetime of damage had been done. Not a single child had survived Mir's lesson for that day. As the guards stood back and admired their handy work, Jahangir ordered phase two of the operation to begin.

The guards proceeded to mutilate the bodies of all of the babies and children. Every carcass was chopped and torn apart and then sown back together as a harr (necklace). Once the children had been sown into human necklaces, the guards were then ordered to place them around the necks of their mothers.

As the guards proceeded to carry out their orders, some of the local people from within the fort had began to arrive at the court. They had been drawn in by all of the noise and commotion caused by the massacre. But none of them had expected to witness such horror.

As the surviving mothers sat in pools of blood, with their dismembered children around their necks, the Subedar once again stood up to address his 'students.'

"The blood of your children is on your hands alone. You chose their fate when you chose Gobind and Nanak over Allah. Those who walk the path of the kafir, are destined to know nothing but pain and suffering!" Mir looked at his prisoners and grew impatient as they continued cry and mourn the loss of their children and babies.

"Silence them!" yelled the Subedar in a rage.

Faithful as ever, Jahangir picked up a child's body part and stuffed it into the mouth of the nearest weeping mother. He then ordered his guards to do the same. Any one still crying or mourning, was to be stopped using the same method.

The crowd of onlookers began to groan in disgust, as they witnessed grieving mothers having the remains of their dead children stuffed into their mouths. "He goes too far," said one. "Barbarism!" yelled another.

"SILENCE!" roared Jahangir. "Or you will all join them!" The threat was enough to silence the crowd, allowing the Subedar to complete his lesson.

"It is never too late my children. Renounce your false prophets and accept the love of Allah in your hearts and you shall be set free this very moment."

Mir looked across the faces of the women before him, yet none of them looked his way or acknowledged his presence. They but closed their eyes and wept in silence for the cruelty their loved ones had just suffered.

"So be it." Mir muttered to himself.

"Put them back to work, no more food, no water, no rest. Let their Guru save them now," commanded Mir, as he tried his best to disguise his disappointment. The Subedar then turned his back to the prisoners and disappeared into his lounge.

"You heard the Subedar Ji! Put them to work!" ordered Jahangir, as he wiped the blood and pieces of flesh from his hands. The Amir looked down at his green kurta top and was annoyed that it had absorbed so much blood. 'I just had this cleaned,' he said to himself, as he left the blood-soaked patio behind and returned to his office.

The remainder of the guards dragged the surviving mothers, wearing their garlands of dead children, back to the stone mills. The guards whipped them until they started to grind their daily quota of grain again. Those prisoners who had been injured were dragged off from the patio and taken to the end field, where they were dumped until more boulders could be found for them.

Ruhi and Suhadna were amongst them.

Chapter 13

The screams of terror and despair from the mothers, sisters and daughters trying to protect their children, had cut across the open fields of the great expanse, and echoed throughout the walls of the mighty fort. Harjit and Jai stopped dead in their tracks, upon hearing the ungodly cries.

Neither of them wanted to acknowledge what those sounds could mean for them both. They looked around for the source of the noise and spotted a crowd of locals walking towards a massive block-like structure, hundreds of feet away. The duo turned off from their current path and headed straight for the largest complex within the fort.

They tried their best not to run and once again moved within the safety of a crowd. As they approached the rear of the towering structure, Harjit and Jai knew they were in the right place, as the building was crawling with guards. The duo cautiously made their way up the rear staircase and proceeded to the observation section of the patio.

The crowd of people that had gathered there, were unusually quiet and that began to worry them both. They pushed their way to the front, until a stone barrier prevented them from going any further.

Not even witnessing men and boys having their heads chopped off could have prepared Harjit and Jai for the sight before them.

They watched the prison guards drag the last of the Sikh women towards a great expanse, littered with oversized stone mills. Each of the prisoners wore a garland of mutilated babies and children around their necks, whilst being forced to grind grain.

Jai stared at the blood-soaked patio floor, still littered with pieces of dead children that had been left behind and then at his friend. Neither of them had the words to express the mixture of feelings, that were assaulting them all at once.

Jai's eyes searched wildly for any sign of his little sister, but there was none. He looked to his friend Harjit, who seemed to have turned to stone. Harjit was staring out into the distance at a single point. Jai followed his friends gaze, to a field furthest to the right and that is when he saw Suhadna.

She was sat up straight, leaning against a pile of discarded bodies in the middle of the field. All around her, lay the bodies of the dead and dying. There were at least twenty other women spread out, with heavy boulders sat upon various parts of their bodies. But it was not clear from there, whether the women underneath the rocks were alive or not.

Two other strangers, pushed through the crowd of stunned onlookers and stood beside their comrades. Kapur looked at the Sikh prisoners and could not stop the tears from forming in his eyes. They were not tears of sorrow, but of anger. He was angry with himself for being too late.

It was a sentiment that the four of them shared. They watched the prisoners grind away at their heavy stone mills, whilst chanting the name of the lord together. Kapur gathered his senses and turned around. He could no longer bare to take in any more suffering. He had spent a lifetime fighting this, yet nothing seemed to change. He closed his eyes and remembered the teachings of his Guru, Nanak. 'Walk the path, by embracing the command of the lord.'

Kapur opened his eyes and understood what needed to be done. He turned to Harjit, who had not moved since he had arrived and placed his hand on his shoulder. Harjit remained still for a moment, before turning around to face the Nawab. Without speaking a word to one another, they looked at Jai and Ikamroop and everyone was in agreement. It was time to take action.

They slowly backed away from the patio, to avoid drawing any attention to themselves and headed straight for the Shahi Akhara, to rendezvous with the other Khalsa warriors.

Across the grounds on the rear side of the people's court, Jahangir entered his office. He was eager to change out of his sticky and wet clothes. The smell of the kafir's blood offended him. Yet, before he could sit down, one of Mir's personal guards appeared and summoned him to their master.

Jahangir closed his eyes for a moment in frustration. 'What now?' he thought to himself, before complying with the command. He promptly followed the guard up the staircase and onto the second floor, where his guards saluted him as he entered into Mir's lounge.

The morning sunlight shone through the large open archways of the Subedar's luxurious chamber, bathing the east side of the room in a warm natural light. Mir was sat having breakfast by the window with his young wife, when Jahangir approached them both.

"Yes, my master. How may I serve you?" asked Jahangir, as he bowed before them and disguised his annoyance at being summoned like a dog.

"You and your men have done well my old friend. But I have one more task for you today," said the Subedar, as he swallowed a bite of his Punjabi style paronta.

"Send word to all of my men across the Punjab. I will pay thirty rupees for every Sikh head brought to my door. But only their heads. No more Sikh's are to be brought to Lahore alive. They are to be killed where they stand. Kill them in their homes. Kill them in their towns and villages. Kill them on the road. I don't care how or where. I want every last one eradicated from this earth," commanded the Subedar, as he dipped the next bite of his paronta into some fresh yogurt and then stuffed it into his mouth.

Jahangir was taken back by the request. "All of them?" he asked cautiously. Mir put down his next bite and studied his commanders face. It was the first time his Amir had ever questioned an order.

Mughalani recognised the dangerous look on her husband's face and saved the Amir's life, by speaking first. "Yes, you heard him, all of them," she said, as she placed a grape in her mouth and smiled warmly at her husband.

Mir noticed the save but decided to forego having his commander executed. It had already been a challenging morning and it was getting increasingly difficult to find good help. But most of all, Mir did not feel like training a new dog again.

"Take as many men as you need, but see it done, today," the Subedar added, before turning his attention back to his breakfast.

"Ji Hukam!" replied Jahangir, who then bowed and turned to leave. But just as he was about to take a step forward, Jahangir paused and looked down at his blood-stained hands and clothes.

"What is it now?" asked Mir, with annoyance.

"Apologies my lord, but what about the prisoners?" Jahangir asked quickly.

Mir had become bored with this topic and made his displeasure known. "I thought I made myself clear! Let them die by the mill! Slowly! Now go!" he yelled, as he finally lost his patience.

Jahangir dared not stay any longer and promptly left their presence. The Amir ordered all the guards in the chamber to follow him downstairs, leaving only the Subedar's personal contingency of guards behind.

Once downstairs, Jahangir assembled all of his lieutenants and relayed the Subedar's orders to his men. "Leave a dozen guards behind to watch the prisoners in the great square. I want every other soldier in this fort, ready to leave here in the next ten minutes. Is that understood!?" thundered the Amir.

"Ji Hukam Sahib!" chimed his men, as they fled out of his office and proceeded to carry out the Subedar's orders.

Outside the Masti gate on the eastern side of the fort, the Nawab's team entered the old wrestling grounds, just as planned. Once they had regrouped with their comrades, the disguised Khalsa warriors moved to a quiet, grassy area of the training grounds to formulate the attack stage of their plan.

They took shade under one of the many trees spread around them. From an outside perspective, they were just a group of scholars enjoying a private debate. Confident that they were not being monitored or watched, Kapur began by first listening to the reports from the other teams.

Once they had shared what they had learnt, the Nawab told them of his team's experience at the horse stables and at the people's court. The other Khalsa warriors sat back in shock and despair, as they learnt about the horrors that had taken place within the walls of the fort.

"Time is no longer on our side," continued Kapur. "The Subedar's last known location was the Diwan e Aam. But we do not know how long he will remain there. Nor do we know how many men he has inside…"

Jai was finding it hard to concentrate on what the Nawab was saying. His thoughts kept taking him back to the blood-soaked patio and to the garlands, made up of babies and children hanging around the necks of their mothers.

"We have to go now!" interrupted Jai, who could no longer contain his feelings of anxiety. The thought of his sister being piled amongst the dead, was too much for him to bear.

"Patience Jai, we need to stick together if we are to have any chance against these guards. We need a plan, they outnumber us by at least ten to one," reasoned Ikamroop. There was something inherently calming about her voice that managed to reign in Jai's anxiety. He took in a deep breath and nodded to show her that he had understood her.

Just as Jai was about to look away, some activity from behind Ikamroop, at the Masti gate caught Jai's eye. "What were those odd's again?" he asked her. Ikamroop and the others turned around to see what he was staring at. The guards seemed to be abandoning their posts in a frenzy, as they ran across the grounds and headed straight for the horse stables.

Jai did not know whether it was a miracle or just a stroke of luck, but finally, something was going in their favour. He looked at his friend. "Er... you can see that too, right?" he asked Harjit skeptically.

Harjit immediately stood up and cast his robes to the ground.

"Like you said, we go now..." replied Harjit, as he unsheathed his sword and began to sprint across the training grounds towards the Masti gate.

"I guess that means we're going now," said Jai, who mimicked his friend's action and bolted off after him.

The others looked to the Nawab for his command. As Kapur watched the two young men sprint away, he discarded his own robes, before issuing a mighty Jaikara, "BOLE SO NIHAL!"

"SAT SRI AKAL!" roared the Khalsa warriors in response, as they too cast off their disguises and charged after Harjit and Jai, with their weapons drawn.

Harjit and Jai breezed past the undefended Masti gate and headed straight for the work fields, to find their loved ones. They did not stop to wait for backup or to consider what resistance they might encounter. They just ran as fast as their legs could carry them.

Just as Jahangir had ordered, only a handful of men now remained behind to guard the Sikh prisoners. The guards were too busy managing their slaves to notice the two young bloody-thirsty men, hurtling towards them at full speed. The two guards closest to Harjit and Jai, were the duo's first targets.

Harjit was the first to reach a guard. His opponent did not even have a chance to lower his spear in defence. By the time the guard felt a sharp prick in the front of his neck, it was already too late. A thin and small Pesh Kabz dagger, had flown through the air and pierced the guard's windpipe, (although Harjit had been aiming for his head).

The guard dropped to his knees and clutched his throat in shock, as Harjit closed the gap between them with his Talwar drawn. Harjit swung his sword from right to left with both hands, as he barreled past the guard. From Jai's perspective, it looked as if

Harjit was striking a baseball. But instead, his sword had cut through the guard's neck, taking his head clear off.

Harjit did not stop. He could not stop. The image of his wife sitting in that end field injured and alone, drove him to a point of madness, beyond all reason. With over a hundred feet and at least a dozen guards between them, Harjit pressed on forwards, towards his wife without looking back.

Luckily, his novice friend was not that far behind him. With his Naag Jeev blade thirsting for blood, Jai sprinted ahead towards the second guard. Seeing the fate of his fallen comrade, Jai's target managed to lower his spear and began a counter charge of his own.

This time however, Jai was able to anticipate the attack. He used the balanced weight of his double-edged sword, to parry the thrust of the attacking spear into the ground. As the guard fumbled with surprise, Jai barged at him with his good shoulder, winding him and knocking him to the ground. Before the guard knew what had hit him, Jai swung his sword with both hands, down upon the guard's torso.

The Naag Jeev Khanda split the guard's chest wide open killing him instantly, whilst spraying Jai with blood. Jai did not stop to fully process what he had done. He simply targeted the next guard and ran straight for him. "RUUHHHI!" he roared out loud, like a madman possessed.

The other guards looked at Jai and then towards Harjit, who had just split another guard into two pieces using his Talwar. The guards were stunned by the ferocity and the viciousness of their attacks.

Seeing a blood-soaked madman running straight towards him with a massive sword, Jai's next target dropped his spear and decided to flee instead. But it was of no use. Jai's longer and stronger legs narrowed the gap between them, like a lion running down a gazelle.

The guard headed straight for the patio stairs in the hope of taking refuge in the people's court, when he felt the sting of the Naag Jeev Khanda, cut the tendons in the back of his leg.

The guard cried out in pain, as he stumbled forward onto the stairs and clutched his leg in agony. Terrified of his attacker, the guard then tried his best to scramble away up the blood-soaked steps. But his efforts were in vain. There was no way of escaping his executioner. Jai swung his Khanda down once more and chopped of the guard's entire leg in one swift motion.

The guard screamed out in pain, as Jai knelt down beside him and withdrew Miri. Holding the Kirpan in his left hand, Jai leaned in close to the guard and looked into his eyes. "Where is my sister?" he asked, devoid of any emotion.

The guard's body shook with pain and fear, and he could not form any words. Without waiting, Jai slit the guards throat with Miri and walked away from the bleeding carcass, as if nothing had happened.

As Jai locked on to his next target, three Khalsa warriors blew past him and went forward to dispatch their own prey.

Ikamroop preferred the lighter Katar's, over the heavier and slower Khanda's and Talwar's. She withdrew her double ten-inch blades and leapt through the air like an acrobat, straight onto the back of another guard, who was running away from her in terror.

Ikamroop showed no mercy, as her razor-sharp blades cut into his shoulders and back multiple times, severing his spine, and mutilating his body. He bled out of several deep gashes before collapsing to the floor, very much dead.

At first, the Sikh prisoners did not understand what was going on. But as they watched the swarm of Khalsa warriors fly in and around them, and kill the remaining guards with ease, they realised what was happening. The remaining three guards fled as fast as they could, but they were no match for their blood thirsty pursuers.

Harjit had almost reached the end field, where he had last seen his wife only a short time ago. "Suhadna!" he shouted out, as loud he could as his eyes scanned the field looking for her. Jai was less than a minute behind his friend, when Harjit finally saw her.

Suhadna was no longer sitting up. His soul mate and the mother of his children, lay on the muddy floor with her head in the lap of her friend, Ruhi Kaur.

Ruhi gently stroked Suhadna's hair, as she stared down at the floor with a blank expression upon her face. There on the floor beside them, were two small bundles, wrapped in blood-soaked cloths. One was the size of a newborn baby, and the other was of a small child.

Harjit ran over to them and knelt by his wife's side. He picked up her hand and held it in his own. It was cold. He looked up at Ruhi with tears in eyes, for any sign of reassurance, but there was none.

Just like his children, his wife was now gone. As the realisation of his loss sunk in, Harjit pulled Suhadna close to his chest and hugged her tight. Closing his eyes, Harjit sobbed into her dead body.

Jai arrived just in time to watch his friend mourn the loss of his family. He ran over to where they were sat and finally saw his younger sister. But his feeling of relief was quickly replaced by one of shock, as he studied Ruhi's appearance.

She looked as if she had been through hell and back. The side of her face was heavily bruised, and she had clearly suffered multiple cuts and wounds during her confinement.

Ruhi looked up, as Jai knelt down beside her. She almost did not recognise her blood covered brother and could barely believe that it was actually him. Reality no longer make sense to her anymore. None of this did. Without saying a word, Jai wrapped his arms around his little sister and hugged her gently, as he breathed a sigh of relief.

Ruhi sat motionless in his arms. A part of her wanted to break down and cry so badly, yet she found herself almost paralysed with grief. She was exhausted, mentally, physically, and spiritually. But worst of all, she felt as if a piece of her had died along with those children. Her mind could not process how she could have gone from holding a newborn child in her hands one day, to seeing that same baby gutted like a fish the next. She could not stop Baani's screams of terror, from echoing in her mind as those beasts tore her apart, limb from limb, in front of her very eyes. The look of pain, fear, and torment on Baani's little face had cut through to the very core of Ruhi's soul.

The longer Jai held her, the more she felt a depth of pain and despair that she never knew existed. Tears began to flow from her eyes, as she dared to feel the true weight of the massacre that had just taken place. The pain was relentless. It continued to hit Ruhi, wave after wave, threatening to drown in her in an ocean of grief.

As Jai held his sister, his friend continued to mourn the passing of his wife and children. It was not the reunion that either of them had imagined.

With her Katar's still dripping wet with warm blood, Ikamroop entered the end field, along with four other Khalsa warriors. They immediately began checking the piles of bodies surrounding them for any survivors, whilst the other Khalsa warriors freed the remaining prisoners from their shackles and chains.

None of them could look upon the remains of the dead children and babies, without feeling a primordial pain, deep within their hearts. The warriors did what they could to comfort the grieving mothers, but nothing that they could say or do, could make what had happened there right.

That is when Kapur approached Harjit, Jai and Ruhi. He stopped beside Harjit and placed his hand upon his shoulder, as he had done once before.

Whilst his heart went out to the young man, Kapur knew that the fight was far from over. As long as Mir was alive, none of them would ever be safe again. "We have to go son," said the Nawab, with a sense of urgency.

Harjit looked up from his wife and stared up at the Nawab, with his bloodshot eyes. Harjit then looked at Ruhi and Jai and then back to the bodies of his wife and children. He placed a gentle kiss on the top of his wife's forehead and then lay her body gently down upon the ground. After covering her face with her blood stained chunni, Harjit turned to address Ruhi.

"Thank you... for being with her... Pehn Ji," choked Harjit, as he tried to suppress his tears. He looked down at his own blood-soaked clothes and removed the gatra from his chest and reached out to Ruhi. She broke from her brothers embrace and turned to her friend's husband.

"This belongs to you," he said, as he placed Piri into her hands.

Ruhi looked down at her Kirpan. It felt like a lifetime had passed since her Dhaddhi Ji had given her that weapon. She thought back to her words. 'Remember, a Kirpan is meant for the defence of those who cannot defend themselves.'

Ruhi wrapped her hand around the cold Jade hilt and withdrew her blade. But this time, the whole world around her did not seem to slow and focus, as it had once done. The was no feeling of electricity. And the colours around her were no brighter or more vivid than they had been a moment before. It was as if all the magic in the world had disappeared.

Ruhi sheathed her blade and painfully rose to her feet. Jai too got to his feet and offered to help her up, but she did not take his hand. Instead, she turned to address the man wearing the blood splattered silver armour. "I am coming with you. No mercy. No surrender. We kill them all," she said coldly, trying her best to suppress her emotions, from overwhelming her again.

The Nawab nodded in agreement, as he looked around at the field of dead women around him. With no time to waste, Kapur called upon his other warriors to regroup, whilst Jai stood by and observed the change in his sister's demeanor. He no longer recognised the young woman standing before him.

"Ru…" he began, but the right words seemed to fail him. Nothing he could say, could change what she had witnessed and what she had lived through. Instead, he looked down at his own Kirpan, before removing it and placing Miri into his sister's hands.

"Here, you're going to need this too. Just don't lose her though, I want her back. Besides, I have this beauty for now…" said Jai, as he showed off his deadly doubled edged Khanda, to his sister.

Ruhi almost smiled at her brothers' gesture but then stopped, as she almost split her bottom lip again. Acknowledging the sentiment, Ruhi accepted the second Kirpan from her brother and strapped it over her shoulder. Despite everything that had just happened, she was still happy to see him. For as long as she could remember, Jai had always watched out for her. Even when they had fought or whenever she would yell at him for being super annoying or lazy, in the end, he was always there for her and that is all that mattered.

Now wearing Miri and Piri on each side, Ruhi rested her hands on each hilt, whilst drawing in deep breaths. Something about having a Kirpan in each hand, helped Ruhi to centre her ever racing mind and for the briefest of moments, she didn't feel as if *all* the magic in the world had truly gone, not just yet.

As the other warriors gathered around the Nawab, Jai hurried over to Harjit, who was still sat beside the remains of his butchered family. Jai extended his arm to his friend. "Come on bro, let's go finish this…"

Harjit looked up. "There is nothing left for me now brother Jai. Go save yourselves and leave me here to die… with them," said a broken hearted Harjit.

Jai could not imagine the darkness and pain that his friend was experiencing. One way or another, the 'Butcher' had slaughtered his friend's entire family, Harpal, Ajay, Suhadna, Baani and Veeraj.

"No bro, I ain't leaving you behind." Jai knelt back down to his friends' level and then leaned in close, so that only Harjit could hear him.

"We are your family now. We started this together, we will end this together. You weren't able to save them, but you can still avenge them. Make these bastards pay for what they have done," said Jai, as he looked to stoke the fire of vengeance within his friends' heart.

Harjit sat in silence for a moment as he contemplated Jai's words and looked at the remains of his dead family.

Reaching for his Talwar, Harjit picked up his sword and then took his friend's hand. "Vengeance," he repeated, as they both stood up ready to finish what they had begun.

"We need to get to Mir before he escapes, otherwise all of this was for nothing," continued Kapur, as Harjit and Jai joined Ruhi, Ikamroop and the other Khalsa warriors in their mid-rescue huddle.

"Nawab Ji, we have scouted the perimeter. There are no more signs of resistance within this enclosure. It is as if all the guards have retreated to a separate engagement," reported Ikamroop.

Whilst this worked greatly to their advantage, the lack of a military presence at the fort was beginning to worry the Nawab. "Did you see any sign of the 'Butcher'?" Kapur asked his soldier. Ikamroop shook her head.

"Our best guess is that he is still somewhere inside the primary complex," she replied, pointing the people's court.

"Don't worry. I know where he will be," said Ruhi, as she looked up towards the second level of the monstrosity standing before them.

"Then it is settled," said Kapur. "Ruhi, Harjit and Jai and I, will intercept the Subedar, whilst the rest of you will lead the

273

prisoners back to the base. Use the back streets and avoid the markets and bazaars. The four of us will deal with Mannu once and for all and then meet you by the river once we're done. If we are not there within half an hour, you are to leave without us. Is that understood?" commanded the Nawab.

"Ji Hukam!" replied Ikamroop, and the Khalsa warriors in unison. But before they left to complete their duties, Ikamroop addressed her father.

"Be careful," she whispered to him. Kapur allowed himself to smile at his adopted daughter before she turned away to carry out his commands.

As the Khalsa warriors began the challenging task of escorting over three hundred survivors from the fort, Ruhi, Jai, Harjit and the Nawab, set off into the Diwan e Aam, to find 'the Butcher' and to bring him to justice once and for all.

With their weapons drawn, Ruhi led the way, as the new squad headed around to the back of the superstructure and straight towards the office of Mir's minion, Jahangir.

Everything looked so different now that the guards had left their posts. As they approached the entrance to Jahangir's office, Ruhi felt anxious at the prospect of going back into the building.

"We need to be careful," said Ruhi, as she looked back, mostly at her brother. Whilst she could not speak for Harjit and the Nawab, she knew her brother was not the most patient of people. "Mir is constantly surrounded by a group of his own personal guards. Once we get past them, we shouldn't have any problem in taking him out," she added.

"I'll go first," volunteered Harjit. Without waiting for approval, Harjit barged straight ahead into the Amir's office and through the door at the end, that led upstairs to the second floor.

"I really wish he would stop doing that," said Jai, as they all rushed in after him.

They bolted up the staircase after Harjit and spilled out into Mir's lounge one by one. To their surprise, they were greeted by eight of the Subedar's guards, who were ready and waiting for them. Without warning, Mir's personal guards charged at Harjit and the others, with their curved Talwar's drawn and all out chaos ensued.

Two of the guards went straight for Harjit, as he was the first to enter the lounge. But that proved to be a costly mistake. Harjit deflected their attacks with his sword and proceeded to hit them with a counterattack of his own. He managed to stab one of them in the stomach, but whilst his blade was stuck in the body of the first guard, the second guard used the opportunity to strike at Harjit's exposed neck.

Luckily for Harjit, his friend was a fast runner. Jai charged towards the second guard and parried his attack with his Naag Jeev Khanda. Sparks flew off from their blades, as they came into contact with one another. It was all the distraction Jai needed, as he used the superior balance and speed of his serrated blade, to cut downwards across the guard's neck, severing his arteries in the process.

Jai was astonished at how easy it was becoming for him, to take the life of another human being. As his dead opponent dropped to the floor, he glanced to see his friend yank his Talwar from the first guards' belly, and then chop of his head in a strikingly violent blow.

Yet, their fight was far from over. As two more guards ran to attack them, Ruhi and Kapur were busy on the other side of the lounge, dealing with some attackers of their own.

But the Nawab was no stranger to warfare. Despite his fifty-four years, he swung and directed his mighty double edged Khanda sword, with the speed and grace of a warrior half his age. Ruhi watched him charge and engage three of the guards at once. Just when it looked like someone was about to land a blow on the Nawab, he managed to avoid the strike at the very last second and deliver a devastating blow of his own. As the Nawab separated limbs like a sculptor working on clay, the leader of the guards headed for the last warrior in the squad, Ruhi.

It had been many years since Ruhi had last handled a weapon properly. But as he advanced towards her with his sword drawn and ready to attack, Ruhi stood planted on the floor, as if she were made from stone. This encounter was very different to the skirmish back at Raichand's haveli and the massacre back on the patio. In those situations, she was purely reacting on instinct.

Whereas here and now, she had a purpose and a focus unlike any she had felt before. A man was coming to rob her of her life, as he had done so to many others before her. With Miri in her left hand and Piri in her right, Ruhi held her ground, as the guard charged straight for her, whilst swinging his sword downwards to split his far smaller opponent into two.

Ruhi watched as he lunged forward and let his blade cut through the air and move closer towards her at an alarming rate. Without thinking or fearing the sting of his blade, she commanded her body flow to the right, as she deflected his attack with Miri. He was far bigger and stronger than she was, yet she used his own momentum against him. As she dodged his lunge, she countered with an attack of her own. She attacked his exposed limbs with the grace and speed of a dancer, cutting and slicing open every piece of exposed flesh her eyes could target.

The guard roared in fury at missing his opponent and swung at her blindly, in a mad rage, as she continued to slice away at him until finally, he dropped to his knees through exhaustion and heavy blood loss. Sensing that he was losing to a girl, enraged the guard even further and he once more summoned all his strength in a vain attempt to stab his opponent. Yet Ruhi simply danced around him, as her blades continued to part open his flesh.

Within seconds, the guard dropped his sword in defeat, as Ruhi moved in closer to finish him off. Looking into his eyes, Ruhi tapped into the darkness raging within her. She then proceeded to stab the guard in the neck with both of her blades and then watched him gargle blood, as the life slowly drained from his eyes.

Jai watched from across the room, as his little sister executed her opponent without feeling or remorse and without mercy. He stopped to look down as his own dead opponents and those of Harjit and Kapur's, when he realised that they had won their mini battle.

But it was also in that moment when he first questioned the true cost of their victory. He had just seen his little sister brutally execute another human being, (as he had just done) and yet, he wasn't sure if that was right or wrong anymore.

As the final guard's head, rolled across the floor, Kapur stood up from delivering his final execution style blow and looked to see if the others in his group were ok. Remarkably, none of them had suffered any injuries, yet critically, there was no sign of the Subedar or his wife.

"Where next!?" the Nawab shouted out to Ruhi, who was stood behind him still savouring her kill. She looked up, as if she had been caught in a trance and quickly scanned the room for Mir and his wife. There was no sign of them. Kapur's squad were the only ones left standing and there was no other way out of there, other than the…

"The Balcony!" she yelled, as she darted for the central doorway.

"No Ru, wait!" called out her brother, but Ruhi did not stop for anyone. She proceeded through the doorway and scanned the balcony for another exit. Just as she had suspected, there was another way out. On the far right-hand side of the balcony, there was a trapdoor protruding from the floor.

'Mir must have used the servant's entrance to escape, when he heard the commotion,' she thought to herself.

Without waiting for the others, Ruhi sheathed her Kirpan's and opened the hatchway that was built into the floor. With only one thought in her mind, Ruhi descended the dirty staircase that spiraled downwards, into the bowels of the court.

Just as her head disappeared below the surface, Jai burst out onto the balcony, followed closely by Harjit and the Nawab. They were all almost distracted by the view of the work fields and the patio floor beneath them, still covered in the blood of children, when Jai spotted the open hatch.

"She must have gone that way. It's the only way down from here," stated Jai, as he pointed to the servant's entrance. The three of them rushed to the hatchway and Kapur paused as Jai started to climb down the stairs after his sister.

"Wait! There is no guarantee that he went that way. You go, watch out for your sister. Harjit and I will clear the rest of this building first, just in case he took a different route," reasoned Kapur.

"Agreed. Good luck," replied Jai, as he hurried down the staircase leaving his friend and the Nawab behind.

Faced with a maze of passages and corridors before her, Ruhi looked for any kind of a sign, that Mir had passed through there with his wife. Only one corridor had light coming from it and whilst it wasn't a certainty, that guess was as good as any. She headed down the middle corridor and ran as fast as her legs could carry her.

The stale air made it hard for her to breath, but the adrenaline pumping through her veins kept her going. The further she ran, the more certain she felt that she was headed in the right direction. With every step forward, Ruhi fought hard to suppress the wondering thoughts that threatened to unravel her. 'What if she was wrong? What if she was too late? What if all of this was for nothing?'

"Nooooo!" she screamed out loud to herself, this was not the time for self-doubt. It was the time for revenge. Ruhi repeated three words back to herself, as she continued to run through the dimly lit corridors. 'Veeraj, Suhadna, Baani.'

With her lungs burning and her feet aching, Ruhi turned the last corner and spotted the silhouette of two people exiting the corridor, less than a hundred feet away from her. It was them; she was sure of it. With her heart pounding in her chest, Ruhi dug down deep and forced her legs into one last sprint.

Hearing rushed footsteps from behind him, Mir turned around and saw a dark purple blur speeding towards them from the distance. Sensing that they were under threat, the Subedar hurried his pregnant wife out of the corridor and into the horse stables, where they looked around for the nearest horse.

The horse stables were virtually empty, as per Mir's own orders. Jahangir had taken as many men and horses as they could spare. But there by the entrance, stood a single golden mare ready to ride. Mir could not believe his luck, as he ran towards it with his wife closely behind him.

"Subhan Allah!" Mir yelled with relief, as he turned around to face his wife. But she was no longer alone. A battered and bruised young Sikh woman stood behind his lady, with one Kirpan pressed to his wife's throat and another pressed against her soft round belly.

Mughalani was trembling with fear, as Ruhi stood close behind her and glared at her husband, the 'Butcher'. Mir's heart sunk into his chest, when he saw the love of his life filled with fear. He looked into Ruhi's eyes and saw a cold hatred reflected back at him, that he knew only too well.

Mir considered his options, which were not many. "Let her go and you will be freed. I give you my word," said Mir confidently, as if he were in charge of the situation.

Ruhi chuckled at the Subedar's arrogance. "You have a pair on you, I'll give you that," replied Ruhi. She applied slightly more pressure upon Mughalani's porcelain skin. Piri dug into the surface of her neck ever so slightly, causing Mughalani to wince in pain and Mir knew that he was running out of time.

"This is just between you and me. Let her go. If it is a fight you want, then I am standing right here," offered Mir, as he rested his hand on the hilt of his jewel encrusted sabre.

Ruhi considered his offer before coming up with a proposal of her own. "How about you drop your sword over there and then kneel on the floor before me, and I will consider not cutting your unborn child from its womb, before sending it and its whore mother to your Jahanam (hell)".

Mir was outraged by the threat of violence against his wife and unborn child. Without thinking, he reached for his sabre, only to be knocked down to the ground by Jai, who had seemingly appeared from nowhere.

Jai pinned Mir to the ground, whilst both Ruhi and Mughalani stood by in shock and awe at his sudden appearance. They had all been so preoccupied with their standoff, that they hadn't noticed him enter the stables through same passage they had used.

As Ruhi struggled to maintain her hold over Mughalani, Jai proceeded to pummel Mir's face into the floor. Mughalani screamed in protest, as she broke away from Ruhi and rushed to her husband's aid.

"No Jai! He's MINE!" shouted Ruhi, as she too lunged forward to stop her brother from robbing her of her retribution. But both of them were too late. Jai already had his snake tipped Khanda up in the air and nothing could prevent him from driving it downwards, straight through the Subedar's chest and out the other side, pinning him into the dirt.

Both Mughalani and Ruhi screamed in protest, as Mir looked at the metre long Khanda protruding from his chest. Mir tried his best to turn his head, to catch one final glimpse of his wife, but the last thing he saw was the roof of a horse stable.

Ruhi was furious and shoved her brother off the tyrant's dead body and proceeded to stab his corpse over and over again, with both of her Kirpan's in fit of rage and blood lust. Seeing her lose her mind and mutilate the dead body, Jai got to his feet and attempted to pull his sister away from the decimated corpse.

"RU! Enough! Stop! He's dead!" Jai yelled, trying to get through to her.

"NO! FUCK YOU! He was mine! He was my kill! It was my revenge! I didn't need your fucking help!" she screamed at her brother.

Jai stood back and was stunned into silence. He looked from his sister to Mughalani, was knelt nearby, crying her eyes out over the death of her husband. Jai caught her attention and motioned her to leave the stables, now.

Mughalani looked at a furious Ruhi and did not need to be told twice. Sensing the danger to her and her unborn child, Mughalani rose to her feet and hobbled as quickly as she could, to the golden mare that was still waiting nearby for its rider.

"Ru…" Jai said calmly, trying to distract his sister from Mughalani's departure. "Look at me. It's over…"

"No! You took this from me, like you take everything! You had no right! You…" but this time, it was Jai who interrupted her.

"You almost killed an innocent woman and a child!" Jai roared in return.

"I saw you holding a *Kirpan* to the belly of an unarmed and defenseless pregnant woman for God's sake. Wake the fuck up Ru! That shit is not ok. It is never ok! I don't care if he was the most evil and twisted motherfucker on the planet. That kid in her belly didn't do anything to you. We are Sikh's! We don't kill innocent people!" yelled Jai, as Mughalani finally mounted the horse and darted for the exit.

Ruhi watched her ride away and then turned back to her brother. "Innocent hey? Some fucking Sikh you are. You ain't no Sikh. And who the fuck are you to decide who lives and dies?" She replied angrily. "How many people have you killed today by the way? He tortured those women! He tortured…. those kids… and where were you? Where were you!?…" Ruhi's voice had begun to crack and break, as she started to realise that she had been crying and that maybe… maybe she had gone too far.

The pain of seeing Baani screaming in terror once again echoed throughout her mind, over and over again, until finally Ruhi could not take anymore. With Piri still in her right hand, she raised the blade in the air and moved to take her own life, in a fit of despair.

Sensing what she was about to do, Jai lunged at his sister and stopped her arm before it could complete its task. "Just let me go, please…" begged Ruhi, as she sobbed uncontrollably. Jai shook the weapons from her hands, until they both fell into dirt below.

"No Ru. Not like this, not like this," said her brother, as he hugged her tight and tried his best not to cry himself. All Jai knew, was that his sister was in unimaginable pain and that he had no idea how to help her. "I'm sorry" he whispered, as she continued to cry into his chest.

Chapter 14

It felt like an eternity before Harjit and Kapur found Ruhi and Jai in the stables. When they first saw the Subedar's body, both were taken back by how many wounds there were on his remains. But then neither of them really cared either. They were just happy to see that he was finally dead. They were more relieved to see that the siblings were still alive.

"Well done, Beti. What you have done here today, will echo through eternity," said the Nawab, as he addressed Ruhi, who was now sat beside her brother, with her head resting on his good shoulder. They were both still staring at the Subedar's dead body. Kapur knelt down beside the corpse and relieved him of his sabre, before presenting it to Ruhi.

"This belongs to you now," said Kapur, as he handed Ruhi the diamond encrusted sword. She looked at her brother, who nodded for her to take it. "Our work here is now done. But we are far from safe here. We need to rendezvous with the others and then figure out how we're going to escort everyone to safety. Come, we have no more time to waste. I need you all," commanded the Nawab, as he helped them both to their feet.

But before Ruhi and Jai could say anything, Harjit spoke next. "Brother Jai and Ruhi Pehn Ji, thank you for what you have done for my family," said the young farmer, as he looked at the both of them. Tears threatened to fall from Ruhi's eyes once more if she spoke, so she just nodded to him instead.

"Come on guys, we're not out of this just yet. You heard the Nawab. We're not done until everyone is safe," said Jai to his sister and friend. Ruhi seemed to have composed herself over the last few minutes. Whilst she was still far from healed, she knew that there were still a lot of women out there depending on them. She picked up her Kirpan's and holstered them back into their covers, before following Harjit and the Nawab.

Jai too retrieved his weapon and took one last look at Mir's mutilated corpse, before turning to leave and joining the others. He watched his sister closely, as they exited the horse stables and headed towards the rendezvous point. 'Please help her Guru Ji,' Jai whispered out loud, as they walked out of the fort and headed for the Shahdara forest.

Despite the hustle and bustle of the busy streets of Lahore, Kapur's squad managed to reach the safety of their camp without incident. Ikamroop was relieved to find her father still alive and in one piece. As per her father's instructions, she had been preparing to leave without them, just in case they did not return in time.

Ikamroop embraced her father, before checking to see if the others had also returned unscathed. Despite not wanting to admit it to herself, she was relieved to see that even Jai was ok.

Ikamroop led her father and the others to the centre of the camp, where they found themselves surrounded by the liberated mothers. The Khalsa warriors were doing their best to share what little provisions they had. Many of the women were drinking fresh water from the river for the first time in months.

It was the first time Jai had truly looked at any of the survivors. Many of them still wore the dead remains of their children around their necks and bodies, and most of them seemed to be suffering from severe malnutrition. Jai looked at his sister in a different light, as she walked amongst them. He slowly began to realise that whatever they had gone through, she had been a part of that experience too. And whether he liked it or not, it will have changed her forever.

Jai followed his sister as she walked through the crowd of survivors and headed towards the banks of the river. He watched her cautiously as she dunked her head into the Ravi and drunk its fresh water. The water began to wash away the dry blood from her forehead and blistered hands.

After quenching her thirst, Ruhi sat herself on the ground and simply watched the currents of the river pass her by. A gentle breeze blew through her blood-stained hair and for a moment, she remembered how it felt to be ten years old and how she used to stare out at the Sutlej, with her Dhaddhi Ji sat beside her.

Just when she thought she was alone, her older brother plonked himself down beside her. "Hey…" Jai began.

"So, we can either just pretend like none of this ever happened OR… we could talk about it… I'm totally cool with either. But I think perhaps… we should probably talk about what just happened, before either of us does something crazy or stupid or something we would totally regret later and by us, I mean you..."

Ruhi looked away from the river currents and stared at her brother in his stupid looking Sufi style turban and his blood-soaked clothes and cracked her bottom lip open when she involuntarily smiled as his stupid attempt to make her feel better.

"I'm sorry about what I said back there too. You aren't a stupid Sikh, and I don't blame you for what happened. If anything, I..." Ruhi struggled to finish her sentence, as she could not express just how much it meant to her, that he had come for her.

"It's ok. I'm just sorry I didn't get to you before all of this..."

A silence fell between the two of them, as they both stared out at the water. There was something inherently calming about watching the water flow past them. Yet both of them knew, that no matter how much water passed them by, nothing could ever erase their memories from the past few days or change what had happened to them.

"So, what do we do now? Where do we go from here?" Ruhi asked, without looking away from the water. Jai turned around and looked behind them. He saw the Nawab and his warriors, preparing to move the crowds of women out from the forest.

"We find a way home. We find a way back to our time. We find Dhaddhi Ji, and we make sure that people never forget what happened here today. I still don't know whether all of this is some kind of a collective nightmare or whether we're really stuck in 1753, but whatever it is, we'll get through it...together. Deal?"

Ruhi looked at her older brother and nodded. "And no more crazy shit, ok? If you go, I ain't staying either, so remember that next time you think about...you know what," added Jai.

Ruhi knew that he was referring to the point where she wanted to take her own life. It was an extreme feeling and a thought that had never crossed her mind before. Yet even as she uttered the word, "Ok," she knew in her heart that it was a lie, as did he.

Jai knew that the horrors she had witnessed, had fundamentally changed his sister in ways in which he could never truly understand. And yet, she was not the only one who was different now. He looked down at his own blood-stained hands and clothes and thought back to all the lives he had taken and all the blood he had spilt with his own two hands.

No matter what path lay before the two of them, the journey they were on had already taken them to some of the darkest corners of their souls and neither of them had come out unscathed.

Jai got to his knees and helped his little sister up. Her physical wounds would take time to heal, but it was the wounds he could not see, that worried him the most. As they rose to their feet, Jai could not help but hug his sister once more. "I love you and don't you forget that you Aloo," he said quickly, in the hope that she wouldn't dwell on his rare display of brotherly affection.

"I love you too bro," Ruhi replied to his surprise. Just as they turned to face the others in the camp, Harjit approached the siblings.

"Are you both ready?" he asked the both of them.

"Sure bro. What's the plan?" Jai asked his friend.

Harjit proceeded to explain to them, that there would be no easy path forward for them no matter which route they chose. Amritsar was the nearest city to them, but at just over thirty miles away, it would not be an easy journey. Especially as the women would have to travel by foot and many hadn't eaten properly in months. There was also still an army of Mir's soldiers and mercenaries out there looking for every Sikh man, woman, and child that they could find.

The Nawab called for silence, as he addressed his warriors and the crowd of liberated Sikh women before him.

"I know that you are you all scared, tired and hungry. I know many of you have lost much and have suffered a great pain at the hands of Mir the 'Butcher' and his men. But he is no longer a part of this world. His soul is with Waheguru now and only the Guru can judge him now. I cannot promise you that the road ahead will be any easier than what you have already endured. But I can promise you that this is not the end for us. All I ask, is that you do not give up. We must persevere, we must continue, and we must survive. I have sent our fastest rider to seek help from Jassa Singh Ahluwalia. But it will be days before Jassa can reach us with his army. We will head to Amritsar and take refuge in Harmandir Sahib (the golden temple) and await Jassa there. My warriors will show you the way. Remember we are not alone. We never have been. Our Guru Ji is with us always and with his blessings, we will prevail. Waheguru Ji Ka Khalsa! Waheguru Ji Ki Fateh!" called out the Nawab, as he finished his speech.

The Sikh women and the Khalsa warriors answered the Nawab, with the same words. "Waheguru Ji Ka Khalsa! Waheguru Ji Ki Fateh!" and began to separate into their smaller groups as ordered.

Ruhi followed Harjit and her brother to the horses secured nearby and she saw her brother's excitement, as he walked up to a black mare and began to stroke her mane. "Hello darling! Miss me? Ru, this is Chittar. Chittar, this is my sister Ruhi," said Jai, excitedly to them both.

"Don't worry, she won't bite," Jai whispered to his horse. Jai helped his sister up on to his trusty mare, as Harjit offered his own saddle to another woman who was struggling to walk.

As the Nawab gave the order to head out, Harjit and Jai led their horses away from the riverbanks and they followed the last group of liberated women, as they all exited the Shahdara forest.

Ruhi looked around one last time to catch a glimpse of the river, as her brother led her and Chittar forward. Whatever lay ahead of them, they were at least together, for now.

You can follow Ishar on:

Instagram: ishar.p.singh

Printed in Great Britain
by Amazon

27635235R00165